W9-DFZ-787

WHAT
HE'S BEEN
MISSING

Also by Grace Octavia

Southern Scandal series
His First Wife
His Third Wife
His Last Wife

Take Her Man
Something She Can Feel
Playing Hard to Get
Should Have Known Better

Reckless
(with Cydney Rax and Niobia Bryant)

Published by Dafina Books

3 1526 04718319 6

WHAT HE'S BEEN MISSING

WITHDRAWN
Harford County Public Library

GRACE OCTAVIA

Dafina
BOOKS

Kensington Publishing Corp.
http://www.kensingtonbooks.com

To the extent that the image or images on the cover of this book depict a person or persons, such person or persons are merely models, and are not intended to portray any character or characters featured in the book.

DAFINA BOOKS are published by

Kensington Publishing Corp.
119 West 40th Street
New York, NY 10018

Copyright © 2012 by Grace Octavia

All rights reserved. No part of this book may be reproduced in any form or by any means without the prior written consent of the Publisher, excepting brief quotes used in reviews.

If you purchased this book without a cover, you should be aware that this book is stolen property. It was reported as "unsold and destroyed" to the Publisher and neither the Author nor the Publisher has received any payment for this "stripped book."

All Kensington Titles, Imprints, and Distributed Lines are available at special quantity discounts for bulk purchases for sales promotions, premiums, fund-raising, and educational or institutional use. Special book excerpts or customized printings can also be created to fit specific needs. For details, write or phone the office of the Kensington special sales manager: Kensington Publishing Corp., 119 West 40th Street, New York, NY 10018, attn: Special Sales Department, Phone: 1-800-221-2647.

Dafina and the Dafina logo Reg. U.S. Pat. & TM Off.

ISBN-13: 978-0-7582-6540-1
ISBN-10: 0-7582-6540-9
First Kensington Trade Edition: December 2012
First Kensington Mass Market Edition: October 2015

eISBN-13: 978-0-7582-7941-5
eISBN-10: 0-7582-7941-8
First Kensington Electronic Edition: December 2012

10 9 8 7 6 5 4 3 2 1

Printed in the United States of America

For those who wait patiently and are ready for love. And for Tony for reminding me that I could feel that way.

Acknowledgments

When I am writing, I often wish I could make the entire world stand still as I run off to a bunker (coffee shop) to finish a novel. That way, I wouldn't appear aloof or distant to those around me, run late when I promised I would be on time, miss things I really wished I could attend, and pass on phone calls that are long overdue. If the world would just stop, I could put it all on hold and come back out when I am done writing, able to catch up like I'd never been gone. This, of course, is impossible. The world keeps going. My nieces get older every year. My friends have dinner parties. My students need me to stop and listen. While I can't always be there or be as attentive as I would like, I want to take this time to thank all of those people in my life for being patient with me and understanding over these last few years as I've tried to make something of my dream of being a writer. While I couldn't possibly name everyone in this short acknowledgment, please know that I appreciate you and cherish the time we do get to spend together. Writing can be a lonely art form. Its very nature requires hours of solitude. And I know that each moment spent doing it is a moment I might have spent on the phone with one of you, being on time to something that was important to you, or being fully present when you really needed me. I thank you for the sacrifice. I adore you for your support.

"I am ready for love . . ."

—India.Arie in "Ready for Love"

I

Scarlet Fever

#**E**picfailure. Two hours before the conclusion of the first decade of the twenty-first century and I was holed up in my loft on the couch . . . again. This shit was getting really old. Three years in a row? And the fourth year back wasn't exactly spent dancing until my feet hurt and popping a bottle of bubbly before belting out "Happy New Year" amidst a crowd of Atlanta's swankiest cosmopolites—I'd met midnight on my knees in the second pew at Mount Moriah in Social Circle with Grammy Annie-Lou.

Looking at me now you'd think I *was* Grammy Annie-Lou. No party. No crystal flute filled to the lip with Krystal. No leprechaun-inspired, obnoxious, blinged-out top hat. Just poor little colored-girl me camped out on the living room couch watching *Love & Basketball* in my "sick and shut-in" lumberjack plaid nightgown, sipping pink Moscato

and eating light-cheese flatbread pizza after taking
my second dose of NyQuil.

So sad to say, I wasn't even having cold or flu
symptoms. It was just my sad-sister cocktail of over-
the-counter drugs. See, I was self-medicating in
hopes that I might be dead asleep by the time the
ball dropped in Manhattan. I didn't even want to
know what it would feel like to see a new year, a
new decade in the new century come to life as I
was thirty-one and all alone in this wretched world.
I know that might sound dramatic, but damn,
something had to give.

Right then, right there on that couch, gorging on
disgusting pizza and half high from a near-overdose
of cold medication and sweet wine, I felt like I was
having the worst New Year's night ever. And not
because I wasn't out at some wack-ass, overpriced
party with an undertalented DJ—I'm old enough
to know that Prince's "party like it's 1999" is all an
illusion once you're right there in the overstuffed
crowd with your feet hurting and some dude wearing eyeliner is feeling on your booty while whispering Prince lyrics in your ear. The sad feeling was
because I didn't have anyone who wanted to take
me to some wack-ass, overpriced party with an undertalented DJ. No one. Not a soul with a deep
voice, muscular arms, and me on his mind felt in-
clined to invite me out to toast the good life.

Those other years there'd been prospects at
least: New Year's Eve '09 the toothless man at the
gas station asked if I wanted to split a bottle of Mad
Dog; New Year's Eve '08 Goldie, the gold-toothed
man who delivered my pizza, asked in the most sincere voice possible if he could come upstairs to give
me a "sweet-tish" (that's how he'd pronounced

"Swedish") massage; New Year's Eve '07 my dead ex-boyfriend Jaheed (he's not really dead; I just prefer to tell people that) stood me up when he, on an emotional whim, decided to go back to his ex-girlfriend and propose to her at midnight (they've since married and divorced). But this New Year's Eve—2010—was going down in history as the year that not even a dentally challenged chap or cheating jerk could stand the idea of having me on his arm.

The most devastating dismal detail of this worst New Year's night ever was that no one would've thought that was my reality. I'm Rachel Winslow. The owner, founder, CEO, and visionary behind Let's Get Married, Atlanta's most formidable, full-service luxury wedding firm. I link the likes of lovers from engagement to honeymoon, making the "most special day they only imagined in high school daydreams" come to life.

I started in the business when I was only six years old and planning the nuptials of Cabbage Patch Kids after school in the high grass in Grammy Annie-Lou's backyard in Social Circle, Georgia. And moved on up to celebrities and Atlanta's elite making romantic promises overlooking the world at the Sun Dial. Last year, a cover story on Let's Get Married in the *Atlanta Journal-Constitution* said, "Winslow just has the touch of love" and noted that my client list is booked for three years (most of those people aren't even engaged yet) and I've grossed $1.25 million since opening in 2008. But I don't do what I do for money or cover-story features and accolades. I do it because I'm still that little girl who celebrated with the newlywed Cabbage Patch couple until my grandmother came out on the back porch—always in her stained peach apron with the ruffle on the bottom—and called me in for supper.

And I really, really believe in love. At first flirty smile—love. At first sexy scent—love. The first moment you see him and you just know from somewhere in your navel that you must have his babies—love. Defy your mama—love. Defy your daddy—love! And who gives a damn if neither one of them ever speaks to you again because "he" is in your life and nothing else really matters right now, does it?—love. Cherry on top—love. Hand-holding on the Ferris wheel—love. Staying in bed all day and you don't even care that your under-arms smell like onions and his breath smells like onions (because he's been kissing your under-arms)—love. Red roses and chocolates on Febru-ary fourteen—love. *Love Jones* with Nia Long standing out in the rain crying just before Larenz Tate sweeps her up into his arms—love. Sappy—love. Yes, clichéd—love. And we don't care if it is clichéd because it's our fairy tale and it can be whatever and however we want it—love. Just—love.

All my life I dreamed I could find it. That I could have it. Be the love story I created. Escape the old myth that professionals in the wedding business are meant to plan for—but not be in—love. But the more New Year's nights I spent alone, the less I thought my dream was possible. And you know what they say: "Whoever you're with at the stroke of midnight on New Year's Eve is the person you'll spend the next year with." Apparently, 2011 wanted to see me solo. Because, just as I'd planned, by midnight I was passed out in my grammy getup.

No new love in sight. Not even the gold-toothed pizza man had tried me that year. Hell, I might've let him upstairs.

Things weren't any better New Year's Day.

At 7:00 AM, my cell phone rang after my best friend sent a text saying I'd better pick up.

"This better be good, Ian."

"You're coming tonight, right?" He sounded like it was 7:00 PM and I had a clue what he was talking about. Actually, I did. While the NyQuil binge still had me a bit foggy, I knew exactly why he was calling. It was his girlfriend Scarlet's twenty-fifth birthday. 1/1/11. How could I forget? Ian had gone on babbling about it every five minutes at each of our weekly Wednesday lunch dates through December.

"What the what?" I groaned loudly to exaggerate the ache of waking, as if I'd been out all night and came staggering in with my stilettos in hand just minutes before he'd texted me. "Coming where? Why?"

"Rachel!"

"It's seven o'clock in the morn—"

"It's not like you went anywhere last night—"

"For your information, I *chose* to have a quiet evening of reflection at home." (Lie.)

"No, you *chose* to stay in the house and sulk. Probably took a gang of NyQuil and fainted on the couch while watching *Love & Basketball* again. Did the pizza man try to get with you this year? I told you to come out with me and Scarlet."

I looked at the NyQuil pill wrappers on the

floor beside the couch; the movie ready to begin again on the flat screen; the empty box of pizza. I hadn't even tried to make it to my bed.

"What do you want, Ian?"

"You're coming to Scarlet's birthday party tonight, right?" Ian was in his car. Probably on his way to or from Scarlet's loft downtown. He was an Africana Studies professor at Emory University and Scarlet was one of his former students turned "international" model and black feminist motivational speaker—whatever that meant. Basically, between Sears catalog photo shoots Scarlet put on a size 0 black turtleneck and Black Power pin, and spoke to poor black women about all the injustices they faced in the world—none of which she herself faced. She's half black and Cuban and grew up in Buckhead with plastic surgeons for parents. Everyone eats up her little "uplift the masses of marginalized black women and girls" routine, though. And Ian has the fullest belly. He thinks Scarlet is the next Rosa Parks and Fannie Lou Hamer . . . and Naomi Campbell, rolled up in one. He says I give her a hard time. But I don't. It's just that . . . well, to be that pretty . . . and that "conscious" . . . all at the same time . . . it's just insulting to the rest of us.

"The party's tonight?" I asked.

"Don't play with me. I need you to be there." Ian had planned the entire party himself. He'd paid for the penthouse suite at the W Hotel and sent out invitations to all of Scarlet's size-0 model/conscious-activist friends. The night was guaranteed to annoy me to death.

"I know. I know. The W. Tonight. Whatever."

"Are you coming early?"

"Don't push it," I said. "And why are you so amped about this anyway?" I knew I didn't exactly sound like a wedding-planning romantic at that point. Really, a brother so excited about shelling out thousands of dollars to celebrate his girlfriend's birthday should've scored high on my romance card. But there was something about Scarlet. I don't know. While I'd never told Ian, I thought she was just putting on an act with the whole "black women rule the world" crusade and, honestly, I didn't think she was good enough for him.

"I'm gonna ask her to marry me."

It was like a missile had fallen from the sky. KA-BOOM! Right between me and the pizza box. The alcohol and acetaminophen in my gut was suddenly shooting up my esophagus.

I was up from the couch and on my feet before I responded.

"What?"

"Yep! Had the ring shipped in from Namibia—I found a nonconflict diamond dealer there, you know how she is about stuff like that." (Instant frown earned from me.)

"You already have a ring?"

"Scarlet's mom was the one who brought it up—us getting married—you know how those Spanish mamas are. She don't play that long-term dating stuff. And at first I was like 'nah,' but then I was like 'ahh' . . . so I just got the ring!"

"You *just got the ring*?" I repeated, mimicking his nonchalance. He sounded like he was going to a linen sale at Macy's.

"Why did you say it like that, Rach? I know how you feel about Scarlet, but I thought you'd at least be happy for me."

"Feel about her?" I rolled my eyes at the thought that I felt anything or anyway about Scarlet. "I don't feel anyway about her." This little leak was so fake—and even with my forced smile Ian couldn't see, I was sure he knew it. "It's just that . . . I thought, you know, that we'd talk about this first. Before you made a decision. And . . . what about that girl? The one you met last week at the conference in New York—at NYU? The one with the books? The writer? I thought you liked her."

"That was one night. A drink. Scarlet's my girlfriend. I love her. I can't imagine my life without her. She completes me." When Ian is confused he has a tendency to speak in clichés. "She's the best thing that's ever happened to—"

"Fine! I'll come," I blurted out to stop him. I couldn't take it anymore. Ian was also as stubborn as a wild boar, and flooding him with questions wouldn't get me anywhere. He was one of those "you catch more flies with honey than vinegar" people.

"Great! Early?"

"Yes, Ian." I sighed. "I'll be there early. I'll be there as your best friend. Supporting you in marrying the best thing that's ever happened to you." (Cue the sarcasm.)

"No way! I'm not going. This is the worst thing that could happen! The worst thing ever!" I grimaced and nodded into the little camera lens perched on top of my computer monitor.

"Lord, what's going on in the ATL? Do I need to get Dame to put me on a plane?"

While Ian was caught up in a cloud of clichés

about his love for Scarlet, I was logging onto my computer to call on the only person who could stop me from completely wigging out over his pending engagement and making a worse situation ... *worser?*

Journey Cash is my former client who was actually already married and living the only life she thought she'd ever have, being a high school teacher and singer in her daddy's church in Tuscaloosa, Alabama, when one of her former students showed up to steal her away from it all. OK, that might all sound a little crazy, so it's important to add that her former student was actually of legal age when he returned to Black Warrior High School to steal his old chorus teacher's heart away—that and the biggest rapper in the country. Damien "Dame" Mitchell wasn't just the toast of Tuscaloosa, but of every town and city all around the world. He had everything—number-one albums, media madness, a cultlike crew following, millions of dollars in the bank and a plan to turn them into billions—seemingly all a man from the projects of a small southern city with one highway in and one highway out could want. But Dame was missing the one person he thought was responsible for all his riches, the first person who inspired him to dream, and he set out on a seemingly impossible quest to get her, too. Well, impossible it was not. When Dame and Journey showed up in my office in 2009, smiling and ready to jump the broom, Journey had just finalized her divorce, was working on her own album, and was about a month pregnant ... with twins. They explained that because of Journey's family, they wanted to say "I do" as soon as possible. Her father, Jethro Cash, was leading the biggest mega church in the South and Journey felt she'd done the family name enough damage by running off with one of her former students—not to mention, her baby brother was living the life of a female stripper in Atlanta and her older brother had been arrested for stealing funds from the church. While a lot of people had children out of wedlock (including Daddy Cash), Journey was certain a "bastard" baby from his only daughter would send her father to an early grave. Dame was willing to pay top dollar to make sure that didn't happen. We had two months to plan the wedding of Journey's dream—in three months, she'd be showing for sure. We spent about every waking hour together for those two months. I actually ended up going to some of Journey's doctor appointments with her when Dame was away. To my surprise, I found a kindred spirit in her. Someone else who'd believed that even though she was imperfect, she deserved perfect love. It found her in the middle of her life and interrupted everything. It could find me, too.

After the wedding, Journey left Atlanta to go on a world tour with Dame, but we actually missed talking to each other every day, so Dame's assistant introduced us to the wonders of video chatting on Skype. I called her when I couldn't stand not being in love. I think she called me when she wanted to remember what it was like before she found it.

"He can't marry her, Journey! Not Scarlet. Scarlet? Not Scarlet! No. He can't." I collapsed and banged my head on my desk to add a little drama.

"Well. Why?" Journey asked. She was sitting before a backdrop of finger paintings and family photos. Since the wedding two years before, Dame and Journey actually had the twins—two little boys (Jessie and Justin)—and a baby girl, Apache. Journey released her first album, *Black Warriors*, and it became an instant classic, but she wanted to take time off to raise the children around their father. That meant that they basically lived in hotels. She tried to keep some semblance of regularity by hanging the children's artwork and pictures everywhere they went.

"I told you before, she's a faker. A phony. She's trying to . . . I don't know . . . get Ian to marry her," I said.

"So you don't think she loves him?" Journey asked.

"No. I don't know . . . Maybe."

"Does he love her?" She leaned in with a little more interest.

"No!" I sucked my teeth. "I don't know . . . Yes? But only because he doesn't know who she really is."

"And you do?" Journey reached down to pick up Apache, who'd just started walking and was grabbing for the keyboard. "Look, you keep saying how much you don't like her, but you can't say why and you haven't even told Ian how you feel about her."

"Because I can't—"

"You can't find anything *really* wrong with her."

"It's just a feeling in my gut that this is wrong. That she's wrong. That she's wrong for him."

One of the twins showed up beside Journey at the laptop. They both looked just like Dame.

"Then who's right for him, Rachel?" Journey flashed an accusing frown.

"Don't get on that again. There's nothing between Ian and me. He's my best friend."

"Well, you be his best friend and just support

him. Be there for him. Instead of being all suspicious about this being the worst thing for him, help him make it the best thing for him. Can you do that?"

"Whatever. Yes. I mean, if this is what he wants . . . whatever," I said. "Marry the fake-ass Angela Davis."

The little boy climbed on the desk in front of Journey and peered into the camera at me. He came in so close all I could see was his mouth.

"Boy, back up from the camera," I heard Journey order before she pulled him back. Then the other twin showed up.

"I hungry, Mama," he said as Journey hustled him back into her lap.

"Oh heavens!" Journey said, trying to manage both of them at the computer and not looking like she was going to be successful. With all of her responsibilities literally mounting up in front of her, my emergency seemed so trivial. "Look, Rachel, duty calls. I need to feed these little people."

"OK."

"But listen, before I go, there's something else I want you to consider."

"What?" I asked.

"Why this bothers you so much."

"He's my best—"

"No, no, no," Journey said. "I don't mean that. I mean, maybe this is less about Ian getting married and more about you *not* getting married. You said it yourself last week. Another year alone. Another Christmas. Another New Year's. Just be certain that you're not trying to stop your friend from getting engaged simply because you're not the friend who's getting engaged."

* * *

The lobby of the midtown hotel where Ian had reserved the suite for Scarlet's birthday party was so full it looked like it was the spectacular New Year's Eve celebration I'd missed the night before. Techno-pop washed into the grand entrance through invisible speakers and a matching modern decor of art deco leather couches and random abstract sculptures provided the perfect backdrop for a thick crowd of leftover partygoers, whose chatter seemed to erupt into uproarious laughter every thirty seconds.

As I snaked through the maze, careful not to drown in someone's martini or tip over in the red six-inch platform heels I'd need to hop out of in three hours and slide on the flip-flops I was carrying in my purse, I realized that the gathering was almost all black men. Impeccably dressed. Irresistibly fine. The brothers were everywhere. It looked like a single black woman's dream—well, any woman's dream. And the few sisters (white and black) who were sprinkled into the mix were beaming like lottery winners, holding onto whatever brothers they could catch.

Taking note, I put my meanest platform stiletto walk into action. I'd pinned my loose natural curls up in a pompadour bang, summoning a bit of Afro-chic glamour, and slid on a simple little black halter dress that let my red heels do all the talking. I knew I looked good when I walked out of the house. And now here was the test of my evaluation. Journey always says, "Anytime is a good time to meet a great man." Unfortunately, most single sisters, especially the successful single sisters, are guilty of giving up on the day-to-day meeting opportunities that present themselves. So they rush when they leave the house—put on little to no makeup, jogging pants, Uggs, and T-shirts that are so old you can hardly read the lettering. They put hats over their hair, shades over their eyes, and frowns on their faces, and go out into the world like they're ready for war. And then wonder why they haven't met anyone or had a date in years. Of course, this is the extreme, but I know I've been guilty of at least five of these counts on a daily basis. Now, taking Grammy Annie-Lou's advice that "Even a barn needs a little paint," I try my best to look my best even when I feel my worst. While I'm the judge and jury of what exactly that best look is before I leave the house, once I'm on the go there's a new sheriff in town. Now, I know I'm a complete neurotic mess, but there's something about the whole process of just knowing men will look at me that all the way fucks with my mind when I'm walking by. I'm always like:

1. What if they look for a second, frown unmoved, and turn away? Death sentence! Does that mean I need to go to the gym? Dye my platinum edges? Stop wearing this darn pink lip gloss?

2. What if they look and smile, but don't say anything? That's better than the death sentence, but a smile isn't getting me anywhere. I didn't spend thirty minutes on my hair to go home with a bag of smiles. Do I try to slow down awkwardly and start up a conversation with a total stranger? He smiled. Right?

3. What if they look, smile, and call me over?

This may seem like the best-case scenario, but it fucks with my head more than the other two. Do I walk over like some needy puppy, making it obvious that I'm on the market and so thirsty to meet a man that I'll stop and talk to random dudes in public? What if I trip? What if I have a booger in my nose?

4. What if no one looks? Now, this is the single-woman's holocaust. You're so lame, you're invisible. Casper. Harry Potter under his magical cape. No one can see you. You've spent hours getting dressed only to realize that no one cares that you're there and, well, no one cares if you leave. Do you then inject yourself into someone's path of vision? Or sit and pretend to enjoy your own company?

Journey says I'm going to have to get over this, that thinking so much only lowers my confidence (how I walk into a room, stand at a bar, and smile while just on my own) and that males thrive on this female confidence. It's what attracts them most. So, twisting through the crowd of men in the lobby at the hotel in my killer red heels, the sugary-sweet positive angel on my left shoulder thought, "Confidence, confidence, confidence," but the what-the-hell-were-you-thinking-walking-out-of-the-house-in-hooker-shoes devil on my right shoulder backed that up with, "Did he just turn his back when he saw me?" and "Oh . . . was that a smile? I knew these shoes were working! Maybe I should go over and say hello. . . . Oh . . . That wasn't a smile. Maybe he has gas." Managing my neurosis some-where in the middle, in my mind I winked and lin-

gered at the smiling brother a bit, but in reality my
nerves sent me rushing to the receptionist so I
could get the number to Scarlet's party suite.

"Big night, huh?" I said after giving the woman
behind the desk Ian's last name and turning back
to drink in the brothers as she looked at her computer.

"Leftovers from last night," she said. "It's a fraternity. They had a ball."

"Really? Wish I had an invitation," I joked, remembering my disaster on the living room couch.
Certainly, one of these men could've used my ser-
vices. "It's not every day that you get to see so
many fine brothers in one place like this." I saw
two of the men greet one another with a fraternity
handshake. Their linked-up arms were so muscular and strong it sent tickles up my spine. Lord, it
had been so long since I'd felt a touch like that.
"Dang," I started, turning back to the receptionist,
who looked a little less impressed than me. "I love
fraternity men. Maybe I should call some of my
girlfriends down here. You think they'll be here all
night?"

"Probably," she said flatly. "But don't bother
calling your girls."

"Why? What?" I spied the dazzling menfolk
once more and then turned back to the receptionist. "What? Oh no. Don't tell me. They're gay! It's
Atlanta! I should've known," I discerned aloud. In
my voice there was a mix of surprise and acknowledgment with a dash of quick understanding. Suddenly, in my mind anyway, I could explain why I'd
gotten no cat calls during my stiletto-clad cat walk
through a sea of men. Of course no one wanted to
holler at me! They're all gay!

"No, they're not gay," the receptionist said.

"What?"

"Not gay. They're not gay. They're transgendered."

"Trans-what?"

"Transgendered." She nodded toward the group, signaling for me to get another peek. "Those fraternity boys used to be sorority girls."

As Grammy Annie-Lou would say, my mouth was picking up flies. That's country people speak for: it was wide open as the landscape before me redeveloped into a new reality.

Armed with the party room number, I'm sure my face was painted in colors called shock red and crimson awe as I made my way back halfway through the strange promenade to get to the elevators. All those muscular arms, perfect jawlines, tight bums in designer suits, the delicious opus of masculine energy was . . . a group of women turned men? I traded my previous saunter for a humble creep. I couldn't care less if no one looked at me now. Wait . . . they weren't checking for me either. . . .

Ian opened the door before I could knock.

"I thought you were coming earlier," he barked in a tight-jawed whisper.

"Umm . . . can I get a hello first?"

Ian was just as I had left him. All height and all muscle. He was six feet nine and so naturally in shape I never once heard him mention going to anyone's gym. When we'd met during orientation freshman year at Florida A&M, I was sure he was a basketball player—I think the team even tried to recruit him—but Ian Dupree's head has always been in his books.

"Yeah . . . whatever . . . *hello*." Ian quickly pulled me into the suite. There was a little sitting area set up before a hallway that led to the main dining room. I could see that the room was already half full.

"People are already here?" I asked.

"It's eight fifteen."

"The party started at eight," I pointed out with surprise in my voice.

Ian gave me one of his looks. He had baby cheeks and penny-colored eyes that matched his skin. He was more cute than handsome. We'd become fast friends after that orientation at FAMU. He loved that I was from the country and didn't ever know anything he was talking about. I loved that he was from New Orleans (a big city to me) and seemed to know everything no one was talking about. With one of his books in his back pocket, we'd walk through campus debating the world. He had all the information. I had the neurotic opinions. Ian never seemed to notice all the girls standing around looking at him with thirsty eyes. I'd play into it. Laugh like he'd just said something really funny, link arms with him, and stare past their needy ciphers like we were so connected we couldn't see them. My roommate said I had a crush on him, but really I just liked the attention of walking around the yard with the cutest guy on campus and I figured I was keeping Ian single until the right woman came along.

"Come on, Ian. Who comes to an eight o'clock party before nine in Atlanta? If the invitation says eight, that means they'll still be setting up at eight. It's just courteous to get there at nine."

"Sure," Ian said. "Well, Scarlet's friends got news

of the proposal, and by seven thirty they were lined up outside like it was the running of the bulls."

Right then, I wanted to say something sweet to congratulate Ian on his big move, but I was still trying to figure out how to convince him to call the proposal off. Journey was right—I had to support my friend, but if he called it off himself, I'd have nothing to support.

"How'd they find out?" I asked.

"I told Scarlet's best friend."

"Yeah, that'll do it." I looked into the room of well-dressed, wide-eyed women and realized that Ian hadn't moved to go inside. "You nervous?"

"Not really . . . I'm just . . . I can't believe this is it. The big step! The *biggest* step!" Ian peered into the room like he was in a trance. There was a cake in the middle of the table. Champagne bottles and flutes were scattered all around. "It's surreal. Kind of exciting. Like bungee jumping or skydiving!" He reached into his back pocket and pulled out a book.

"What's that?"

"It's called *The Psychology of Love*. I've been reading it all day and it says that it's normal for people to feel like this before making such a big decision to move forward."

Ian was pacing and rolling the little book up in his hands.

"Feel like what?"

"Feel like—" Ian stopped and looked at me like I'd asked the dumbest question in the world. "Nervous! Yes, Rach, I'm nervous! I mean, I really love Scarlet, but this is a lot." He looked so helpless.

"Ian—" I snatched the book and threw it to the floor. "Look, this is about love. Not something you read in a book. Not jumping from a plane in a parachute or a bridge with a rope tied to your waist. It's about experiencing the kind of love that makes you feel so free that you're flying and you can't even worry about where your feet will land, because you don't intend on ever touching the ground again. That's what getting engaged is about," I say, lost in the moment as I considered the concept for myself. "Finding an angel that's so wonderful, so amazing, that you want to fly with her forever. That you want to ask her to fly with you forever."

"Damn, Rach! Can you ask Scarlet to marry me?"

"Oh loverboy!" One of the girls from inside of the party who I thought was Scarlet's roommate poked her head outside of the dining room. "I just got word that Scarlet's on her way upstairs. It's show time!"

A collection of cheers jabbed into my gut as the girl came out and pulled Ian and me into the party.

"Let's go," she insisted.

A massive crystal chandelier perched atop the circular mahogany dining table set glints of brilliant light over the heads of the sixteen smiling, overdressed people scattered around the room. I was able to count so quickly because everyone was coupled up. All of Scarlet's friends were in that particular mid-twentyish age range where their perky breasts and ability to stay up all night helped them snag a mid-thirtyish age range brother who was so amazed he could still get a girl so young he immediately gave her the title "girlfriend" and took her everywhere he went, like a new puppy or fast car. Unfortunately, in two years they'd all find out that these men had no intention of marrying them. And end up at age thirty jaded and alone. I was speaking from experience.

"You didn't tell me there'd only be couples here," I whispered to Ian, but really I should've expected this. There was something about people in their mid-twenties and late thirties and not wanting to go anywhere alone.

"She's getting off the elevator!" someone shouted and everyone started to duck down and hide beneath and behind things.

Ian grabbed my hand and pulled me beneath the table. For a second, I looked into his eyes. In the shaded darkness he looked like a little boy playing hide-and-seek. Suddenly I remembered every small, magical moment I'd ever had with this man. Breakups. Breakdowns. He'd always been there for me. My confidant. My homie. My best friend.

"You ready for this?" I asked, not letting go of his hand.

He looked at me and winked with the nervousness he'd had just minutes ago gone from his face.

"Yes," he said. "I am." He winked again. "I do."

Ian's birthday surprise cover plan, as he'd told me over lunch the week before, was for Scarlet's best friend, who was visiting from California, to say she needed to stop by her hotel room to pick up something. They'd open the door, we'd jump out. Everyone would be excited.

This all went off without a snag, but when I saw Scarlet decked out in a black fascinator hat with purple ostrich feathers poking out the top, I knew she was clued in to both the party and Ian's ring.

No woman would waste a hat that obnoxious on dinner with her girlfriend.

Still, Scarlet was the perfect pretender. She placed her skinny fingers over her skinny lips and squealed like a little piglet.

"For me?" she said like Scarlett O'Hara. "All this just for me?"

Someone pushed Ian to the front like a lamb to slaughter.

"You did this for me, baby?" Scarlet batted her little eyes at Ian.

"Yes, honey. Happy Birthday!" Ian kissed Scarlet on the cheek and the crowd cooed like a room full of babies. They even made him do it again so they could get a picture.

Scarlet pulled Ian by the hand around the room as she sighed and squealed with her friends about the surprise party. I poured myself a generous flute of champagne and spied from the darkest corner I could find to watch Ian for the look of love Journey had asked about. He was smiling big. Had his arm around Scarlet's shoulder and rubbed just a little when she was talking and not paying attention to him.

"Rachel! You're Rachel Winslow! Right?" One of the women, who'd been left solo when her boyfriend went to huddle with the rest of the guys by the wall window that let all the twinkling lights from midtown Atlanta traffic into the room, had walked over to my corner.

"Yes," I said, putting the flute down on the little wooden table beside me.

"I'm Jennifer. Scarlet told me Ian was friends with you. Amazing. I saw you on the *Wendy Williams Show* in December."

"November."

"What?"

"The show aired in November," I pointed out over a cackle coming from Scarlet across the room. Ian's hand fell to her waist.

"Oh. OK." Jennifer took a sip from her flute as if that was all she had to say. Or maybe that was the point in the conversation where I was supposed to ask her something, but I didn't because I knew what was coming next. She turned to look longingly at her boyfriend standing in the huddle like he was a football field away. "You here by yourself?" she asked. "No date?"

"No," I said. "I'm a friend of Ian's. And I'm here with you guys."

"No . . ." Jennifer laughed a little. "You know what I mean. Like 'alone.' Like with no date."

"You got me! No date tonight!" I picked up my flute and sipped the last little bit of champagne left so I'd have an excuse to walk away.

"How brave of you, sister! I remember those days. Being single and just out there. Living life out loud!" She turned back to stare into the huddle. "But then I found my man and everything in my life changed." Her voice sank way too deep for a cocktail party conversation. I just love him so much."

"Yay for love." I pumped my fist and sounded decidedly obnoxious. "You're so lucky. How long have you two been together."

"Three months! But it feels like three lifetimes." She waved at him like he was going to try to escape if she forgot to keep an eye on him. "You know, they say the true way to build a strong black nation is to get married. Have a family."

"Really? Where'd you hear that?"

"A class I'm taking . . . grad school."

Ian's hand had retreated to his pocket. Scarlet slipped away and was taking pictures with her girlfriends again.

"Don't worry. Your ship is coming in for sure. Your life is all about love. You breathe it every day." Jennifer leaned into me. "It must be hard seeing all those people in love when you're not."

Ian turned around in my gaze and gave me a weak smile before shrugging his shoulders.

"I mean, you do want love, right?" Jennifer asked. "You're not like . . . you know . . . a—"

"Yes, I want love," I said. "But something real. Not just someone I can take to cocktail parties and pose in pictures with."

"Oh yeah," Jennifer said distantly and just then I realized she wasn't listening to a word I was saying. "Hey, can you hold my purse?" She turned and handed me her little hot pink clutch before rushing over to grab her boyfriend's hand and dragging him into one of the pictures that had claimed Ian as well.

From where I was standing behind them, I could see Ian reach into his back pocket and finger his book. His head tilted away from Scarlet, he pulled the book up a bit, then pushed it back down when she laced her arm around his waist.

"My sister!" Scarlet came to me with her arms outstretched after dispersing from the photo op. "So glad you could make it out to my little surprise birthday party!" She hugged me so tightly it felt like a chiropractic back adjustment. Ian nearly had to pull us apart.

"Oh, Ian was so excited. I wanted to support

him. To support both of you," I said, watching Ian. The confidence he'd grown in his eyes was wavering. I saw bungee cords in his pupils.

"Yeah, this beautiful black man!" Scarlet pinched Ian's cheek. "I can't believe he planned all this behind my back. Such a blessing. But it's no wonder. You know, I've been so busy organizing the girls I mentor at the Sankofa Institute. That keeps me away so much. I'm just happy my loving kingman puts up with all my volunteer work."

"Ian's always been quite the understanding *kingman*. My bestie," I said, nudging Ian in the gut.

He nodded rather mechanically. When Ian and Scarlet had started dating he used to complain about some of her half-baked ideas about the world, about politics and revolution. She was in a place where we used to be when we were in our early twenties and still thinking we could save the world by building one house with Habitat for Humanity. Then we'd gotten real jobs and had bigger fish to fry. Not that we didn't want to build the house. That was important work. But our days bragging about it were long gone. And time to commit to it was just plain limited. Sometimes Ian dragged me out for drinks to get away from Scarlet's philosophizing about things she only half understood.

"*My* kingman." Scarlet pinched his cheek again. "What about you, Rachel? Do you think you could find some time to come down to the institute to work with the girls? I know you're really busy with your business and all, but they could use someone like you there—you know, you grew up poor in the country, first in your family to go to college—that kind of thing. They'd relate to you."

Scarlet was holding my arm the entire time she

spoke. Ian had pulled that little book out of his back pocket and I was thinking maybe it wasn't me she should be holding onto.

"You OK, Ian?" I asked.

"Yeah. Yeah." He fanned himself with the little book. "Just a little hot in here."

"Yeah, babe." Scarlet fanned Ian with one hand without stopping to look at him. "Speaking of hot, Ian tells me you have a new beau who kept you out last night so you couldn't join us at Masquerade." She grinned at me with pursed lips like I was her old aunty who'd somehow stumbled upon a boyfriend.

"Really? I have a beau?"

"Yeah, that's what Ian said." She was pointing at him now, but still not looking. "It's not true?" Now she was looking like I was her old aunt who'd just been pushed in front of a bus. Her black and purple fascinator suddenly became a funeral mourning hat. She shot me a complimentary sad face.

Ian rolled his eyes to suggest that I simply agree with Scarlet.

"Oh . . . beau? Beau? You mean a boyfriend?" I asked.

"Yes, a boyfriend!" Scarlet's smile returned.

"Yes, I do have a boyfriend. See, I don't speak French," I said with a bit of hidden sarcasm I was sure would make Ian laugh, but he didn't.

He rolled up his little book some more. Wiped a bead of sweat from his forehead.

Scarlet frowned and then smiled tightly like maybe I'd just been disinvited from visiting the Institute on account of my not knowing what "beau" meant.

"Ian, you sure you're all right?" I asked again. The color was slipping from his face.

Scarlet finally turned to him.

"Actually, you know what, Rachel, can I talk to you in the other room?" Ian asked.

"But we're about to cut the cake," Scarlet said. "I mean . . . aren't you all about to cut the cake for me?"

"In a minute, babe," Ian said. "I just need to talk to Rachel."

"But what about my big birthday surprise?" Scarlet smirked coyly like a seven-year-old. I'd seen Ian fall to his knees for this display from her before.

"In a second, hon," he said in a way that clearly shocked both Scarlet and me. "Rach—" He grabbed my arm and pulled me out of the room before Scarlet could find another reason to disagree.

On the other side of the suite was a king-sized bedroom Ian had decorated with rose petals all over the floor and bed, and white taper candles on the nightstand. It was clichéd, but much more than I'd ever expect from Ian.

"What's up with you?" I asked, standing alone in the room with Ian after he'd closed the door behind us. "And why in the world did you lie and tell Scarlet I had a boyfriend?"

"I can't do this, Rach! I can't!" He threw the book onto the bed.

"Can't what?" I knew what I was thinking he was saying, but I needed to confirm that he was saying what I was thinking.

"I can't!"

"Can't what?"

"You know I didn't even tell my parents? Who gets engaged without telling their parents? I can't.

They're gonna hate this. They're gonna hate her. My mother hasn't even met Scarlet. Oh shit!"

"Can't what?"

"And you know why I haven't told them about her? I didn't because I was afraid—I was afraid they'd try to talk me out of it."

"Out of what?"

"Asking Scarlet to marry me, Rach," Ian said, falling onto the bed. "I can't ask her to marry me."

"You can't?" (Hiding my excitement here was quite difficult. But considering the distraught look on Ian's face, with him laid out on the bed like a man about to undergo open heart surgery, I couldn't break out the streamers and balloons just yet.)

"It's just not right. There's something that's not right!"

I stood in front of Ian on the bed with my arms crossed.

"What's not right? This morning you called me all excited about the ring from Namibia. What happened?"

"Don't play with me, Rachel. You know she's not right for me. Maybe now isn't the time." Ian shot up and stood beside me. "There's something missing. Something just missing from us."

"Something like what?"

A rap sounded at the door and one of Scarlet's happy friends poked her head into the room.

"We're almost ready for the surprise!" she whispered. "About to cut the cake, too!"

Ian was frozen.

"We'll be out in a minute," I said.

She closed the door slowly and reluctantly.

I looked back at Ian. We'd been in these kinds

of standoffs together in the past: sophomore year when he caught his girlfriend cheating on him with some muscly Omega in a bar in Tallahassee and I had to stop him from going off and losing his first fight; senior year when I was cheating on my boyfriend with a muscly Omega in a motel room in Tallahassee and called Ian from the bathroom for help when my boyfriend knocked on the door (ten minutes later, Ian pulled up in back of the motel and I climbed out the bathroom window).

"What are you going to do?" I asked.

"I can't do it, Rachel." Ian looked into my eyes.

"I'll get you out of here if you want me to. We'll walk right out the door. But I need you to be clear about what you're doing," I said. "That girl in there—all those people in there are expecting you to get down on one knee and propose."

"I know."

We looked to the balcony outside the glass doors beside the bed.

"It's the tenth floor," he said mordantly and we laughed.

"And we're a little too old to be escaping from hotel rooms."

Ian walked to the doors and looked outside.

"I can't do this to Scarlet," he said. "I know you hate her, but it'll really hurt her. She's worth more to me than that."

"I don't hate—"

"She'll be devastated. I don't want to be that guy in her past. The one who—made her jaded like most of the other women I know."

And there was Ian being the man I knew—always complex. Always caring for someone else. Sometimes, I thought that was what kept him going with Scarlet—for all of her perfection, she needed him for something. To hold her hand. To be her cherry on top.

"So?"

Ian turned back to me.

"You know," he started, "Scarlet obviously knows about the ring—"

"Obviously—"

"But she doesn't know that I know that she knows. She still thinks it's supposed to be a surprise."

I nodded along with his twisted thinking.

"And—"

This time the friend didn't knock. She burst into the door and grabbed Ian.

"It's time," she whined . . . or growled.

I grabbed for Ian's other hand, but he leaned into the girl.

"Don't worry," Ian said. "I know what to do."

These black people had formed an actual runway from the bedroom to the dining table where the lit birthday cake was waiting beside a beaming Scarlet. The shiny silver cake knife was on the table beside the cake. Everything was quiet and slow-moving as the friend led us down the gauntlet to the sacrificial table. Like we were mobsters walking into the coffee shop in Little Italy where we were about to become made men—or dead men. Folks were holding out iPhones ready to snap pictures and record the scene. Whatever Ian had up his sleeve, I hoped it was good. Suddenly, that tenth-floor balcony escape wasn't looking too bad. Scarlet was from Buckhead, but she was still a sister. There was no telling what she'd do in this situation. Too bad I'd disobeyed Grammy Annie-Lou's advice and left home without my framing knife—I felt the bottom of my purse to be sure.

"Happy birthday to you—happy birthday to you!" they all sang so happily once Ian had made his way to Scarlet.

The color in Ian's face was gone. He was a white man. Was he planning to faint? Good stuff.

Scarlet blew out the candles. Posed for more pictures. Thanked everyone for such a nice surprise. The place got quiet as a funeral parlor.

The girlfriend beside Ian nudged him—visibly.

He ignored her, but then she said, "And Ian, don't you have a surprise for Scarlet?"

"A surprise?" Ian smiled and everyone laughed like he was a dear old dad holding out on the keys to some sixteen-year-old's first car. "Yes, I do have a surprise—a surprise for my sweetheart." He took Scarlet's had and the cameras started rolling.

"Really?" Scarlet shrugged like she was completely caught off guard.

"Yes. Scarlet," Ian said, "I love you and I want to know if you would—" He stopped.

"What, baby?" Scarlet pushed. "What do you want to know?"

Was he about to ask her anyway? Now I was about to pretend faint. Was that the plan?

"I want to know if you would join me"—he paused again—"on a two-week vacation to"—he did a little two-step that impressed no one in the crowd—"Hawaii!"

"Hawaii?" Scarlet repeated with a half smile on her face, her left hand mistakenly extended. "Hawaii?"

"Hawaii?" The word was said in different ways around the room—none good.

"Hawaii!" I cheered and clapped like I was going. "Oh . . . that's so great!"

Had Scarlet's eyes have been guns, she would've shot bullets right through my neck.

Ian clapped along with me for the big sell.

"All inclusive!" he added. "Drinks and food!"

"Yo, that's what's up?" her roommate's boyfriend said before the roommate elbowed him in the gut. "What? That must've cost the brother a grip." He raised his glass and then, like hostages unsure of what else to do, everyone else did, too, one by one—everyone but Scarlet. She was looking at her boyfriend and thinking so hard I could see her brain moving around beneath her pretty little hat.

"So?" the roommate's boyfriend opened again. "Do you want to go to Hawaii?"

"Yeah, do you?" someone else behind me asked.

Scarlet looked down at her feet pensively. There was no way to know if she'd started to cry. Her shoulders were shaking. She took one of Ian's hands into both of hers.

Ian looked at me for a second and I knew he felt terrible.

"Do you?" someone else asked.

"Ian," Scarlet said with her eyes moving from her feet right to Ian's eyes. "You know, I think I would like to take that all-inclusive trip with you to Hawaii."

Ian's face brightened. All around me let out the breath they'd been holding in.

"I would like to go," Scarlet went on, "but . . . but only if it's as husband and wife."

"What?" I'm nearly certain this was me.

"What I'm trying to say, Ian, is that it's 2011. I'm an independent, educated, and successful sister.

And I'm not ashamed to say that I'm in love with you and I want to marry you. Times have changed and, as a woman, I want to ask you to be my husband."

The cameras around me started rolling again as Scarlet tried to get down on one knee to ask Ian to marry her.

Shocked as he was, Ian's mouth was just as wide as mine had been in the lobby earlier, but he didn't let Scarlet get down on her knee. He pulled her back up: "Will you marry me?" she asked.

I was standing there praying to God and everything holy that Ian said yes. Really, I'd actually seen this a few times in my years working in nuptials, and when a woman proposes and a man declines, there's simply no savvy recovery. She leaves there let down and goes to the insane asylum and then from there to her grave. I didn't want him to marry Scarlet, but to say no right then would ruin her and the dreams of every woman in that room. He could say yes now and then no later.

And when I looked at Ian, I knew this was what he was about to do—the first part, anyway—because he was looking at Scarlet like she was all new and smelling like spring again. His color was back. His hands were confident at his sides. He looked, well, happy.

"Yes," he said. "I will marry you."

It would take me some years to understand that Ian didn't say yes to Scarlet just because he couldn't say no. Birds of a feather flock together and, as I was looking for love, Ian wanted to believe he was already in love. That the feelings that had him rolling up that poor little book weren't real doubt, but real fear—something that would dissipate, go away, once he realized that he was doing the right thing. Right or wrong, so many of my clients, so many of my friends, had gone to the altar using the same logic. Thinking that the love they wanted would conquer all. I wouldn't admit it myself, but if I was in the same position—ready to get married and had the person I thought I loved standing in front of me asking for my hand in marriage—I might've done the same thing.

In the end, only time would give the answers in Ian's case. As the crowd of awkward smiles closed in upon him and Scarlet, cheering, I realized that the time for questions was over. I picked up a champagne flute and joined in. Kissed Scarlet on the cheek and winked softly at Ian. Posed for pictures, slid off my heels, and walked to my car, vowing to never again bring up the escape plan we'd discussed in the bedroom at the W Hotel.

2
"No 'Settle for' Man"

#IlovewhatIdobut: But when you love love like I do, it's hard to listen to two people who probably aren't in love and shouldn't be getting married, explain why they're in love and are getting married.

"I would fucking kill someone for her! You know what I'm sayin'? Shoot a nigga right between his eyes, yo!"

Alarm Clock is a rapper who seems to like to remain on my client list. After Journey and Dame introduced us a few years ago, I'd arranged every detail for his first two marriages to a backup dancer and video model respectively, and now he was in my office for our first consultation to plan his third.

I'd opened the meeting by asking the pair how they met. Donnica, a beautiful girl with a body that made me promise myself that I'd go to the gym as soon as I left the office, was a nail technician where Alarm's last child's mother (not a wife) was getting a pedicure in Miami. She'd volunteered to give Alarm a shoulder massage in a back room while he waited for his baby mama.

My second question was why they'd fallen in love with each other.

Alarm always seemed to equate love with murder. He knew he was in love with his first wife because he was going to kill her if she tried to leave him (he eventually left her), he knew he loved his second wife because he'd die trying to protect her from harm (he didn't), he knew he loved Donnica because he'd kill someone for her.

"Know what I'm saying?" he asked me.

"Well, no. I actually don't know what you're saying" I said, sitting on the opposite side of my desk in my midtown office with Alarm and Donnica. They were my third of four consults before lunch and I was getting tired of nodding along. Actually loving the couple whose wedding you're planning is kind of like finding a really great book you know you'll forever cherish and remember. When it happens, it makes the less likable and "well, I could've done something much better with all that time" books bearable and actually a great litmus test through which to determine how much you actually love what you love.

I actually liked Alarm Clock. While he seemed infatuated with murder in both his music and conversation, he was like me. He wanted to find love and still believed it was possible. After four children and two failed marriages, he was still willing to say "I do." It wasn't the most gangster thing he could do with his time, but he was trying.

"What about you, Ms. Grant—Donnica?" I turned to the bride with the two-million-dollar ring on her airbrushed French manicured fingernails. "Why did you fall in love with Zachariah?" (Rappers always have the funniest first names.)

"He real good to his sons. I ain't got no kids, but grandmamma always told me that if you want to know how a man will treat you, watch how he treat his mama and his kids."

And although Donnica's grandmother's advice seemed to assume every man her granddaughter would meet would already have children, it was sound rhetoric that made me believe these two had a chance, so I said, "That's great advice. Now tell me: how do you two envision your wedding day?" I already knew what Alarm envisioned, but I didn't want to bring up the past—and then this happened:

Donnica: "We got to have a chocolate fountain! Fruit at a chocolate fountain."

Forget the music, forget the women, forget the pants hanging down below their asses—the only problem I have with rappers is how they spend their money. Yes, you can get a Maybach if you have the money, but don't get Burberry's signature print spray-painted on the hood. Yes, you can move into an eastside estate, but your first order of business need not be to install inside and outside basketball courts and a pitbull kennel. Yes, you can get married at Musha Cay, the most luxurious and expensive private island in the southern Bahamas, but no, you won't have a chocolate fountain—not if I'm planning it. Golden Corral has a chocolate fountain. My home church in Social Circle had a chocolate fountain at the Easter revival. They sell chocolate fountains at CVS. It's over. Let it go.

"I saw a chocolate fountain on *Real Housewives of*

Atlanta, and I wanted one at my wedding," Donnica went on.

"Will you shut the fuck up about that damn chocolate fountain?" Zachariah spat out, sounding more like Alarm Clock. "I told you my girl Rachel gonna plan everything. Keep shit classy. Fucking chocolate fountain is mad ghetto. Tell her, Rachel."

Alarm sat up and pointed at me.

"Well, no," I delicately answered, looking at Donnica, who was holding onto Alarm like she and I were two hens in a house with one rooster. "I wouldn't say it's ghetto to want a chocolate fountain. I'm just sure we can come up with something a little more sophisticated together." Something that speaks to where this couple is going (a divorce paper fountain?). "To where you're going, Donnica."

"What you mean?" she asked.

"Well, sweetheart, you're about to be married to one of the most powerful performers in the world," I said. "You won't be trying to snag a rich man like those allegedly married women on all those reality shows. You've got one. You're it. You're better than a chocolate fountain."

Alarm grinned while Donnica looked into nowhere at the possibilities.

"That's why I fucks with you, Rachel!" Alarm said. "See, baby, you gotta think about where we going!"

Donnica nodded and then asked, "Whatever . . . well, what about the horse and carriage? I always wanted to have a horse and carriage at my wedding. You know, with one of those pumpkin carriages that lights up—like in Cinderella?"

"What the fuck?" Alarm fell back, deflated, in his seat.

"What? What the fuck is wrong with that?" Donnica snapped back at Alarm. "It's my fucking wedding. She fucking asked. Fuck! I don't understand why we got to be answering all these fucking questions anyway. Uggh." Donnica sucked her teeth, rolled her neck, and looked out the window in disgust.

"Well, Donnica, the thing is, I work on inspiration. You tell me what you like and I use what I know to finesse it into something you'll love. Something you'll never forget."

"Fuck. I don't see why we couldn't just get married in Miami anyway," Donnica said, getting up from the chair and walking to the window with a sad, pouty face.

"Oh shit." Alarm sank farther and spoke so only I could hear him. "Here we go with this again."

Donnica started crying and went on about wanting everyone in Liberty City to see her marry her prince charming. And how it wasn't right that all her cousins couldn't be there.

Alarm was shaking his head at first, but then he started looking at her like he was a man in love. He got up and went over to the window.

I sat back and watched the drama unfold. Planning a wedding is very emotional. Most of my clients, even the best ones, have these moments right in front of me. It's usually best to just sit back and let it happen.

He grabbed for her. She pushed him away. He kissed her shoulder. She cried some more. He kissed her chin. She shuddered. They started kissing like that was how you had an orgasm.

Just as I was about to throw my bottled water on them, Krista, my assistant who'd probably heard the overuse of "fuck" a few minutes ago, poked her head into the doorway and announced my next consult.

A. J. Holmes had quickly become the most popular black face in news when he got his own show on CNN. Everyone was sad that he'd replaced the network's first black female to have her own show, Sasha Bellamy, after she got a little power hungry and ended up getting fired, but A. J. was to news what Obama had been to politics—what everyone wanted to see, when everyone wanted to see it. Somehow, even through television, you had a sense that you knew him, that you liked him, that he was a great guy who really cared about the world.

I was more than excited when one of my clients called the day before my meeting with A. J. to request what I call a "trade out" with A. J. Because my calendar is booked for three years solid, many clients who aren't engaged yet but pay annually to keep their spot "trade out" as a gift to a newly engaged friend. In return, the client gets the first next spot available on my calendar and a refund of the money they've paid, so long as the new client pays in full before the consult.

While I was in a NyQuil coma, A. J. had asked his fiancée Dawn to marry him on national television during a CNN taping of the ball drop at Times Square. Getting him on my list as a trade out was a godsend. The space he was taking was promised during the fourth quarter of the year. The winter wedding of CNN's darling star. The press would be all over it. I'd be booked for three more years now. But that wasn't what interested me most.

"So how did you two meet?" I asked, looking at A. J. and Dawn in my office.

When they'd walked in, his hand was on the small of her back. He waited for her to sit down. When Krista offered them something to drink, he asked Dawn what she wanted and then requested two of the same.

Dawn didn't look like what I'd expect A. J. to go for—a man who literally had his hand on the remote control to the world. She looked a little homely. Had on a respectable Target dress with actual flesh-toned stockings and blush on her cheeks. But still, just by looking at her, it was easy to know what he loved about her. "Going for" someone and "loving someone" were two different things. Being in this business for so many years, I'd learned fast that there was no formula to explain how and why people made their choices in love. Sure, the rappers and newly famed actors and ballplayers typically went for the Barbie types, but the ones I found who were truly in love at the altar picked what you must have thought they'd want their mother or some version of her to have looked like when she was their age and getting married. Soft eyes. A humble smile. Shoulders not low or high but right in line with his.

"I was married before," Dawn said, pursing her lips like she was in confession. "And right in the middle of my divorce, this man came in and threw me a life vest. He saved me." Dawn put her hand on A. J.'s knee.

"Well, that was after she beat up one of my

coworkers," A. J. said and they laughed like she'd just said something I wasn't supposed to hear.

"I did not beat her up!" Dawn's eyes and smile were on A. J. and then she turned to me. "His coworker, my college roommate, who shall remain nameless, was having an affair with my husband . . . and I came to the job to gently ask her to back off."

"Wow!" I said. "Sounds like some drama there!"

"Yeah, it sure was, but even through that, I saw my baby and was like, yeah, she's what I've been looking for. What I've been missing." A. J. lifted Dawn's hand from his knee and kissed it. "See, I was dating at the time, but none of those relationships seemed to be going where I wanted them to go. A few dinners here. A movie. A play. Whatever. A broken promise. It just didn't feel right. But as soon as I saw Dawn I just knew. She was everything I was looking for. She loves her children and she loved her marriage enough to put everything on the line to fight for it. You don't find that nowadays. And she was just like me. Real. No pretense. I know everything I need to know about her by looking into her eyes."

There was quiet while I was trying to catch my breath as I thought, "Is he for real?"

"Wow," I said again. "I guess you just answered my second question, A. J." I grinned and turned to Dawn. "What do you love about A. J.?"

Dawn's eyes pooled with tears, as though she and A. J. were at the altar and I was officiating. A. J. rubbed her back as she wiped a few tears sneaking from the corners of her eyes. When she spoke, her voice was fractured and honest.

"I didn't think this was love. I can't explain it. I

just didn't even think this was what love was," she said. "Like everyday. Someone who cares and listens to my needs and, my God, takes me seriously. Holds me. And doesn't stop. It's every day. I don't have to ask. He showed me that love isn't connected to power. That it should be free, and accessible, and honorable. And that gave me the permission to give him all of that back and not even think about the result. He's given me a real love that I can give back. And being through what I've been through, that's more than a reason to say I love this man."

My eyes were as glassy as Dawn's. I was without words again for the second time after sitting with this pair for less than ten minutes. Was she serious? This was it. This was why I was doing what I was doing. People always ask me what the difference is between couples who make it five months and those who make it a lifetime—well, here it is. Honesty. Surrendering your heart.

A. J. and Dawn explained that they wanted a small wedding. One that Dawn's twins could enjoy and remember. Nothing too fancy or exotic. But they wanted the best. And they heard I could give that to them.

"So when are you thinking about doing this?" I asked, already envisioning these two jumping the broom at an old plantation house in the North Georgia Mountains where their entire family could stay over the night before. I looked up from the pad I'd been writing on. "I only do one wedding a season—it allows me to focus. Your trade slot is in the winter. Any dates you've been considering?" I looked directly at Dawn. Usually the brides had such details.

But A. J. answered, "Well, we were considering New Year's Eve."

"Yes. One year exactly from the engagement," Dawn added.

"I see. Well, I don't commonly take appointments during the holidays," I said. "It's a personal limitation. I try to keep that time open so I can spend it with family. Friends. You understand?"

"Oh . . . We didn't even think of that," Dawn said. "Of course." She laughed. "Why wouldn't you? While we were out getting engaged on New Year's Eve, you were probably out somewhere fabulous. A ball with your"—she looked at my bare ring finger—"boyfriend?"

"Not exactly," I said. "But—"

The magical couple looked into me with eager, hopeful eyes. I so, too, wanted to be playing on their team.

"But—close." (What was that?)

"Ohhh!" they both gasped.

"I knew it!" A. J. said. "You probably have half the guys in the city chasing you. The one you love is so lucky."

"That was so sweet to say," Dawn said to A. J. She turned and kissed him on the cheek.

He leaned into her and put his hand over her hand on his leg.

"We understand," Dawn went on. "You have to keep some limitations. We were just thinking: it's a new year, and we want to have the wedding on that day to symbolize our new life. Us starting out together, as a family, in our new lives."

When Dawn said "family," the twosome nestled closer together.

"We'll just think of another date," A. J. said. "Maybe in October?"

I hate the entire month of October. It's a month of nothing. It comes in between the beautiful unraveling of summer in September and the final push of fall in November. Basically, all it does is hold people waiting until its very last day so they can dress up like demons and witches. It was an in-between thing. A. J. and Dawn were on to something. They needed a beginning.

"I'll look into some things," I said before Dawn could answer A. J.'s question about October. "See what I can do about New Year's."

"Really?" Dawn looked like she was about to pop out of her seat and hug me. "Seriously? For us?"

"Yes. I'll see about it. I'll give you two a call later this week to confirm."

Dawn jumped out of her seat. She came around to my seat and hugged me tightly.

"I just had to give you a hug. Thank you so much," she said, pulling me to my feet.

Then A. J. came around, too, and all three of us were hugging.

"Thank you," he said.

"It's no problem, really," I said in their embrace.

"Thank you."

"Thank you."

I felt like we'd all just gotten engaged.

My first love had driven a red Ford pickup truck—big time in Social Circle in 1990. His name was Chauncey Billups. He was big and strong and so black Grammy Annie-Lou wouldn't let him sit on our front steps—in the country, after you pass a certain age, sitting on a girl's front step is a sign you're courting her and Grammy Annie-Lou wasn't having that. When I was thirteen, Grammy Annie-Lou told me Chauncey and his people were too "damn black and country"—all that when his house was less than a mile from ours, which in Social Circle meant our families once lived on the same plantation. They just lived a little farther back from the Irving plantation house that was now separated from the rest of our homes by fences and dirt roads and served as a museum and café for visitors coming to Social Circle to buy sweet onions and see the "old South."

Grammy Annie-Lou's house was closer to the plantation because her grandfather had been the blacksmith for old "master" Redeem Irving, whom he'd actually grown up with, and had become his card partner who always "won low"—how they say we got our last name. Family myth says Reedem and my great-great-grandfather were actually half-brothers. Chauncey Billups's family lived farther from the house. His great-great-grandparents were sharecroppers and every line of his family since were farmers—he'd actually be the first in his family to go to college when he left Social Circle to go to the University of Georgia and become an agricultural scientist. Well, Grammy Annie-Lou didn't know anything about the University of Georgia being in Chauncey's future when we were fifteen and making eyes at each other in school. And she didn't want to hear anything about "that black Billups boy." But, as they say, "What you want the least will come to you the easiest." I was my mother's only child. She died when I was just three months old. Social Circle in the 1980s was like the rest of the world in the 1880s, so my father immediately tried to marry someone else, but it didn't work. His heart was too broken so he went home to live with his mama. By the time I was a teenager, I was ready to rebel and tired of the two of them fawning all over me. Chauncey was just what I wanted.

He'd just gotten his driver's license and his father gave him his old rusty red Ford that had been sitting in their backyard since forever. But Chauncey fixed it up and got it on the road. One day, he drove up to my house and didn't come up on the stoop, but he honked the horn and said, "Hey, little gal, you wanna ride?" Shit, I was in that car faster than a fly. We went everywhere. And soon we were secret boyfriend and girlfriend. He took my virginity in the front seat, and I didn't know anything about birth control, so I got pregnant. I also didn't know anything about being pregnant, so I didn't know what was going on until I was sitting in church between my father and Grammy Annie-Lou and saw red everywhere on my dress. Grammy Annie-Lou dragged me to the bathroom thinking it was my period, but I wouldn't stop bleeding. The blood was everywhere. Soon the bathroom was filled with women. Mama Billups, too. They didn't tell me what was going on. They had me stand over the top of the toilet with my legs wide apart. I remember that Grammy Annie-Lou didn't look worried anymore. She looked afraid. They all did. When we walked outside the bathroom on our way to my father's car, he was standing right at the door. "Who done this to you?" he demanded. "You tell your father!" Grammy Annie-Lou pushed him back. "Leave her alone, Robert. Now is not the time. We've got to get this girl to the hospital. Move back!" She pushed again and the women made a circle around me.

The next morning, I woke up in my bed with a bedpan on the nightstand. At the hospital, the doctor had said I'd had a miscarriage. Grammy Annie-Lou was asleep in a chair beside the bed. I heard my father's voice out front on the porch. He wasn't yelling, but I could hear his anger. I limped—for no reason other than that I thought I should—to the window. Chauncey was standing at the foot of the steps. My father was at the top. The old red Ford was parked in the dirt road in front of the steps. I pressed my ear to the window so I could hear. "You took my best thing from me. The only thing I have that's worth anything. The only thing I love," my father said. "A man can't take something from another man without paying for it." Chauncey didn't respond. I looked to see him stand straighter. "You ruined my girl," my father said. "What are you going to do?" Chauncey looked at me in the window. "You look at me, son," my father said. "My daughter ain't about to be no one's good-time gal, so you can take your eyes off her. After high school, she's going off to college. She's too smart to be around here with you. But there's still the matter of what you owe me." Chauncey's eyes left me. He looked down at his pocket. He slid his right hand into his right pocket and pulled out the keys to the Ford. He threw them to my father and that was that. Chauncey obeyed the old-school code and never spoke to me again. My father parked the pickup behind Grammy Annie-Lou's house and never once moved it. Grass and wild onions grew high up under the hood and soon it seemed to be eaten alive by the earth. Our old dog, King, the world's only fat German shepherd, slept under the bed in back.

At my father's funeral last year, Grammy Annie-Lou handed me a piece of folded-up napkin paper. My father had written his will in blue ink on the inside. He owned three things and gave them all to me: a set of tools, King, and the old red Ford. I left the tools and King in Social Circle, but a few months ago, I had the truck hauled to Atlanta with dreams of fixing it up and maybe even giving it back to Chauncey. My father's words were spoken in sadness and tradition and no pickup could ever make up for what that experience did to me . . . to all three of us. And it wasn't all Chauncey's fault. I think my father realized both of those things at some point. But he couldn't return the truck. And Chauncey wouldn't have taken it anyway, back then.

For the last three months, Bird, the owner of the West End auto body shop where the tow truck driver suggested I deliver the Ford, had been working on it, rebuilding everything under that hood that had rotted during all that time out in the yard, making big plans for the red candy paint exterior and bigger plans for the white leather seats and sound system.

"Gonna need to send off for those valves. Can't use what they got at the store. New stuff is crap. Can't put new stuff on an old thing," Bird said, after explaining a list of problems he was having with the engine he'd just finished rebuilding. As usual, the point of the speech was that he needed more parts and more time and more money. He was so particular about everything with the truck, excited about getting it back to its original condition with its original parts.

"And how much are these valves and such going to cost me?" I asked Bird. We were standing in front of the truck in the shop's garage. He'd just finished rolling out from underneath the hood and had some kind of black oil zigzagging down his forehead. He wasn't in shape but had the arms of a man who lifted many heavy things. Looking at him, it was hard not to imagine what those things might be—if maybe I could be one. Maybe it was the tattoos all over his arms. Or his tight T-shirts that showed every mark of hard work on his chest. The seemingly endless reserve of sweat that glistened over his arms whenever I saw him.

"How much you got, Miss Lady?" Bird leaned against the hood and crossed his legs. When he moved like that, it reminded me of Chauncey and the country-boy flirtation he'd used to get me into that truck. Bird tried the same thing. Every week when I stopped by Bird's Auto on Tuesday during my lunch break, he'd lean against the truck with his two gold chains hanging from his neck and ask me out. I wasn't fool enough to fall for his advances. It wasn't anything to take to heart. He was a "cat caller," meaning he'd make a call at any cat . . . any cat.

"Depends on how much you need," I said, matching his tone. It was just our play.

"All that money you got," he said, looking me over from heel to head, "ain't nothing to you. What you got, a million in the bank?"

"Maybe. Maybe not. But it's not truck-fixing money either way."

"Hum . . ." Bird reached out and pinched my

elbow. "When you gonna let me take you out, Miss Lady? You so pretty."

"Come on. You ask me that every week."

"And every week you turn me down."

"So why do you keep asking?"

" 'Cause you keep coming back." Bird pinched my elbow again and wiped the last little trickle of grease from his forehead with his elbow. "Real question is, why you keep saying no?"

"Because, Mr. Bird, I don't mix business with pleasure. And I'm a woman of my word."

Bird chuckled and went inside to get a printout of my invoice from his receptionist. I chuckled, too, and turned to get a look at my real car waiting in the parking lot outside the garage. Ian had just pulled up beside it and was stepping out of his car.

"Ian? What are you doing here?" I looked at my watch. "Is it Wednesday?"

"No, it's not Wednesday," he said, stopping in front of me. "Just wanted to see you. Stopped by the office and Krista said you were over here in the hood." He looked over my shoulder at the truck. "Man, I can't believe you're really fixing that old thing up. I thought you were joking."

"No, I was serious. I'll be on the road in no time."

"Yeah, sitting on the side of the road while you call AAA to come pick you up," he said with a smirk. Ian lectured on Tuesdays, so he was wearing his standard young professor attire: a shirt and tie with a thick retro cardigan with leather patches on the sleeves; jeans; and a paperboy hat. Last year, one of his students took a picture of him lecturing and e-mailed it to a local newspaper that deemed Ian the "sexiest professor in Atlanta" in a special edition of the newspaper. Ian pretended that he hated the idea, but that didn't stop him from collecting at least ten copies and stashing them in his office.

"Very nice, Mr. I Need a New Car Every Year," I teased.

"You're damn skippy! I work too hard dealing with these bad-ass college students to be driving around in something old. I'll take riding in luxury from here to there, please. What, the black man can't have new things?"

"Nothing wrong with old things," Bird said, appearing from behind me with the invoice in hand. "You know what they say about old cars? When the world comes to an end—you know, we drop them bombs on one another and we're all burned to smithereens—two things will be left: roaches and old cars. Built tough." Bird knocked on the hood of the Ford and then extended his hand to Ian. The oil and cuts and whatever on his hand were the perfect contrast to Ian's paws that had hardly managed any upsets aside from a paper cut while grading essays. "I'm Bird, this beautiful lady's mechanic."

"I'm Ian—this crazy lady's friend." Ian tightened his jawline. I guessed he was trying to seem bigger.

"Ian? The brother who's getting married? Congrats, man!" The handshake turned into a brotherly grip with Ian cutting his eyes at me.

"Oh, Rachel is talking about me?"

"I was just telling Bird how excited I am for you," I said.

"No worries, man," Bird said. "Most people don't know it, but the garage is just like a barbershop at times. Me and Miss Lady talk about a little bit of everything. And sometimes a lot of nothing."

Bird and his muscular arms were flirting with me again and my eyes were flirting back.

"Sure," Ian interrupted, poking his head between us—me and the arms. "Hey, 'Miss Lady,' can I talk to you in private for a minute?" he asked. "Bird, it'll only take a moment, then she's all yours and you two can talk about whatever you like."

Bird nodded and Ian pulled me into the parking lot.

"Talk about desperate," Ian said, after pulling me halfway across the parking lot.

"He's not desperate," I said. "He's just country."

Bird was still standing in front of the truck waving at me.

"I wasn't talking about him!"

"What?" I looked at Ian. "I am not desperate! According to you, I'm dating someone. Right?"

"What?"

"That's what you told Scarlet."

"Oh, that was nothing. She was trying to hook you up with some dude."

"And?"

"And I knew you wouldn't like him, so I told her you were dating someone."

"How could you be so sure I wouldn't like him?" I asked.

"He's a plastic surgeon. One of Scarlet's dad's golf buddies. Has his own practice." Ian was trying so hard to make all of these traits sound uninteresting.

"And? Sounds like prince charming to me!"

"You don't like those types of guys," he said. "He's too successful for you."

(If I'd had a burning poker, Ian would be missing an eye right now.)

"What the fuck is that bullshit supposed to mean?"

"Whoa!" Ian threw up his hands. "Don't shank a brother in the West End now. I didn't mean it however you took it."

"There aren't too many ways to mean it and take it," I pointed out.

"You know what you do with types like that," Ian said. "Like that last guy, the doctor from Morehouse . . . What was his name? Prescott? The one who was all 'doctors without borders' and 'try to save the world'?"

"Preston Alcott," I answered.

Ian stepped back and smiled before we started laughing. There was no need to retell the story. I fell hard for Preston Alcott on the first date. He had a fast car, and like Tracy Chapman, I wanted a ticket to anywhere he went. He knew fine art, fine food, history, politics. He was rich. Had manicured hands. Good teeth. Great bones. Curly hair (I'm country, so I like curly hair—whatever). He wasn't like anything I knew. A lot of men in Atlanta have money now. A lot of men in Atlanta drive Bentleys and live in penthouses. But Preston didn't do it like it was new. Like it mattered to him. He was just prime rib. And he liked me! Now, I admit that I slept with him on the first date—but it wasn't for naught. The next morning, before he drove me home, he asked me out again. He was going to the mayor's ball and wanted me to be his date. I nearly died. Nearly fainted and just died. I was a long way from Chauncey and that pickup truck. Of course I said yes. The only problem was that while Preston had been asleep, I'd gone through his house (just a little detective work to see if he really was who he'd claimed to be) and found pictures of his former fiancée. She was a pretty thing. A long neck and cherry-shaped eyes. What bothered me, though—and I suppose I was looking because Preston had called me "thick" in bed—was that she couldn't have been over a size 0. Her arms looked like golf clubs. Her fingers, cocktail straws. And there Preston was, sliding a huge rock on one of those straws in a picture he'd stashed in his desk drawer. I wanted a huge rock! I looked down at my chubby fingers and thus began the craziness. I had ten days to lose twenty pounds for the mayor's ball. I'd make my grand, high-society debut on the arms of *The* Dr. Preston Alcott! Krista suggested I try this lemonade and cayenne pepper diet. It was ridiculous, had me dreaming of cheeseburgers and fried eggs all week, but I kept Preston in my mind and I did it. I lost the twenty pounds in ten days, and the morning of the dance, I was model gaunt and could fit into a size 6. I shimmied into Preston's arms and thought I was Halle Berry. Until the middle of the night. Then I was feeling lightheaded. Then I fainted.

"That situation is in the past," I protested the memory of Preston looking so embarrassed as he helped get me onto a gurney in the middle of the dance floor at the mayor's ball. "It was just too much pressure to be perfect."

"Pressure you placed on yourself," Ian said.

"Men like Preston expect that. They want you to be perfect," I said.

"I (You) hate them," Ian and I said together.

"So what am I supposed to do? Be single for the rest of my life?" I asked.

"No, you got me!" Ian answered. "And I'm a doctor, too!"

"Yeah, right! And where have you been anyway? I haven't heard from you since the big proposal at the hotel weeks ago."

"Scarlet has had me everywhere," Ian said. "Dinners. The engagement party—"

"Engagement party? You didn't invite me?"

"Oh, it was small. Just some folks at her parents' house."

"That was fast," I said.

"Yeah, seems like everything is moving pretty quickly." Ian's face went nervous. He seemed to drift away. "My Scarlet sure knows what she wants."

"Do you?"

"I'm fine!" He raised his voice as he refocused on me. "No need to revisit what happened at the hotel. It was just nerves. I love Scarlet. And I'm ready to get married."

"Being ready to get married is no reason to marry someone."

"Are we going to do this? Are you really going to force me to have this conversation in front of"—he turned and pointed at the sign over the shop— "Big Bird's Auto Body?"

"Well, you—"

"I'm in love! I'm getting married."

"OK!" I held up my hands in surrender.

"And . . . speaking of the wedding . . ." Ian smiled at me.

"I wasn't talking about the wedding. No one was talking about any wedding," I said. I knew this was coming. But Ian knew my rule: I don't plan friends' weddings. No mixing business with pleasure; it always goes wrong.

"Come on, Rach! You know I have to ask."

"And you know my rule." I started walking back to the garage.

"I know, and I told Scarlet, but why can't you at least talk to her about it?" He grabbed my arm.

"About what?"

"About planning our wedding," Ian said.

"I can't. I won't," I said.

"Won't?" Ian followed me closer to the garage. "That sounds like more than principles."

"Ian, I just don't do that."

"It's all Scarlet is talking about. She's telling everyone my best friend is planning the wedding."

"What? She's telling people that? You need to tell her I'm not doing it."

"I think it'll come off better if she hears it from you. If I say it, she'll think it's because you don't like her—"

"Well, I—"

"But if you say it, she'll know it's not personal." He made it sound so simple, but I knew better.

"This is a setup," I said.

"How about over dinner tonight? My treat. Parish at eight?" He pulled the keys from his pocket like it was a done deal.

"Parish? Tonight? I can't!"

"You can't?" Ian frowned in disbelief. "Why?"

"Because I—I—"

"You what?"

"I have a date!"

"Whatever!" Ian laughed like he expected me to join in. "A date? There's no way!"

"No way?"

"You tell me everything. I would know."

"Well, maybe right now you don't know," I teased like we were in a school yard.

"Why wouldn't I know?" Ian stepped in close to me like a bouncer.

"Because . . . because I just made the date."

"You just made a date?" Ian smirked.

"Yeah!"

"With?"

I looked around and there was Bird still grinning at me from the red truck.

"Him!" I pointed to Bird.

"Him?" Ian looked at Bird.

Bird waved.

"Fine," Ian said. "If that's what you want. Fine. How about tomorrow? Lunch?"

"Lunch? That's our lunch. We always go alone. No one else," I said.

"Just this one time," he said. "So you can tell Scarlet about your rule, and she can get it out of her head and we can be done with it."

I exhaled as I watched Bird cleaning a tool he was holding at his waist.

"I'll do it," I said.

"Great! Same place as always?"

"Same place," I said. "Same time."

"Good. I'll tell Scar," Ian said, taking out his phone as he started walking back to his car. "And have a good time"—he pointed at the sign—"Big Bird."

"So, you're a woman of your word?" Bird said when Ian was gone. "Guess I'll see you tonight."

*   *   *

I spent the rest of the afternoon trying to think of how I could get out of the date with Bird, but the truth was, I didn't have anything else to do. Either I'd sit at home or go out to confirm what I already knew: there was no way anything between Bird and me would develop. We were just too different. I kept reminding myself that I wasn't making love plans. But it wasn't bad to have some plans. And what harm could he be? He was named after one of nature's most splendid creatures . . . and the most popular puppet on Sesame Street. Maybe he was the man I'd been waiting for. The one to sweep me off my feet. Be full of surprises I couldn't imagine. Sure, he seemed to like gold jewelry and obviously had some kind of s-curl kit in his hair. But I could change that. Love is meant to prevail against all odds!

Still, in case I couldn't change those things and the date was a disaster, I told Bird to pick me up at the office at five o'clock. That was the only address he'd had on file at the shop and there was no sense giving him my home address.

Of course, he showed up in a Ford. One older than mine. Shiny and purple and big. He pulled tight to the corner on Peachtree in front of the building where I was standing with Krista. I kept telling her I was all right and I'd see her in the office the next day, but she insisted on reviewing every single detail of the work day while scrolling through messages on her cell phone. I think she was just waiting to see my date, though, because when Bird pulled up in that purple car, she nearly squealed like a preschooler who'd just found an Easter egg in the school yard. "This is your date?"

"He's just my mechanic," I said dryly. "We're just kicking it."

Bird turned off the ignition. I was hoping he'd stay in the car, not make some grand scene, giving Krista something to grin about (I could already see that he was wearing the gold chains), but he got out of the car and walked slowly around the butt so Krista could see his matching brown silk slacks and shirt. A thicker gold chain was around his wrist. Two rings were on one hand. He stepped onto the curb and I introduced him to Krista and her nosy half grin.

"You look beautiful," Bird said to me after shaking Krista's hand.

"I'm just wearing what I had on earlier at the shop," I said passively.

"Well, you look more beautiful in it now." He smiled and took my work bag before leaving me alone with Krista on the curb.

"Yeah, he's your date," Krista affirmed with full backing. She was always trying to link me up with someone, trying to help me escape "the marriage planner's curse."

"Please, it's not even like that. It's not that serious."

"Tell him." Krista nodded at Big Bird, in the car and ready to go. He'd leaned over and opened my door. "See you tomorrow. I'll expect a full report. Good luck."

As always, the conversation with Bird was simple, light banter. Nothing too deep. We rode up Peachtree talking about his car, my car, his love of cars, of Fords. Listening to him talk reminded me of my uncles and my father, the old men at my church who stood around talking about Jesus, sports, and cars all day. He wasn't that much older than me, but his style, how he spoke, and what he spoke about was decidedly dated. He was from a farm town smaller than Social Circle and laughed like it. His cologne was sweet and heavy and all over the car. I rolled my window down.

I hated to jump the gun—I mean, the man had jumped out of the car to grab my bag and had opened my door (two things fewer than half of my dates in the last three years ever thought to do)—but listening to him and looking at him and smelling him sitting across from me in that purple Ford only confirmed how different Bird and I were. Besides our country backgrounds and Chauncey's truck parked in Bird's garage, I was sure we didn't have anything in common. Shit, I know how bad that sounds—*really, really bad.* But, that was the thing about the blue-collar brothers like Bird—the ones Oprah and Tyler Perry seemed to endlessly suggest successful single sisters flock toward like an available dick in the veritable glass case—although he was single enough, nice enough, and found me attractive enough, we lived in two different worlds.

I hadn't eaten lunch and I was starving, so when Bird asked if I liked seafood, I perked up in my seat and smiled yes, but I should've asked a few more questions. On my side of town, seafood meant lobster and oysters, a filet of sole on the back patio at Fontaine's or the Oceanaire, but that purple Ford bypassed any place I knew of that served any kind of seafood I normally ate and stopped in front of a huge barn with a parking lot out front. Pickup trucks and old Cutlasses, even a few old

Cadillacs, were in the spaces. Men with cornrows in their hair and chains around their necks just like Bird's sat on the hoods as they sipped on bottles in brown paper bags. A few women were sprinkled around, but their hair was just like the boys. One was wearing a red spandex body suit with a stomach that stuck out so far it swung right over her vagina. And I was thinking she should've gone with the cornrows like the rest of the women out there because from across the parking lot and inside the car with Bird, I could see her weave tracks.

"This is where we're going?" I asked, trying not to sound as irritated as I felt. "I thought you said we were going for seafood."

"Yeah, baby girl," Bird said, turning off the car. "This is Bigelow's. They have the best fried whiting sandwiches in the A." He looked at me. "Something wrong? You want to go someplace else?"

"No," I said, not wanting to offend Bird. "I've just never been here before."

"Oh, don't worry. You with Bird. These just some folks from around here. Ain't nobody gonna touch you."

"I'm not worried about someone touching me. You say that like I'm afraid."

"You sure look afraid."

Bird got out and walked around to open my door. I heard a few people call out his name and when I got out of the car I saw every eye of every woman in the lot glued on me.

"Bird got himself a lady friend!" someone shouted loud enough so it was clear that she wanted me to hear her.

I looked at Bird as he helped me out of the car.

"Don't you mind her none. She's just toying with me. Ain't nothing," he said.

The inside of the bar looked as could be expected from outside. It was nothing but a big space with a bar and tables and chairs around it that looked like they came from some abandoned chicken shack. Toward the back of the room, one of those cheap snap-together parquet floors was supposed to be the dance floor. While it wasn't late enough for the floor to be packed there were enough people to call it a party. The DJ was playing the same old blues standards Bird had been singing along to in the car.

"They serve food here?" I asked, following close behind Bird. He'd taken my hand and was heading to the bar. The lights were dim and a few of the seats were already occupied with folks sipping on beers and bouncing their heads really slow to the music.

"Good food. The best food." Bird sat down on a barstool and the waitress came right over like she knew him.

She was a skinny woman. No older than me. Had gold teeth and a big smile that made you look at them. Her navel was pierced. Someone's name was tattooed beneath it. I could see this because her jeans were hanging just above her pelvis.

"Birdie Boo!" She gave Bird a high five over the bar. "See you got some company." She smiled at me and flashed the golden teeth.

"I'm Rachel!" I said before Bird could introduce us. I've learned that it's always best to be very friendly to other women when I'm with a man they know. It cuts out a lot of bullshit. They know you're not the enemy.

"Nice to meet you, Rachel Boo! I'm Ronnie." She winked at me and then looked back at Bird. "Guess you done got too good for us over here. Ain't been here to see about me since the weekend." She pouted at him the way I pouted at Ian.

"Been trying to make money, so I can tip you real good," Bird said and Ronnie rolled her eyes playfully. "What now? What you got to say now?"

"I'll take that," she said. "I was just looking for you to say thank you for Western Unioning that money down to Jake for his school books. He needed it for real. And I ain't had no way to get it to him."

"No problem," Bird said. "Don't mention it. I got Jake long as he got those grades up."

Ronnie turned to me and said, "My boy Jake in his second year of college down at Tennessee State University." She nodded to Bird. "This man here sends him money every semester for books and what not. Don't know what we'd do without him."

"I don't know how you have a son in college," I said. "You can't be over thirty-five."

"I had him real young. I was just a baby myself. Ain't had no business giving birth to nothing at all. But I got lucky. Jake smarter than a roomful of doctors. Got a full scholarship. I just got to send money for his dorm and books. If it wasn't for people like Bird, I'd have to find me a pole to swing on at the Clermont Lounge—'cause my boy staying at the school."

"You always talking about swinging on a pole," Bird joked. "You know damn well you ain't about to take your clothes off at the old timey strip club.

Need to take these drink orders. Get my food ready. All this talking you doing."

Ronnie hissed at Bird and turned to me.

"Now I know what this fool eating and sipping on. What you want, Ms. Lady?"

"Well, Bird tells me you have seafood," I said.

"We got fish."

"What kinds?"

"We got whiting and porgies."

"Oh . . . How is it prepared?"

I could feel Bird staring at me.

"Both fried," Ronnie answered.

"No blackened?"

"Fried. On white bread."

"Wheat bread?"

"Fried. On white bread. I can bring you extra hot sauce."

"Sounds great."

"Now, what you want to drink?" Ronnie asked.

"Do you have any wine?"

"Not none I would be drinking," she said, leaning into me. "I'd stick to the liquor. Manager don't spend a lot of money on the wine. Don't nobody here drink it."

"OK."

"What you got a taste for? Blue Mother Fucker? Sex on the Beach? Pretty Asshole?"

I didn't understand anything she was saying, so I went with the best option: "Surprise me."

Ronnie disappeared into a room behind the bar that looked like a kitchen.

"You ain't know what she was talking about," Bird pointed out.

"Nope," I said and we both laughed.

"Well, don't be surprised if the drink she makes

you has you out on that dance floor grooving like MC Hammer in like ten minutes. She's been working in this little bar for a long time and they don't serve light drinks."

"Well, I can hold my—"

"No, you did not bring some heifer up in here!" said a woman I'd noticed staring at Bird's back from the other side of the bar, coming up behind Bird. She was petite but thick. She had an attitude in her face. Her lips were scrunched up like she'd just bitten into a piece of sour candy. She had on an out-of-season rainbow print dress with matching, too-long acrylic nails.

Bird closed his eyes for a second when he heard her voice. He didn't even turn around to see her. "Don't start this shit," he said tiredly, looking down at the floor beneath his barstool.

I didn't know if I should look at the woman or get up and walk out. She was eyeballing me hard and didn't look like she meant to say anything good. She was obviously one of Bird's lady friends.

"Start shit? No, you started shit when you brought this"—she waved her nails at me—"thing up in here. Up in our spot." She was in her early twenties. I could tell by the way her tits sat up in the dress with no bra, and sweat underneath them.

Now, I may not have been raised ghetto, but I was certainly raised country. I noticed that she'd called me "this" and the country girl in me was ready to "go cow tipping" on her ass, but I hadn't had a fight in fifteen years and I wasn't about to go to jail for fighting over my mechanic, who, by the way, clearly wasn't trying to correct Ms. Thing and tell her my name—well, maybe that was a good thing.

"This ain't our spot," Bird said.

"The mother fuck it ain't. You ain't been around me or your kids. And they miss they daddy."

I guess Rainbow dress saw my eyes narrow, because she announced, "Both of your kids." (I honestly expected a higher number.)

"Jazz, give it a break."

"First of all, you get my mother-fucking name right—it's Jazamaraya. And second of all, I'll give it a break when you give me my mother-fucking child support! Don't make me take your ass to court again."

Bird actually looked like he was about to start laughing. He turned to Jaza finally and said, "Please stop. You're embarrassing me."

"I'm embarrassing you? No! You're embarrassing me! Up in here with this . . . this . . . this . . . white girl."

"Hold up!" The country girl in me would not be exorcised another minute. Now, I admit that I'd gone bourgeoisie, and I wasn't trying to get locked up, but there was no way I was going to just sit there and let her call me a white girl to my face. She'd gone in on me and it was no longer about Bird and his kids and not paying child support.

"Hold up?" Jaza started laughing. "I think we got us a fighter!" She threw her purse down on the floor and went right into a fighting position. I was about to get off my stool, but Bird got up and stood in front of me.

Jaza fell laughing into his seat. "I got her ass! I got her ass good!" she said, laughing.

"What?" I was up and ready to climb over Bird to get at her.

"Whoa!" Bird said, holding me in my seat. "See,

Jazz, she's taking you seriously. I told you to stop playing."

"Playing?" I said.

Ronnie came over, shaking her head at Jazmine, and set our drinks on the counter.

"I'm Jazmine. Bird's baby cousin." Jazmine reached over Bird's shoulder to shake my hand.

It took me a second and a long look into Bird's eyes before I could believe it and shake her hand. "Your cousin?"

"Baby cousin," Bird said. "Immature baby cousin." He turned around to her.

"No. Actress baby cousin." She rolled her eyes at Bird and looked around at me. "I'm about to be in a Tyler Perry movie soon . . . as soon as he discovers me. Getting ready for my audition. Cousin Bird here pays for my acting classes downtown. I like to show him that he's getting his money's worth. What you think?"

"I was convinced," I admitted. "I was ready to fight you."

"Wow!" Jazmine said and her eyes sparkled. "I'm going to get an Oscar before I turn twenty-five. That's my goal. If I can believe it, I can achieve it. So, what you do?"

"I—"

"Jazmine, get out of her business. Don't you have somewhere else you need to be?" Bird said.

"Yeah. Right here." Jazmine rolled her eyes.

"I'm a wedding planner."

"Wow! Like on *Bridezilla*?"

"Not exactly. But I have met a few bridezillas in my time."

The DJ started playing the "Cha Cha Slide" and half the people at the bar ran to the dance floor.

"Oh, that's my song!" Jazmine started doing the line steps right in front of our barstools.

"Well, why don't you go do it then . . . like, on the dance floor?" Bird pointed to the lines forming in front of the DJ.

Jazmine rolled her eyes and sucked her teeth. She looked at me like I was her best friend. "You want to dance with me?" she asked.

"No, she doesn't," Bird jumped in. He turned to me. "Just ignore her. My aunt dropped Jazmine on her head when she was a baby," he joked.

"That story is not true," Jazmine said. "There was a carpet on that floor."

We all laughed at her wit and she pulled my arm.

"Come on, girl. You look like you need to dance. All tight in the stuffy suit. Let's rock the house," she said.

"I'm not the best dancer," I pointed out. (In fact, I was the worst dancer. I knew the "Cha Cha Slide," but I preferred to do it alone . . . in my home.)

"Well, from looking at you, you don't know anyone here, so this is the best place to start working on your smooth moves." Jazmine wouldn't let go of my arm.

"You know what? I'll go." (This was the liquor I'd been sipping on talking.) "But only if Bird comes with me."

Jazmine grabbed Bird's arm then, too.

"Hell no," Bird protested. "Ain't nothing but women on that dance floor."

"There are dudes, too." Jazmine pointed to a few men in the back of the line looking at women's butts.

"You two can go. I'll be here waiting on my fish sandwich," Bird said.

The waitress seemed to come from out of nowhere to push him on. "Those sandwiches won't be up for ten more minutes. You know Slim is slow as shit back there. I'll hold the sandwiches for you."

"Please!" Jazmine pulled us a little more.

"It's just one song," I said to Bird.

"And it's almost freaking over, all the deliberating ya'll doing."

Bird slid his drink onto the bar.

"Just one song," he said. "And if the other brothers leave the floor, I'm out."

The good thing about line dancing is that all of the moves are already preplanned. All you have to do is follow along. Work on memory. Problem is, I have the worst dance-move memory. Whenever I get on a dance floor—like for the Wobble, the Electric Slide, even the Tootsie Roll—my goal is to get behind the best dancer and just do what she does. Luckily, Jazmine was the best dancer in Bigelow's. I stood behind her and she was my instant choreographer. The only problem was that she was changing half the moves and freestyling and whatnot. I almost knocked a few people down following her. Bird, of course, stood behind me and did more booty watching than moving. When the dance turned to the back, he just stood there and moved his hands to the beat.

The bad thing about line dancing is that the songs are always longer than you can ever be prepared for. And after every dance, you feel like sitting down, but the beat starts up again and you can't seem to get off the dance floor. Lord, how long were we out there, me sweating and feeling the hairs on the back of my neck curling up. And it was funny, too—Bird must've seen the little sweat droplets rolling down my neck, because he started dabbing at them with a napkin. Soon, to save my energy, I just did the dance in place in front of him. And when the song went off we stayed there and danced together one more time.

Some man in a purple silk two-piece outfit (which, along with gold chains, was apparently the standard outfit for men in Bigelow's) grabbed Jazmine and pulled her to the middle of the floor, where she made it clear that she believed she was starring in her very own movie titled *Dance Fever*.

Bird and I went back to the bar where our hot fish sandwiches were waiting for us. He was obviously one of the most popular men in the bar. He could hardly take two steps without someone grabbing his arm and whispering in his ear. It was interesting, because in that place I seemed more like I was hanging onto him. Women looked at me like I was lucky to be with him. They whispered when I walked by and poked out their asses to get him to look in their direction.

Ignoring the pool of grease in the bottom of the fish basket that likely made the sandwich as tasty as it was, I replenished every calorie I'd burned on the dance floor, tearing through the sandwich like it was my last meal. Bird and I could hardly talk, the food was so good. I ate until there was one little last bite and gave up.

Bird finished his sandwich and then reached over for mine.

We laughed as he scarfed it down and pounded on his full belly like Tarzan.

"You know, Bird, you're a cool guy," I said.

"Why, thank you. I aim to please."

"And I am pleased. I'll admit it—at first I was a little nervous about hanging out with you."

"Nervous?" He looked puzzled. "About me?"

"Not really about you . . . more like us . . . I wasn't sure if we'd have anything in common," I said delicately.

"Oh. We're both black and breathing. Isn't that enough?"

"You know what I mean. But I'm happy I was able to look past it. You're pretty cool. I've enjoyed hanging out with you. I certainly haven't seen this side of Atlanta." I looked around the bar. "But I could get used to it."

Bird kind of squinted and then looked at me like I was some naïve schoolgirl. "Sure, baby girl. I'll give you a list of spots to check out."

"A list?" The offer sounded so distant. "Oh, I see how it is."

"How it is? What's wrong with a list?"

"It's just the way you said it—kind of like you don't intend to go those places with me."

Here was Bird's opportunity to say of course he intended to take me those places and ask me out on a second date. But, as they say, opportunity is only available to those who seek it.

He said, "Sure, we can hang out again." His voice was even more distant this time. Suddenly, he was looking at me like some crazy old lady he'd met at a bus stop. The conversation had morphed from his chance to invite me out again to me seeming like I was asking him out. And the worst part was that I wasn't sure that I wasn't asking him out. Whiting sandwiches at Bigelow's was the most action I'd seen in months.

"Sure?" I repeated the same distant way he had. "And there it is again."

"I'm not sure what you're getting at."

"I just thought that—you know—that you'd ask me out again. Like on a date. Not just to hang out. Hanging out is for friends." (Oh no! Where was this going? I had the feeling that I was about to humiliate myself, but I couldn't stop myself. Ronnie's drink was talking to me.)

"Oh . . ." (Bird looked like he was sensing the same thing and didn't want me to make an ass of myself.)

"It's nothing. You don't have to explain." I put my hands up defensively. "I just noticed that your voice changed and—"

"I'm sorry, Rachel, but I just wanted to take you out. You're a beautiful woman. I like beautiful women. But I wasn't looking for anything serious with you. Did you think that?"

(There really isn't any other way to answer this question without sounding insane.)

"No, I didn't, but . . . I . . . I guess I did. . . . I mean, I didn't think I wanted to, but . . . you asked me out, so I thought maybe you wanted to—" Thank God Bird stopped me from talking right then, because as I kept rambling, I was about to start crying at any moment.

"Oh, so you thought I was just all in love with you?" This wasn't exactly the kind of interruption I was looking for.

"No, it's not like that. I was just thinking that since you asked me out, that you, you know, liked me like that."

"I do like you, but not like that. We're different."

"Different?" I repeated as if I hadn't been thinking the exact same thing just hours before when he showed up in front of my office in his brown silk two-piece. What a difference a few open doors and free food can make in the heart of a single woman.

"Yeah. We're different. You just said it a minute ago. Is it different because I'm saying it now?" Bird paused and slid his beer onto the bar beside my drink. "It's like, I work and live on the southside. You only come to the southside to get your car fixed."

"So?"

"So . . . I don't plan on leaving the southside. Do you plan on leaving Buckhead or Alpharetta or wherever you live? I noticed that you didn't even let me pick you up at your house."

"I can explain that—I'm—"

"It's not a big deal. See, I know that when sisters like you date men like me, it's not exactly your first choice. I'm more like the man you settle on. The brother you consider getting with right before you start dating white men—or after you realize the white men won't marry you."

"That's not true and I—"

"Rachel, it's fine. Don't insult my intelligence by trying to explain. I may not have gone to college, but I'm pretty bright," Bird said. "You see me every week working on cars. I have greasy hands and shit all over my shirt. I know that's not what you want. You want one of those Morehouse men who wear suit jackets to work and can impress your friends with his credentials—like your boy who came by the shop today. That's cool. You can have that."

"I'm open to try anything," I said and I didn't know how crazy that would sound until I heard it come from my mouth.

"I don't want anyone to 'try' me." He held up his hands to put invisible quotes around try. "I want what everyone else wants. What you want. For someone to choose me. Now, I've asked you out dozens of times. And that's just the flirt in me. I'm a man. If I see a beautiful woman, I'm on it. If you wanted to go out with me, you would've said yes a long time ago. Not just when your boy was there and you wanted to impress him or something."

"He's my friend. I wasn't trying to impress him," I offered.

"Well, we can be friends, too, baby girl. We can go out. We can hang hard. But I won't be your settlement man. When I find my woman, she'll be looking for everything I am. And then, I'll shower her with everything I have." Bird smiled. "And that's a whole lot. Car repairs don't come cheap. My wife won't have anything to do but make sure her man's belly is filled when he gets home."

The bartender came back to our end of the bar. "Another round, Bird?" she asked.

"Why not?" Bird said, clinking his beer bottle against my glass. "I got it."

For the rest of the night, Bird kept the conversation going. He'd gained the upper hand and I felt smaller than the fly that had landed in my drink. In the car ride on the way back to the office to get my car, I wanted to pop in my earphones and listen to my iPhone. To disappear never to be heard from again. Only, I knew that was too far from the truth. We'd see each other again, and those times would be even more uncomfortable and awkward than this. He offered to walk me into the garage to get my car, but I shot back with a firm "No!" and jumped out at the curb on Peachtree where he'd picked me up earlier.

"Give me a call to let me know when you've made it home safely," he said before pulling off.

I agreed, but we both knew I wasn't picking up the phone to call him ever again unless it was about my truck.

From the red light in front of my building, I could see the light on in my living room. Flashes of color, probably from the television, bounced off the window where the light above was just dim enough. Grammy Annie-Lou and Ian were the only people with keys to my place. Pulling into my parking space, I was sure it was the latter, as Grammy Annie-Lou hated coming into the city for anything but revivals and funerals. So, if it wasn't Ian, the only other person who could have my living room light on and the television going was a burglar, who took time to check out my DVR collection.

"Welcome home, Ms. Winslow. Dr. Dupree is upstairs," said Jeremy, the front doorman and elevator operator as he gave me a lift to my floor in the raw freight elevator that once carried mattresses when the building was a mattress factory. Some years ago, following an Atlanta trend pushed by new socialites and the avant-garde, a developer had purchased the abandoned space, rezoned it, and built condos he could sell quickly to those hoping to be on the cutting edge, and live in the city with a little bit more space and style than those stuck in apartments and condos. There were forty units in the building, and all forty residents seemed to be the same—except for Mrs. Jackson, an old woman that moved onto my floor after her son almost lost his unit to foreclosure. Still, the rest of us were young, entrepreneurs, financially secure, and single. Jeremy, a twenty-six-year-old doctoral philosophy student who wore spikes in his brown hair and jumped the curb on his skateboard as he waited for residents to arrive, was the perfect punctuation to the post-hipster vibe in the building.

"Wonderful," I replied to Jeremy's observation. Certainly, as a doorman, he knew that he ought to tell me that a man, even if he knew that man was my best friend and said man had a key to my place, was waiting upstairs for me. Lord only knows what he'd seen over the years. One of the units on the top floor was occupied by a strip club owner, who wasn't shy about bringing work home.

"Two visits in one day?" I announced, walking into my place. Ian had left the door unlocked. "To what do I owe all this attention?"

"Figured you'd want to talk after your date." Ian was laid out on my couch. His naked feet were up and crossed on one end and his head was resting over his hands on the other. His tie was loose, but he was still wearing the same clothes from earlier at the car shop. I knew that he hadn't been home yet.

"Talk? I can call you on the phone to talk to you." I put my work bag and purse on the dining room table that was across the room from the couch and television.

"I figured you'd need a little extra attention tonight."

"Why?"

"After your date with Sparrow. If things went bad, you know?"

"Bird. His name is Bird," I said. "And no, I don't need any extra attention." I rolled my eyes and started walking toward the kitchen. "Everything was fine."

"I already made your tea. Thought you'd want the coconut chai," Ian called.

In the kitchen, I looked at the stove. The tea pot had steam coming from the spout. The warm, sweet scent of my favorite tea was wafting over-head. It was exactly what I wanted. What I always had after one of those dates that flat-lined for no reason I understood. I rolled my eyes again.

"I was going to make the ginger, but I thought it would be a coconut chai night," Ian said, now standing in the doorway of the kitchen behind me. "I mean, after I saw Dragonfly Jones, I . . . Well, we know the track record."

My eyeroll was decidedly dramatic as we walked back into the living room. "Bird. His name is Bird," I said, sulking and looking up at the black and white printing of a Kara Walker silhouette of an African woman with angel wings hanging over the couch. Maybe something in the coconut chai air was breaking me down. "And I hate you."

"Ahhhh." Ian stretched out his arms and pulled me into a hug. "Was it that bad?" He pushed my head into his chest dramatically though I resisted. "Tell daddy everything."

To anyone watching, this skit of pain and comfort that Ian and I had performed many times might look bizarre or even suggestive of something more, but it was just us. As the best friend of a female, Ian had to be my comforter, my stand-in daddy and shoe picker. For every reason I hated him for assuming my date would likely be a flipping flop, I backed it up with a rationalization. I needed that shoulder to lean on. Someone waiting to listen to me when I got home. Someone who knew the right tea. At the right time.

"Men suck," I proclaimed a little later after I'd had two cups of tea and told Ian all about Bird and his "no settlements" statement.

"I know, but dude kind of has a point," Ian said.

I angrily flipped my legs off of his lap and placed them on the floor. We'd been sitting on the couch and he'd volunteered to give me a foot massage.

"What?" Ian asked.

"What fracking point? There's no point. It was just an excuse."

"Come on, Rach. You know that guy wasn't for you. You should be happy he didn't just sleep with you and dip out."

"Why would he do that?"

"Because no guy wants to be that guy with the girl who's obviously settling—maybe to sleep with her, but not long term. All of her friends and family hate you. She always knows she can do better. And worse, someone who is better might come along and snatch her," he said. "The point is, he just wasn't your type and he knows it."

"Blah. Blah. Blah," I grumbled. "My type? What's the sense in having a type if no one fits that type? And what is my type?"

"Someone who's equally yoked with you. A man

like the one in your favorite India.Arie song, 'Ready for Love.' "

That song described everything I ever dreamed of in a man. Anytime and every time someone asked me what I was looking for in a future husband, I quoted the song, because if I could have just those things in a mate, I figured everything else Ian had listed would fall into place. I'd hazed Ian a million times, making him listen to the song with me as I cried over some man who'd broken my heart. He kind of knew the words by default.

"And he'll be someone who can teach you new things. Sweep you off your feet. Treat you like the queen you are," Ian added. "Because you deserve it."

"I'm thinking that those men don't exist anymore, E," I said. "Everyone knows it. They say I need to 'date down,' date white, or be a polygamist—did I tell you Keisha from undergrad shares her husband with three other women? One in Africa?"

"No, you didn't tell me that," he replied. "And yes, they do exist." He pulled me over from my side of the couch and tucked me under his right arm like a kid he was about to read a book to. "And one will come along. And he will find you. And he will love you. And you won't have to settle. And he'll have to deal with big daddy."

I played right into my part. "Do you think I'm too picky?" I asked.

"No, I think you're just right."

I slid Ian's half-empty tea mug of brandy from his hands and took a sip.

"What about you—do you think Scarlet is settling on you?" I asked.

"Hell no. I follow Parakeet on that tip. I'm no one's settlement."

"So you two are equally yoked?"

Ian paused. "I wouldn't say that. Scarlet is younger. Still trying to figure herself out."

"So you're the one settling?"

"No such thing for a man. A man can marry a woman who works at Burger King if he wants to and he can support her at his level," Ian said.

"But a woman can't?"

"Hell no," Ian said. "Not if she doesn't want problems. And that mix would definitely lead to problems."

"What's in it for the man who's settling, then?"

"Well, first, I am not settling," he said. "I am marrying the woman I love. And second, I am fine with the fact that I know where Scarlet is going. How she thinks. She may not be on my level right now, but she'll get there once she figures it out. Or we'll figure it out together." Ian snatched the brandy back from me. "Nosy ass."

3

"Scarlet Don't Know Nothing 'Bout Planning No Wedding!"

#Ihateoverachievers. I have always aimed to be the best at whatever I get myself involved in and I encourage that kind of commitment from the people around me, but after my disaster of a date with the last single and nonhomosexual male in all of Atlanta, who seemed to be attracted to me before I announced that I was attracted to him, I was in no mood to listen to another speech about how Scarlet was set to save the world, one little black girl at a time. The bad luck that had chased me into the new year could give a tiny lab rat's ass about my mood, though, so there she was sitting beside Ian in the booth at the back of Fado, the Irish pub where Ian and I had lunch once a week. Most Wednesdays Ian and I debated politics and black power. He was a conservative liberal and I was a conscious conservative. We both wanted to do away with welfare, but we couldn't agree on what to do with all those poor people who'd been failed by weak school systems, predatory financial institutions, and broken communities that offered little in the way of proper food options and services. One day, Shane, our standing waiter for three years, said he was sure we could run the country if we ran for president and vice president—then we argued over who'd take the top role. None of that would happen with Scarlet there, though. She was sitting so close to Ian it looked like they were fused at the hip. And, like any betrothed woman, all she wanted to talk about was one thing: her wedding. . . .

"Well, Ian and I were talking about the wedding, and while I was seriously thinking he would want you to be his best man—with you two being best friends"—Scarlet laughed and took a sip of the lemon water she'd ordered for lunch; apparently the diet was already in effect—"we decided to do a barter system and my cousin Steve is going to be one of the groomsmen and I want you to be one of the bridesmen—I mean, maids."

Ian kicked me under the table and I realized I was staring at Scarlet.

"Really? Wow!" I snapped. "I'd be honored."

"Awesome!" Scarlet smiled.

"Ian, who's the best man?" I asked. "Don't tell me it's Xavier! You're just asking for trouble. He'll probably try to sleep with half the bridesmaids." Xavier was Ian's college roommate and one of the top male whores on campus. And that designation was for good reason. Xavier was a beefcake, a mocha chocolate version of Ian. Sometimes I felt bad for some of the other guys on campus when Ian and Xavier were together. It just didn't seem fair that they got so much attention. And even less fair that unlike Ian, Xavier was clearly primed to take advantage of the situation. No one's girlfriend was safe.

"Nah, X is my dog, so he'll be in the wedding, but my cousin Elon will be the best man."

"Oh, Elon. Fine-ass youngun." I grinned and batted my eyes. Elon was twenty-one and mixed with every race in New Orleans. He had silky tan skin and a thick New Orleans accent. His father had run out on his mother when he was young, so Ian was the male role model in his life. He lived in New Orleans, but came to stay with Ian most summers.

"And half your age."

"Don't hate on my cougar possibilities. That boy is a man! And I have an entire year to get slim and trim to make him my boo," I joked.

"A year? Wait, Ian, you didn't tell her?" Scarlet looked at Ian.

"Tell me what?"

"We moved the wedding up," Scarlet said.

"Moved it up?"

"It's in May," Ian revealed.

"Ian, I can't believe you didn't tell her."

"We just decided this last night," Ian said to Scarlet.

"Well, ya'll talk all the time."

"May? May? That's . . . in four months." I'd been counting it up in my head.

"Three and a half," Scarlet said.

I peeked at her ring. It looked like she'd had it polished already.

I said, "Why? That's crazy. It takes at least nine months to plan a decent wedding—one that's not going to break your pockets."

"We kind of wanted to get it out of the way before I leave for the Congo," Scarlet said, and in her eyes I could tell that she'd expected me to know what she was talking about. "You didn't tell her about my trip either?" She turned and poked at Ian.

"Scarlet is going to the Congo this summer to work at an orphanage for girls," Ian blurted out quickly.

"It's not just an orphanage," Scarlet said. "It's a rehabilitation clinic for girls who had their limbs severed during home invasions by the rebel tribes."

"Wow! That's heavy. How'd you get into that?" I asked.

"It's through my graduate program."

"You're in graduate school?"

Scarlet shot a stare at Ian. "Well, not right now," she said. "I start in the fall. This is just a summer pilot program they have going. Anyway, Ian and I are so excited to be getting married that we figured, hey"—she threw her hands up and the look on her face forced Ian to do the same—"we might as well just do it before I leave." She looked at Ian.

"Yeah, we might as well!" he confirmed with his voice as obnoxiously fake as Scarlet's.

I still couldn't piece together why in the world he was putting himself through this whole thing. But, like Journey said, it was his life. I was just there for support. Who cared what they did as long as it didn't involve me?

"And I guess that brings us to why we invited you

here today," Scarlet said. "Ian told me that you don't plan weddings for friends, but I was just hoping, just hoping you would find a way in your heart to reconsider your rule."

"Scarlet, I'm sorry to let you—"

"Wait"—Scarlet cut me off—"before you finish, let me say this: Ian's your best friend. You two have known each other for so long. It just wouldn't be right for anyone else to plan his wedding. Not our wedding. We're all about to be family. And family has to be there for one another. Now, I know you have your rule, but you also have a heart and that heart has to have some love for your family. If you're everything Ian says you are, it just has to." Scarlet pursed her glossed lips together and looked at me like I was holding the plug to her mama on a life support machine. I felt like Ian with all those cameras flashing on him at the birthday party. I could either let everyone down or be the life of the party.

"It's just my policy—"

"Please, just this once?" Scarlet held out her hands together in prayer and closed her eyes.

I looked at Ian bug-eyed, but all he could do was shrug his shoulders.

"In three and a half months?" I said.

"I know it's short, but I was thinking that for someone with your expertise, with your skill—I mean, you're a master. Ian always says how amazing you are at what you do." She was playing me like an African drum, but it felt so good. "You'll have total control. We'll follow your lead." Scarlet looked at me with glassy eyes.

"OK," I said, knowing what she'd just said was a lie. "As long as we keep it small and tasteful."

"That's what I was thinking," Scarlet said.

"Where are you two thinking about having it? I can have Krista look for dates once I get back to the office. It won't be very warm here in three months, so someplace inside is best in case it gets too cold at night. Or we could do a tent." I'd gone right into work mode and pulled out my iPad.

"Oh, I can't get married in Atlanta," Ian said. "I have to get married at home in New Orleans."

I looked up from my iPad. "What?"

"I keep telling him that we can just have the wedding here. Have his people come to Atlanta. It's halfway between New Orleans and Miami. It's only fair. But he insists."

"Scarlet, my mother would have a heart attack if I brought a woman into this family outside of her church."

"Oh, you mean your mother whom I haven't even met yet?" Scarlet asked. "And I thought we decided that we weren't doing it in a church."

"I was raised in the church!"

"Do you know what the Catholic Church did to those Africans during Middle Passage? Raping little boys and girls?"

"Yes, I know. I taught you that when you took my class!"

Shane, the waiter, was standing by the bar and he turned to us when he heard Ian's voice go up.

"Y'all quiet down with all that," I said. "We can talk about this later."

"Ain't nothing to talk about," Ian said. "I have to get married in New Orleans."

"Fine," Scarlet agreed.

"And my father's Zydeco band has to play at the reception."

"What?" Scarlet nearly knocked her water over, but I caught it.

As they continued their bickering session, I signaled for Shane to come with the bill. What in the hell had I just agreed to?

"Why does your father's band have to play at *our* wedding?"

"Because it's my culture. The man might die if he doesn't play at my wedding. Die, Scarlet! Die."

"Well, I might die if I have to listen to Zydeco all night."

"Who said anything about all night? We'll play other music."

"Like salsa? My parents like salsa."

"Salsa? Why would anyone be listening to salsa in New Orleans?"

"Why not?"

"Because it's New Orleans!"

This went on for another ten minutes before I excused myself to go to the bathroom and walked out the back door.

"So please explain to me how you took my advice to mind your business and strictly be there to support your friend to mean that you should plan the wedding. That's just not what I had in mind." Journey was sitting in a chair bottle-feeding Apache. They were both in their nightclothes. It was bedtime for me and the middle of the night where they were in South Africa. I was lying in bed with my laptop and had signed on just to see if Journey might be up. Luckily Apache wasn't sleeping through the night because of all of the travel, so Journey was up trying to coax her back to sleep.

"She played me, Journey. Played me. I went from being against the wedding, to being in the wedding, to planning the whole thing."

"She's good."

"Really good." I added another pillow behind my back.

"So how are you feeling?"

"I don't feel anything. I mean, I've been trying to take myself out of the equation and just look at Scarlet and Ian like any other two people who are engaged. They fit the bill . . . I guess. Listening to them argue today, sounding like two people in love . . . I think I might have felt a little—"

"Jealous?" Journey looked at me like she was a detective who'd just cracked a case.

"No, Journey! That's not it. I'm . . . I do want love. I want to get married and argue about where the wedding is going to be and what kind of music we're going to play, but I know it's not my turn. Not my time. It's Ian's time. I just don't want to see him get hurt. He's such a good guy. So sweet and caring. Always there for me. And he'll be a great father. Probably will have his son reading before he can sit up," I said jokingly, but Journey still had her sharp eyes on me. "What? Why are you looking at me like that?"

"Why do you think?"

"Stop it, Journey!"

"No, you stop it, because you started it."

"You know what? Fine! I'll admit it. Ian is the perfect man for me. He's everything I want. He's into everything I'm into. He enlightens me. He's my rock. I'm his rock. It's all there," I listed.

"And he's fine as shit," Journey whispered, looking over her shoulder for Dame.

"He looks all right."

"And he ain't poor!"

"Yes, he makes a decent living," I said. "But that ship has sailed. It left the dock a long, long time ago and it won't return."

"You sure?"

"I'm beyond sure. I'm committed."

Journey started laughing and the bottle slid from Apache's little mouth a bit. The baby girl whined at her mother until she got the bottle readjusted correctly.

"Why did you laugh?" I asked.

"Because you just said that you're committed to not being in love with someone. That's insane. I think I said the same kind of thing right before I ended up sleeping with my former student. Now I have three children with him and follow him around the world. Did you see my baby on the cover of *Rolling Stone* last month?"

"Wonderful," I said. "Good for you. But that has nothing to do with me."

"Maybe not. Maybe." Journey pulled the empty bottle from Apache's mouth and put her over her shoulder for a burp. "Have you ever thought about how committed Ian is to nothing happening between you two?"

"He's marrying someone else. Obviously, he's committed to nothing happening between us."

"Maybe he's just too afraid to admit it. Maybe he's thinking there's no way you two could ever get together, so he's going with the next best thing."

"Settling?"

"I wouldn't say that he's settling. Think about it: if he marries Scarlet, he can still have you in his life. While she's out in Ghana or wherever the hell she's going, and modeling and saving the world, he'll still be home with you. Lunch. Stopping by the office. Using his key to get into your place. Foot massages. He'll have two wives—one he's sure he can have and another he's sure he wants. You said it yourself a while ago—whenever he wants to talk politics, and culture, art and music, his heart and soul, he comes to his equal. When he wants to have someone on his arm, someone to sweat him and beg him to stick around, he goes to his girl."

"Well, I didn't exactly put it like that, but that's some deep old shit, J!"

"Girl, please. Don't go listening to me. I'm just trying to figure this here thing out. Who knows what's going on in his mind. You're just going to have to wait and listen. Watch for the signs. If he comes to you, let him. If not, remain committed to not being in love with him."

"I'll take the latter for five thousand, Journey Trebek!" I said. "I don't love no damn Ian Dupree. That's my boy! OK? You got that? *Capisce?* Can you hear me now?" I got in close on the camera so she could see the silly expression on my face.

"I hear you. I'm just wondering if you hear yourself."

Journey rocked Apache back to sleep on her shoulder. The baby's tiny body went limp and every limb looked so heavy I wondered how Journey held her up.

Grammy Annie-Lou had been leaving messages on my voice mail for days. But between getting the front staging of Ian and Scarlet's wedding in New

Orleans together (reservations in, Web site up, and invitations out) and Alarm Clock and Donnica to actually set a date (Alarm Clock had been growing cold on the idea of losing his bachelorhood to the nail technician he'd been ready to kill over in my office), I hadn't had time to call her back. Grammy Annie-Lou liked talking on the phone for hours—and all about nothing. And I knew that if I called her back, I'd end up on the phone listening to intel about some woman at the church who was making moves on the pastor or her recent doctor's appointment. I figured I could bypass all that by waiting until she was a little more specific in her voice mail message. She was old and didn't really understand the concept of the voice mail system, so when she actually left a message, it was short and direct: "It's your grandmother—Annie-Lou. Call me. Hear?" She'd pause and then I'd hear every noise in the background before she figured out how to hang up the phone. In contrast, when it was important, she'd push herself and actually let me in on the purpose of her call and leave explicit direction. Such purpose and direction came on the morning of the day most single women dread more than Thanksgiving, Christmas, New Year's, and their birthday combined. . . .

On February fourteen, I woke up ready to do what any other reasonable single sister did to ensure the day would be a forgettable success: take the back streets to the office to avoid seeing anything red, mylar, or flowery; go into my office and shut the door; refuse all calls, e-mails, and texts from anyone who might acknowledge what day it was; take the back streets back home from the office; call the pizza man and order a light-cheese flatbread pizza; take two doses of NyQuil, and pass out on the couch while watching reruns of *Law and Order: SVU*—all to pretend it wasn't Valentine's Day.

Because I'd been blasting Nina Simone's *Little Girl Blue* while I was in the shower that morning, I didn't hear the phone ringing, but when I got out and checked the voice mail, it was Grammy Annie-Lou with purpose and direction: "Hey, baby. I done called you so many times. Guess you too busy in that city to call me. Well, I was calling about King. Think he need to be put down. He old. Been acting funny the last few days. Won't eat. Last night he done climbed under the porch and won't come out. I left some turkey necks on the stoop after dinner last night and come out here this morning. They is still here. I was going to take him out in the yard later to give him rest. But he your dog. I'll wait for you to come see about him. Hear? It's your grandmother—Annie-Lou. Call me."

I called her right back. By "give him rest," she meant that she was going to shoot him with a shotgun. King was old as hell, but he probably just had worms, an easy fifteen-dollar shot at the vet would cure that. Grammy Annie-Lou was from a different time. She didn't believe in walking dogs on a leash, keeping them in the house, or feeding them anything but scraps from the table—which was probably how King had gotten sick (that and he was the oldest dog in Georgia). I told her that I'd be there in an hour and then called Krista to tell her that I wouldn't be in.

In the car on the way to Social Circle, I forgot that it was Valentine's Day. Red and mylar balloons and flowery bouquets were set up in storefronts and riding in the backseats and butts of delivery trucks, but I noticed none of it. I kept thinking of King sleeping under the back of that old red Ford. He seemed to love and appreciate the truck more than anyone else. At night in the summer, when it was cool outside and what seemed like millions of stars in the sky were shining bright over Grammy Annie-Lou's old farmhouse, King would climb up on the hood of the truck and howl at the moon. Sitting on the front stoop beside me, my daddy would always say, "Even the laziest country dog in the world can't ignore the beauty of the moon." He'd put his arm around me and we'd listen to King's song.

"Morning, beautiful," Ian said after I picked up the phone. "Happy Monday."

"Very funny," I replied. He knew I didn't want to hear anyone say the words "Valentine's" and "Day" together on February fourteen.

"I figured I'd give you a call before you went into the office. How are you? You're already out of the house? Sounds like you're in your car."

"Yeah. On my way to Social Circle."

"Oh. You're going to see my boo Annie-Lou? You think she'll make me one of her boysenberry pies?" Ian said. "Let me call my grandma on the other line." (He was seriously about to click over. Grammy Annie-Lou seldom sent me back to Atlanta without a pie for Ian.)

"I doubt it," I said.

"What? No pie? Damn!" Ian laughed but stopped quickly when he noticed my silence. "Everything OK?"

"She thinks something's wrong with King. Wants to put him down."

"Well, he is five hundred years old," Ian pointed out.

"That doesn't mean he has to die," I protested.

"Rach, are you crying?"

"No." (Lie.)

"You need me to meet you there?"

"No." I wiped my tears. "It's probably nothing. I'll just take him to the vet and get him a shot. Probably worms. You know how that old woman just feeds him anything! I put five hundred dollars worth of organic dog food in the shed and she feeds him turkey necks from her greens. King is fine. Just need to get him to the vet."

"You sure?"

"Yes," I said. "Anyway, I know you have a bunch of stuff to do. Scarlet probably has you putting in some work."

"Nah. We're just having dinner at this vegan spot in the West End. She wanted to use the day to support a black-owned business."

"Figures."

"What?" Ian was laughing again.

"Just classic Scarlet," I said. "She'll get over all that once she's out in the real world and gets a real job. You can only be militant for so long. Once you have bills to pay, you realize that the revolution isn't cheap."

"Sure the hell ain't," Ian agreed. "Speaking of the revolution, let me get off the phone, so I can finish grading these papers in time for my class. These kids will organize a *coup d'etat* if I don't give these papers back today."

"Cool."

"And Rachel—"

"What?"

"Happy Monday again."

Grammy Annie-Lou had three wigs: her church wig, her doctor's-office wig, and the wig she put on when she had company. I knew something was wrong when I got to the end of the winding dirt path that led visitors from the road to her house and she was sitting on the porch in her rocking chair with her thin, gray plats exposed. It was cold outside, so she had on a coat, but at the bottom I saw a housedress hanging out over the old winter boots she always wore around the yard.

When I was small, Grammy Annie-Lou seemed larger than life. She was a tall woman with wide hips and hands bigger than my father's. I'd once seen her mount a horse with no help from a man or step. She seemed to just fly up in the air and land on his back. Dug her heels into his sides and they took off down the road like the men did in all those Westerns. Mr. Durbin, a white man who always stopped by the house when I was a little girl, was beside me in front of the house. I wouldn't have believed what I was seeing if he hadn't been right there to confirm it. He spat some red tobacco onto the dirt and said in a way that I probably shouldn't have heard, "You have to respect a woman like that." When Mr. Durbin died, Grammy Annie-Lou didn't go to the funeral, but he left her everything he had. My father said they were lovers. She never once admitted it.

Over the years, Grammy Annie-Lou's stature, her ability to climb a horse and take off down the dirt road had declined. She seemed so much smaller and slower. Like what she was, the woman who had to be respected, was fading away with time. I didn't know if it was because I was getting taller or she was getting smaller. I imagined that one day she'd be so small I'd be able pick her up in my arms and carry her to her bed. I'd do that willingly.

"Hey, Pop out," she said, her arms shaking a little with age and extended to me as she came down the steps to greet me. The house behind her looked like something from an old Civil War movie. It was big and yellow. Had ten windows in the front and a white porch that wrapped all the way around it. It was in the middle of five acres of land my great-great grandfather purchased outright with money he'd saved before the Civil War. Grammy Annie-Lou would tell anyone who'd listen that her grandfather said, "Not one of my seeds gon' be planted in soil that won't let it pop out and see all the world." She always said I was the "pop out."

"Hey, Grammy." I kissed her on the cheek and inhaled every scent she could offer in a hug. "Where's your hair? And why don't you have anything on your legs? It's cold out here." I had on a coat and a hat, but I was still cold.

"You mind your eyes, Miss Ann!" she said, laughing. "We got business out here. I been waiting for you." She pointed to the cold plate of neck bones. "See? See? King ain't ate a thing."

"He's probably sick." I walked to the porch and got down on my knees to see him. All I could make out was shadows and some old stacks of bricks. I got up and walked around to the other side of the steps to see if I could spy him out over there. "You sure he's still under here?"

"I'm old, but not dumb, Pop out."

I looked up at her and rolled my eyes. "I didn't say you were dumb." I squinted a little at something round in the back corner. "You got a flashlight?"

"Yes," she said. "But you don't need it. Go on and call him."

I looked back at the roundness in the corner. "King," I called, but it sounded more like I was just saying the word than calling him to come to me. "King!" I looked up at Grammy Annie-Lou.

She shrugged her shoulders.

"King!" I waited a second. "King!"

The roundness moved just a little.

I got up again to go around to the back of the porch, so I could get closer to him, maybe coax him out with my voice.

"I'll go on and get the shotgun in case he come out," Grammy Annie-Lou announced, going in the other direction and up the steps into the house.

"You ain't gonna need it," I said. "He's sick. I'm just gonna take him to the doctor."

"He sick 'cause he old. Time to put him down. That's the best thing to do."

Grammy Annie-Lou went into the house to get her shotgun that she kept underneath her bed.

"King!" I called as I walked around the porch. "King! King!" As I shouted, I thought of how odd it sounded to hear my voice so loud. In the city, I hardly called anything out so firmly, so directly. Maybe I'd yell at someone cutting me off in traffic, but that was quick and out of anger. Here, in Social Circle, I could scream out loud and no one would care, because no one would hear. Not for a long way. "King! King!"

I got as close to King under the backside of the

porch as I could and tried to crawl under the porch, thinking I could maybe pet him or ease him out. It was so cold out there, I was hoping he hadn't gotten stuck and was freezing to death.

On my hands and knees, I got a few inches cleared under the porch, with my breasts nearly scraping the ground.

King moved a little. Let out a loud sigh.

"King," I called a little softer. My fingers were freezing. I could see his little eyes. Smell him even through the cold. "Here, boy! Here!"—that's how I'd called him when he was young and we'd learned every inch of my family's five acres on expeditions that included two chunks of cornbread I'd stuffed into my pockets—one for me and one for King. "Here, boy! Here!" I got closer to the little eyes. Dirt was everywhere. There was a pinching ant on my hand, but I knew better than to panic or it would pinch me for sure. "Here, boy! Here!" I got closer to the little eyes.

King moved back. Sighed louder.

"King! It's me! Rachel! I know you know me." When I was close enough to him, I reached out. "Here, boy! Here!" I reached. I inched in some more. I reached. When I almost got to King, he let out a low growl at first, but then he snapped and snarled and barked so loud I flinched. The ant bit my hand and I hollered. King growled and snarled and barked again. This time he didn't stop. Forgetting I was under the porch, I went to stand and hit my head on one of the beams. I might've been knocked out and probably had a mild concussion, but I kept moving. So fast, I crawled back from the little eyes until I could see the sun on my hands.

"Pop out, you know better than to crawl under

the porch with that dog!" Grammy Annie-Lou was waiting for me with the shotgun. "That's how you got bit when you was five."

"Thanks for reminding me."

"Lord, what's that on your hand?" She grabbed my hand. Blood was dripping from the sides.

"I got bit."

"King? He ain't never bit nobody before!"

"No. It was an ant."

The blood was covering a little mound where the ant had dug into me trying to defend itself.

"Can't believe an ant done all this," she said, inspecting the bite. "I told Juan not to be buying that cheap fertilizer from Walmart. Turning all the ants here to crazy. I think they ships it from China. Ain't nothing good gonna come to America from China. They hate us. Why would you buy a bunch of cheap stuff from people who hate you? Poison you for sure. Now we got overgrown pinching ants. You know Walmart is the devil?"

"I know," I said. I'd heard her position on Walmart before. After her best friend Claudine had to close her dress shop downtown when "we got a Walmart" (that's how people in the country announce it when a Walmart comes to town) and she couldn't beat their prices, Grammy Annie-Lou has been talking about how Walmart is the devil in some way or another.

"Let me go in the house to get something for this overgrown pinching ant bite," she said, handing me the shotgun. "I'll be right out."

I bent down and looked under the porch for King again.

He'd turned around to face the front of the house.

"Whatever," I said, slumping down against the side of the porch, and set the rifle on the dirt between my legs.

There was a small lake that Grammy Annie-Lou liked to call the Winslow River in the back of the house. My father had always pointed out that it wasn't even on the maps of Georgia. He also pointed out that he'd fallen in love with my mother on Winslow River. He'd taught her how to pitch two pebbles at one time and watch the ripples bounce against one another. To him, it was just a game he'd played in the tiny lake in his mother's backyard. But to my mother, it was how she could explain everything in the world. He'd once told me she'd said, "We all connected. All of us. One person hurt, we all hurt. One person happy, we all happy." He hadn't understood what she was saying at the time. They were just twelve years old and my father had been held back two grades in school. He didn't even know why my mother was talking to him, but he never let her out of his sight after she explained the ripples in Winslow River that way. He said that what she'd said made it seem less like a little lake and more like a big river. The same was true about Social Circle, Georgia. The world. He married her the day after her high school graduation. He dropped out of high school and got a job two months later when they discovered that she was pregnant with me. When I came along, he said that times were hard and nothing came easy, but those were the best months of his life with my mother. Just watching her hold me and sing to me made him love her so much he knew he'd never want to live without her. And three months after I was born, when she died of an infection she prob-

ably got when she delivered me, he didn't want to
live. And he was about to kill himself. Had strung
the rope up over the low beam in the barn nearly a
half mile away from Grammy Annie-Lou's house.
He was about to climb to the loft and jump out
with the rope around his neck when he heard
King barking. King was just a puppy then. He was
the sickly runt in a litter of puppies one of the dea-
cons at the church had been selling in the parking
lot one afternoon after Sunday School. On account of my father being nineteen and a widower
with a baby, the deacon just gave King to him,
thinking the dog might live just long enough to
help my father through his pain. When my father
heard King's bark for the first time in that barn
when he was about to hang himself from the low
beam, he knew something was wrong. "What is it,
boy?" he called to King from the loft. King slipped
underneath the barn doors and started barking
wildly. "What is it?" my father repeated. And when
he would tell the story, he'd always say, "And then
King just stopped barking. He looked into my eyes
in a way that told me to listen. And so, I did. Then
I heard—it was you, Rachel. You was just three
months old, up in your cradle in Grammy Annie-
Lou's bedroom, crying your little eyes out, screaming so loud for your daddy to come home. No way
I should've heard you. No way the stupid runt
should've known to come and get me. I walked out
of that barn and moved your cradle down to my
room. No way I'd leave you again."

"King, I need you to come out from under this
porch," I said, crying and still looking at the lake.
"I need you to just come out and get in the car

with me, so I can take you to the doctor. I need you not to fuss at me. I know you mad. I know I left you here. But if you don't stop this, we gonna have to put you down." I kicked the shotgun to the side and pulled my knees to my chest. Buried my head in the palm of my hands to hide my tears from no one. I didn't even know why I was crying. King was older than midnight. He had one good eye and six good teeth left—and that was the situation the last time I'd seen him on Christmas. There was no reason for him to still be alive. And probably no one really cared if he died. "Please come out, King! Please!" I started sobbing so loudly, I wondered if Juan, the boy who helped my grandmother fix things around the farm, could hear me from the barn.

"Rachel." I heard my name called so softly it sounded like I was in heaven with my mother and father.

I looked up and there was Ian, the sun shining behind his head.

"Ian?"

"Yeah." He knelt down beside me. He had on his work clothes and glasses. The same hat he was in at Bird's.

"What are you doing here?"

"You sounded like you really needed me," he said. "I canceled class and hit the road. I saw Ma Lou in the house. She told me you were back here."

"I didn't mean for you to do that."

"I didn't mean for you to ask me."

I fell into his arms, crying harder and telling him about the ant under the porch with King.

"You can't climb under a porch with a dog," Ian repeated my grandmother's advice to make me laugh.

"I know that," I said. "But how else am I supposed to get him? He won't come out when I call him."

"Well, he went under the porch to get away from people," Ian said. He stood up and started looking around.

"What are you looking for?"

"A stick or something."

"You're going to poke him out?"

He looked at me. "Just watch me work." He looked around and went to pick up a long branch that had fallen from the pear tree on the side of the house. "You got something of your father's? Like a shirt or jacket?"

Grammy Annie-Lou walked around to us with a napkin and peroxide in her hands. I knew she'd seen Ian because she'd changed into a baby blue sweatsuit and had on her church wig.

"I got some of his old clothes still in his room," she said.

"Good," Ian said. "Just get one of his shirts. A dirty one if you have it."

Grammy Annie-Lou set the things in her hand on the porch and went back into the house.

"What do you need my father's shirt for?" I asked.

"I figure the old dog probably misses his master. It's almost a year since your father passed away. Right?"

I thought about it and Ian was right. It had been eleven months.

"If King smells your father, that might make him

excited enough to come out," Ian said. "It's worth a shot."

Grammy Annie-Lou reappeared with an old denim shirt in her hands. It was my father's favorite.

I stood up and watched Ian wrap the shirt around the stick.

He pushed the stick under the porch and Grammy Annie-Lou and I started calling King again.

"King! King!"

"Here, boy! Here, boy!"

"King! King!"

There was rustling. Ian pulled the stick out and we waited. King didn't come out.

I kept calling, though.

"Here, boy! Here, boy! Papa came back for you. You better come on and see him. Here, boy! Here, boy!"

There was more rustling. No King.

Ian was about to push the shirt wrapped around the stick back under the porch again, but then King crawled out and we cheered like he was just being born.

"Here, boy! Here, boy!" I said, setting the shirt on King's shoulder.

He didn't lick at me or wag his tail. He looked like an old country dog who'd been hiding under the porch and not eating. He was shaking and dirty. So cold. I could feel his ribs. Smell something like death in his mouth. I was crying, but smiling. Holding him in my arms. I looked up at Grammy Annie-Lou and Ian. They had worry on their faces.

"Ian and I are going to take him to the vet," I said confidently. "He'll be fine. It'll all be fine."

"Pop out, I know you is sad because that's your daddy's dog, but he don't need no doctor," Grammy Annie-Lou said. "He needs his rest."

I looked at the shotgun in the dirt and started crying harder again.

"I'll go with her to the vet, Ma Lou," Ian said. "Don't worry about it."

"You is some kind of man to my grandbaby," Grammy Annie-Lou said, sliding her arm around Ian's waist. "Take a real man to make a woman right when she's wrong."

Ian beamed so brightly I felt King roll his eyes.

"I'll have two pies ready for you when you come back from the doctor's and they put the dog down," she said.

"They aren't going to put him down," I said, holding King tighter and covering his ears. "He just has worms and needs a shot."

The doctor told us we needed to put King down.

I cried like he was my best friend. I cried like I never knew how much I loved that lazy dog. I cried like I missed a mother I'd known. I cried like I never mourned my father.

I signed the paperwork giving the doctor the right to inject poison into King's body. I knew Grammy Annie-Lou would say that the shotgun would've been cheaper, but I didn't want to see the shotgun, hear the shot and know that my father's dog was bleeding from his head. With the injection, I could imagine he was sleeping. Dreaming about the red truck and my father.

When it was done and King's heart had stopped

beating beneath my ear on the cool metal table, where the only veterinarian in Social Circle had laid his body, Ian helped me up and walked me out to the waiting room that instantly became a funeral parlor. I fell to the floor and wailed so hard the vet and his secretary went to wait in the office.

Ian got down on the floor and rocked me so close to his heart I felt it beating.

He was right. I didn't mean for him to come. But I needed him to be there.

"I left him here," I cried into Ian's shoulder. "I should've taken him with me."

"To Atlanta?" Ian laughed to make me aware of how I sounded. "You think King would've fit in at Piedmont Park with the Chihuahuas and bulldogs?"

"Don't talk bad about my dog!" I said.

"I'm sorry. I was just pointing out that he was where he was supposed to be. King wasn't a leash dog. Not all dogs are meant to be tied to a person like that. He was out here free. Could come and go as he pleased. He chose to stay until he couldn't stay anymore."

"He was a good dog," I said. "Had my back."

"That's what a good dog is supposed to do."

I watched Ian so closely in the car on the way back to Grammy Annie-Lou's. I was still thinking about King, but I couldn't help but remember what Journey said about me committing to not love him. Grammy Annie-Lou was right: he was so good to me. So supportive. So loving. I wondered if I'd let him slip by me. If he'd let me slip by him.

I slid my hand over his on the armrest between the seats. We smiled at each other the rest of the way.

When we got to the house, Grammy Annie-Lou had cooked everything she could find and had lain it out on the dining room table. There were ribs and greens. Macaroni and cheese and yams.

Ian started rubbing his belly and she giggled so deeply I knew they were in love.

"Pies in the oven. Be ready in an hour, but then it needs to cool," she said and it was easy to imagine that it was how she'd sounded when she'd offered my grandfather a plate long before I was born.

"No worries," Ian said, sitting in one of the dining room chairs before the massive afternoon meal. "I got all night."

"All night? Don't you have to get back to Atlanta for your Valentine's date with Scarlet?" I asked when Grammy Annie-Lou went back into the kitchen.

"Canceled it," he said nonchalantly.

"Canceled what? You can't cancel a Valentine's Day dinner with your fiancée—unless you want to die!"

"It's not my life you should be worried about," Ian said, laughing. "She didn't sound too happy that you had an emergency!"

"Ian! That's awful. Go back to Atlanta and be with your fiancée. I can bring the pie."

"Rachel, I'm where I want to be. I'll see Scarlet tonight when I get home." Ian reached down and unbuttoned his belt. "But now, we eat!"

4

"Pretty in Pink"

#Youneverreallyknowwhosomeoneisuntil . . . you help that someone plan a wedding. As the old cliché goes: there's something about weddings and funerals—they bring out the worst and sometimes the best in people. Too often, I've learned that weddings bring out the worst . . . in women. Maybe it's because most women start planning for their weddings the moment that first Barbie doll is slid into their soft little hands and they consider, without even being told, that finding a Ken and getting a Barbie Dream House after the perfect sunset wedding is the most desired chain of events in a woman's life. And by the time they actually get to that perfect sunset wedding—if they get to that wedding—most women are raving lunatics trying to make a day in their real adult life match up with the expectations of their seven-year-old imagination. I wish the outcome was more pleasant. But it never is. As amazing and beautiful and wonderful as the actual day can be, it'll only come close to being a representation of that imagined day. And the frazzled female walking down the aisle, crying because it all turned out worse than she expected or better than she believed, is just a fragment of the lovely human being she was before her future husband put a ring on her finger. If he's super lucky, time and epiphany will return that woman he only proposed to because he thought she'd never change. Luckily, most of these men wait it out, though. They give in and give out, sit on the sidelines, and agree to whatever they need to just to get her down the aisle and things back to normal.

I wasn't having any delusions that this set of events would be different with Scarlet. It didn't matter what she'd told me about me having total control and her and Ian following my lead. At the end of the day, I was the wedding planner and it was her wedding. She'd transform like all of the other transformers I'd seen. I just wondered what she'd transform into. Would she be the nitpicking, worry-wart, drama queen, or full-on bridezilla? And how would Ian handle it all?

One month before the wedding, and Krista and I came up with the answer to the first question. Scarlet wasn't in any of those common categories. Oh no. Ms. Scarlet outlived and outshined all who came before her. In the short time we had to plan her destination wedding in a town she knew nothing about and on a quarter of the budget we were used to working with, and while we were planning another celebrity wedding in just weeks, in private e-mails and on Post-it notes around the office Scarlet became known as "Two Face." The name—which Krista came up with in homage to the Batman comic book character Harvey Dent after a vial of acid thrown on the left side of his face left him horribly disfigured and forced his dormant split personality to the surface—perfectly described Scarlet's hourly changes of heart. One hour, she'd be in a meeting with me, all granola and Mama Africa, trying to save the world and refusing to have wedding bouquets ordered from shops that wouldn't guarantee that workers, from picking to delivery, were paid above minimum wage. The next hour, she'd send a text to Krista all hard and harsh in all caps and with no periods and smiley faces at the end, demanding only the best orchids and saying her father would pay top dollar. Krista would forward the text to me with an intro: Two Face strikes again.

After the day King died in Social Circle and Ian held me in his arms tight like he was my father and knew just how to love me at that moment, it was hard for me to watch and witness and work around all of this. I knew in that car on the way back from the vet that I was in love with Ian. I'd known for a long time that I was in love with Ian. I just couldn't admit it to myself. I was happy, I was comfortable with the way things were—the way they'd been. I didn't want to break what hadn't been broken. Thinking about it that way, I wondered if maybe the same way Ian had been enjoying two pies, I was also getting water from two wells. I was single and so sad about it. But I was never really alone when Ian was around. Bad date: he'd always be there. Need a comforter: I didn't even have to call. He was my boy-best-friend. And having him in that category maybe made him better than any other man in my life. Like Journey said about me, he wasn't going anywhere. But with Scarlet's regime picking up the pace, I wondered how long that would be true. I also started to wonder how long I could keep my secret from Ian. If I needed to.

Scarlet's mother was out of town at a conference the morning of Scarlet's final dress fitting. Scarlet called me before sunrise crying—literally crying— and begging me to go with her. She didn't want to take any of her friends, saying she wanted them to see her dress for the first time at the wedding. Ian was out of the question and Scarlet's father was busy at his practice. Half asleep, I was so eager to get her sobs off my phone that I agreed to meet her at the Buckhead Dress Studio first thing in the morning. When I said yes, she cheered like a cry-ing child who'd just been given a candy bar. I could literally hear the tears dry up through the phone.

"Thank you! Thank you! Thank you!" she cried. "You're the best. I know why Ian loves you so much."

I hung up the phone and told Krista she'd have to have the intern take over the office for the day. There was no way I was sitting through that fitting alone with Two Face.

Scarlet was waiting outside the shop in Ian's car. My heart skipped a beat when Krista and I pulled up.

"I can't believe we're still going through with this wedding," Krista said, parking in a spot beside Ian's car. All of my epiphanies about Ian hadn't been self-generated. Over after-work margaritas a few days after the day in Social Circle, I'd told Krista about sliding my hand over Ian's in the car. How he didn't move. How he'd said, "Rachel, I'm where I want to be."

"What am I supposed to say?" I asked. "Hey Scarlet, I can't plan your wedding anymore. I fell in love with your fiancé when my dog died?"

"You could start there."

"Ian would be so confused. He'd probably move to Afghanistan and join a madrasah."

"Or admit that he loves you and take the ring from Two Face," Krista said, pointing at Scarlet waving at us excitedly from inside the other car.

"Oh God!" I cried. "What the fuck am I doing?"

"I don't know," Krista said. "Look, why don't you let me take over on this one? I can lead. You're in the wedding. It doesn't make sense for you to be the lead planner. What are you going to do on the day of the wedding?"

"I'll think about it."

Scarlet had e-mailed me pictures of herself in her wedding dress when she picked it out. I commonly go to fittings with my local clients. I like seeing the dresses and imagining what they'd look like floating down an aisle draped in purple Peruvian lilies or terra-cotta royal roses. It inspires me as I plan. And it also helps me to bond with the bride, who most times never imagines I'd even ask to come.

I didn't request an invite to Scarlet's picking, but I did ask for shots. The Hotel St. La Rho, where Ian and Scarlet's wedding would be, had two reception halls: one with windows all along the back, another with a view of the sky from a window on top of the dance floor. I thought that seeing Scarlet's dress and picturing how the lights from the pier one block away from the hotel might look crawling over her shoulders or imagining the moon kissing her forehead could help me decide which setting to ink. The picture had been of a contemporary Monique Lhuillier that looked more like it was for the two-month marriage of a Hollywood starlet than for a future graduate student and UN Ambassador. I went with the lights on her back.

The staff at the Buckhead Dress Studio knew me, so they had a full spread of drinks and food awaiting Scarlet. Her dress wasn't cheap, but I knew that red-carpet treatment wasn't without reason. They were spoiling her in front of me in hopes that I'd send other clients their way.

Scarlet downed two glasses of Perrier-Jouët before following the studio attendant into the fitting room.

"Two Face," Krista whispered to me on the couch where we were sitting and not touching any of the food or drinks—after seeing the burnt orange mermaid dress Scarlet had me walking down the aisle in, I'd committed to losing seventy-five pounds by the wedding. "I hate to see what she's like when she's drunk."

"You guys ready?" Scarlet called from inside the dressing room.

"Jesus, please be a fence," Krista said and I elbowed her.

"Yes! Come on out," I answered Scarlet.

The attendant, a short Italian woman who hardly spoke English and had pins darting up the front of her right sleeve, walked out of the little room first and held out her hands dramatically toward the door. "The bride," she announced.

Scarlet walked out, all smiles, and I went from being the least anxious person in the room to the most confused.

The bride, who was supposed to be dressed in white, was dressed in pink.

"Pink?" Krista confirmed my vision.

"It's rose." Scarlet's smile evaporated and her face looked more like mine and Krista's. She looked at me with her shoulders ready to slump. "You like it?"

"What . . . ? Why . . . ?" I was at a loss for words. It was the same ML from the picture she'd sent, but it was a new color. And Scarlet really did look beautiful in it, but colorful wedding dresses just never went over well.

"It's my signature color. My favorite," Scarlet whined and I had the sense that if someone didn't say something nice fast, she'd run out of the store in the dress and right into traffic. The fragile girl in front of me needed me to approve.

"Beautiful! Molto bello!" The little Italian woman must've sensed it, too. She kissed her fingers.

Krista and I gave her a "butt-out" glower and she stepped out of the fitting area apologetically.

"You hate it?" Scarlet's eyes were already red.

"But you sent me a picture of a white dress," I said, avoiding answering the question. I got up and walked over to her. She looked so desperate standing in front of the couch alone.

"I had it dyed. Ian loves this color on me."

"Well, it's your wedding. It's not necessary to wear your favorite color at your wedding," I said, feeling ridiculous for having to point that out and afraid that if I mentioned white, Scarlet would go into some speech about "purity" and "male domination"—only pink (rose) wasn't any better than white. She looked like a girl going to her first dance. The quaint yet elegant event I'd planned was about to look like a 1980s prom.

Living up to her nickname, Scarlet tried to stand her ground. She put her hands on her hips defiantly. "This is what I want! There's nothing wrong with it." She sounded like she was about to have a tantrum.

Krista and I looked at each other.

"We're not saying there's anything wrong with it," Krista said carefully. "It's just that in our history, most times when we see colored wedding dresses, it doesn't come off quite as beautiful as the bride intended. We don't want you to go for this and then be disappointed on your wedding day."

"But it's my day!" Scarlet cried and ran back into the fitting room.

"What the hell?" Krista said. "Did Angela Davis just have a breakdown over a pink wedding dress?"

The attendant came back in and headed to help Scarlet out of her dress.

I stopped her. "Let me get her," I said.

I knocked on the door. "Can I come in?"

"It's open."

I opened the door. Scarlet was still in the dress and sitting on a dressing stool with her elbows on her knees.

"You might want to stop crying. Don't want to damage your ML," I said, trying to get her to laugh. I'd been in this position so many times. Weddings are emotional events. And women are emotional beings. For most weddings, I was more of a clinical psychologist than a wedding planner. Scarlet just needed a human touch. A reminder of what the wedding was all about and who she was. The only problem was that this wasn't just any wedding and any bride. After my epiphany, I'd been going on pure instinct, maneuvering the wedding planning for Ian. But was I capable of talking his fiancée into not freaking out and becoming the Goliath of all monster brides? A more conniving and diabolical person would take advantage of the situation and use Scarlet's mania to her benefit. Maybe push her over the ledge and make Ian see her for who she really was: a little girl in a pink dress. But . . . I'm a professional and I was raised better than that.

"I thought it would be pretty. Different," Scarlet cried, ignoring my comment about stains. "Ian likes it when I'm different."

I sat down on the floor in front of the mirror Scarlet was facing.

"I think you look pretty," I offered.

"You do?" Scarlet looked at me.

"Your skin . . . the rose does compliment it," I said. "It's just different. And what we fear, what Krista was explaining, is that if you wear something different, people will be so busy looking at your dress, they won't notice you."

"I only care what Ian thinks."

"And if you like it and he loves it, then I say go for it."

"You think so?"

"Mama Dupree won't be happy about it, but like you said, this is your wedding. If you choose this dress, Krista and I will make sure every detail, from the lighting to the candles, complements it. We'll make it work."

"Thank you, Rachel," Scarlet said, jumping up

and falling over on the floor to give me a hug. "I knew you would understand."

A week before the wedding and I was hiding out. I'd turned everything over to Krista and used the excuse of focusing on Alarm Clock and Donnica's big day to get away from Ian's calls and e-mails. I stopped answering the phone. I couldn't face him. Not with what I knew. With what I was feeling. I had to keep my distance. I was afraid to say anything to him, thinking everything would just come out of my mouth in one embarrassing ramble.

I felt like I was about to burst, though. I had no outlet. Journey hadn't signed on to video chat in weeks. She was probably moving around and dealing with Dame's schedule. Sometimes I wondered if she resented him, how she had to keep his career first until he had a break and she could get back into the studio to start singing again.

I started sending her e-mails to keep her caught up on my drama. I figured she could at least read them and send me good vibes from wherever she was in the world. Scarlet had already moved in with Ian and she'd told Krista that they were talking about turning the office I'd decorated into a nursery. A nursery? For what?

One night, after looking at pictures of Ian and me in our FAMU yearbook, when I was about to get into my car and drive over to his place, my computer started ringing on my desk in the living room and Journey in her newly twisted dreadlocks showed up on the screen.

"Thank God!" I said, sitting at the desk. "I was about to do something crazy."

"Yeah. I finally got to sit down and read your e-mails. We've been on the road," she said.

Dame was walking around in the background rocking Apache in his arms. He was wearing basketball shorts and a white tee. It was always interesting to see rappers, who appear larger than life in music videos and on magazine covers, living and just moving about in their everyday lives. They were fathers and husbands. Sons and brothers. Just like everybody else.

Dame handed Journey a Pampers. "I think Apache needs to be changed. You smell that?"

"Yes. Change her." Journey rolled her eyes at me and tried to hand the Pampers back to Dame, but he wouldn't take it.

"I'm holding Apache," he said.

"Then you can change her." She tried to hand him the Pampers again, but Dame backed up.

"I don't change diapers. That's the agreement." He bent down over Journey's shoulder. "Oh hey, Rachel! Wassup?"

"I'm good," I said. "How are you?"

"Being a black man in the world. It's a hard job. Got my wifey over here trying to emasculate a brother by making me change diapers." When Journey and Dame got married, he had locs down his back, but now his head was shaved clean. He looked a little older.

"*Your* kids' diapers!" Journey exclaimed. "Your kids that you made. Why is this so hard?"

"A man wasn't meant to handle doo-doo," Dame said, backing up.

"So a woman is meant to handle doo-doo?" Journey asked.

"Someone has to do it. What do you think, Rachel?"

"I don't know," I said, holding up my hands defensively. "I'm not getting into it."

"What she meant to say is go and change your child's diaper. Damn!" Journey held out the Pampers to Dame again.

He snatched it roguishly and walked away.

She leaned into the camera and whispered, "It's like I have four kids sometimes."

"I heard that," Dame hollered in the background.

Journey repositioned herself and took a deep breath.

"So, Ms. Winslow, enough of the woes of a roadie housewife. What's up with you? How are you holding up?"

In one of the e-mails, I'd told Journey about the car ride in Social Circle and that rose dress.

"I love him," I said. "I'm in love with Ian."

"Finally, we have full acceptance!" Journey cheered. "So what are you going to do?"

"Put on my orange dress and watch him get married."

"So you're sure that's what he wants?"

"I already told you, he's made his decision. There's nothing I can do about it," I said. "I'm miserable. I just can't believe he's really going to marry her. He can't see her bullshit. You know, I called the school to see about that program in the Congo. . . . There is no program. I think she made it up."

"You called the school?" Journey grimaced like she now had the full picture of my foolery.

"I only called because I needed to know that I wasn't crazy. I knew something was up with her."

"Did you tell Ian?"

"No."

"So what was the point? Now you know your best friend is marrying a woman who's been lying about who she really is and you're not going to do anything about it?"

"It's too late. Anything I do now will look crazy," I said.

"Maybe it's not too late." Journey looked at me mischievously.

"The wedding is next week," I reminded her. "That's too late. He's not going to change his mind right now. The invitations are out. The families are on their way. It would take an act of God for him to call it off at this point."

"Or an act of love."

"No. There's no way I'm putting my hand on that."

"I'm not telling you to go break up the brother's wedding," Journey said. "Like I said before, I just want you to wait and listen. If he comes to you, be open to it . . . but you have to be present and available in case it happens."

"So you're saying I should avail myself to break up his wedding."

"I'm saying you shouldn't let him settle. And you shouldn't let yourself settle. I know what that's all about. I was there. It ain't pretty," Journey said, referring to her first marriage.

"How did you know, J, that you'd found the person who was worth risking everything for?"

"We loved each other equally. One day, I realized that the same way he was running to me, I wanted to run to him. I wanted him. He had to get me there, but I did. And I knew getting him wouldn't be easy, but it was worth it. It's all worth it. Life is too short not to take risks for love."

Dame walked back into view and kissed Journey on the shoulder.

"Can I go to bed now?" he asked.

"After you give me some sugar," she said.

They pecked and then Dame turned to me.

"Night, Rachel," he said.

"Night, Dame."

5

"Laisser Les Bons Temps Rouler"

#don'tmixbusinesswithpleasure. I know I shouldn't have. I *probably* shouldn't have. But I did. Because I had to. And I was paying for it. The first—and consequently what I thought was the last—time I'd planned a wedding for a friend, it turned into an unpaid fiasco where my constant bickering with my godsister over her Louis Vuitton emblem theme that she insisted on splashing over every element of the wedding (including her bridesmaids' dresses and her groom's bowtie) led to an ugly court battle, the conclusion of our friendship, and some jail time (she cursed out the judge for siding with me and calling her wedding idea tacky). Still, here I was, on my way to the same altar. Or so it felt. There was less drama, but I had the same gut feeling. That I had to act. And that my action could be disastrous. Things could get ugly. I could lose a friend.

This time my best friend. And who knew about jail time. Nothing could be predicted in the Big Easy.

I kept considering the possibilities on the flight into New Orleans with Krista. Everything felt wrong. And I needed to do what was right. But for whom? If Journey was right and I waited for the sign, the perfect time to open up to Ian about how I felt, I could fix it. I could have him. Make him see that I was what he'd been missing. But if I didn't, if I stuck to the plan, did my job, and did what I was supposed to do, he'd go his way and I'd go mine—back to my lonely couch. More pizza. More NyQuil. Only this time, I'd know for sure what I could've had and who I could've had it with. The man of my dreams. My best friend. I couldn't stand thinking of those odds.

In the car ride over to the hotel, Krista was turning through her stack of invoices and lists, last-minute changes Scarlet had called into the office before we left Atlanta. Krista kept pulling me in for a signature or response to something she was complaining or excited about, but I was in my head and she knew it. She didn't even wait for me to respond.

"Dress is here," she said once, clicking off her phone.

"Ian's parents have checked in." She clicked off the phone again. "I wonder if the hotel is giving out those gift bags we shipped." She looked in my direction, but didn't wait for me to open my mouth before adding, "I'll call Lori; she's the new manager. Did you know they have a new manager?" She pulled out her phone and then she was talking to Lori.

A few seconds later: "Check on the bags!" She looked out the tinted window of the Lincoln. "God, I love this city. Smells like crap, but it's so alive. Like a big-ass party." She peered deeper at something I pretended to spy as well and then she reached into her purse. She turned to me with a little clear box with little orange pellets inside. "Tic Tac?" She held it out to me.

"I'm fine," I said distantly.

"Humph."

If my feelings weren't making things bad enough, public opinion would.

After Krista and I checked into our rooms, we rang each guest to personally welcome them to New Orleans for the Dupree wedding and remind them of the welcoming reception Let's Get Married was hosting in the penthouse suite. Three associates I commonly took to destination weddings to help with service and details had flown in early to set things up with hotel staff.

"There's our girl," Ian's mother, Gwendolin, said, reaching for me when I walked into the suite with Krista. She was a dark-skinned woman with high cheekbones and an unforgettable air of importance in her voice. What was interesting about that pompous tone, though, was that Ian had grown up just as poor in New Orleans as I had. Mrs. Dupree had worked for her mother's housekeeping business and Mr. Dupree had played the trombone at a Ninth Ward shack nightclub that had been washed away with Hurricane Katrina. Still, Mr. Dupree was Creole and Ms. Dupree could prove her Indian blood with one look at her face. To them, that about made them royalty. They acted the part, and raised Ian to believe it.

"Hello," I said, returning Mrs. Dupree's dainty embrace and smiling at Mr. Dupree standing beside her.

Always dramatic and lively in the fashion of a true New Orleans man, Mr. Dupree insisted on kissing my hand. He was as tall as Ian, but had a potbelly filled with liquor to prove that he was serious about his music.

I introduced them to Krista and made sure one of the staffers filled Mr. Dupree's cup to the brim with Jim Beam. Some of the other guests were sprinkled around the room chatting and eating shrimp cocktail.

"How have you been, darling?" Mrs. Dupree asked. "We haven't seen you since last summer when we came to Atlanta for Ian's lecture at that college."

"Emerson," Mr. Dupree tried to add.

"Emory," I said, correcting him lightly. They could never remember where Ian taught. Their only care was that it was at a college. "And I'm fine. Just working hard. What about you two? I know you're excited about tomorrow."

Krista excused herself to see about a missing pot of shrimp étouffée.

"Excited? I suppose." Mrs. Dupree clasped her hands at her breasts in a way that added a layer to her statement. "I'm about to have me some grandbabies soon. Finally. Before my hair goes all gray!"

"Ain't nothing wrong with the hair on your head, Gwennie. Your worrying about it is what's making it gray," Mr. Dupree said. "Worry makes nothing but mess."

"Well, I guess you were very worried about your hair, then," Mrs. Dupree joked, swiping the big bald field at the top of her husband's head. They laughed and Mr. Dupree said something in French I think Mrs. Dupree half understood. She turned back to me and said, "Well, my boy is happy. I guess that's what matters. Now, have you met Ms. Scarlet's parents?"

"Not yet," I said, but I sensed her frostiness, so I added, "but I hear they're great people—according to Ian. He's pretty good at judging people."

"From Miami?" she quizzed suspiciously, begging me to confirm what she already knew. "Doctors?"

"Yes," I confirmed.

"Hum." She shot her nose up. "Hope they don't think they're coming in here to run something. They're in New Orleans. We have our ways."

"I understand," I said.

"I didn't even want to stay in this hotel," she said. "And we have room. They could've stayed with us."

"Please, Gwennie!" Mr. Dupree said. "What, you want to have the whole wedding party there, too? The wedding in the backyard?"

"That's how we did it in our day!"

"Things have changed, beloved. These kids don't want no crawfish out de crik!"

"I wouldn't mind that," I said, laughing.

"Speaking of," Mr. Dupree started and I knew what was coming next: "When are you getting married?"

"Well, I'm not rushing things. Just waiting to meet—"

"Oh, Erskine, mind your business!" Mrs. Dupree cut in. "She'll get married when she pleases! Right?"

"Yes," I said, happy she'd stopped me.

She leaned in and whispered in our trio, "I was hoping Ian would marry you! Perfect match, if you ask me."

"And no one asked you!" Mr. Dupree said.

Mrs. Dupree frowned at him and continued with a speech about the connection she'd seen between Ian and me since she'd met me during Parent's Weekend freshman year at FAMU.

"When Ian called and said he was getting married, I just knew who he was talking about," she concluded before the suite door swung open and loud noises broke up our little meeting. "I'd've been proud to have you as my daughter-in-law."

"Thank you," I said in my business voice to avoid crying and shaking in her arms. I turned to the source of the noise and excused myself with a nod. "I'm sure these are the groom's men."

Xavier Hamilton had been Ian's roommate all four years in undergrad. He was a lion-hearted Chicagoan whose voice could always be heard before he was seen. With a big laugh and bigger biceps, he didn't have to do much to attract the girls Ian had ignored. And after he made drum major of the Marching 100, no one could tell him anything. He became the unofficial king of campus.

Now he was easily the center of attention in the middle of the spectacle of fine men in casual suits that interrupted the moderated chatter in the suite. An unlit cigar in his hand, he was laughing the loudest and clearly in the middle of some tawdry tale that had the men around him at attention. I literally felt the women in the room strike a pose to look at him.

Jennifer, one of the women from Scarlet's birthday party, whose boyfriend was standing beside Xavier, started playing with her earring and whispered something to the woman beside her.

"Rachel Winslow! The baddest chick on the Yard!" Xavier said, coming over to me. He grabbed three shrimp from a platter and devoured them as he hugged me.

Jennifer kept whispering.

"Hey, X," I said. "Don't get on me. You were the true player!"

"Well, you know how I do!" Xavier grinned and looked right at my breasts—right through my dress.

"Yeah, I've heard." I'd actually met Xavier before I met Ian. He'd been standing outside the freshman girls' dorm when I was moving in and asked me to lunch. He took me to a wing's spot off campus and refused to pay for my food until I kissed him. I didn't, and I never heard from him again. When we realized we had Ian in common, he decided it was OK for him to be my friend, even though I hadn't kissed him. He'd moved onto bigger fish by then. Still, he made it a point to make a pass at me whenever he saw me.

"The million-dollar lady! I see you set this shit up real proper like for our boy!"

"I wouldn't have it any other way," I lied.

"I can't believe this fool is getting married. But I saw Scarlet. She's banging."

"Yeah, I guess that's reason enough to marry her," I joked, turning to be sure Ian's parents didn't hear Xavier's foolishness. Luckily, they'd moved on to chat up Ian's uncle, Uncle Cat, who was a spectacle all his own.

"So what's going on with you? You breaking motherfuckers' hearts in the A? I know they stay on their knees for you," Xavier said. He owned two McDonald's on the southside of Chicago and had an MBA from Wharton, but he'd kept his hood and swagger. It amounted to this rare mix of street corner and boardroom shine, with deep pockets and charm to back it up. I'd be lying if I said it wasn't sexy. But he was still Xavier and my side eye on him from the first flop at the wing spot was permanent.

"I do OK," I replied.

"No ring, though." He pointed at my naked ring finger. "I guess you're still available." Xavier looked at my breasts again and slid the cigar into Chapstick-shiny lips.

"Baybee girl, baybee girl! Look at those thick legs!" Uncle Cat invited himself into the conversation just as Krista popped her head into the suite to signal for me to come outside. We always escorted the bride and groom into the welcoming reception with the best man and matron of honor.

"Hi, Uncle Cat!" I said while signaling to Krista that I'd need a minute. "So glad to see you."

"Well, prove it to me!" Uncle Cat, who got his name on account of his metallic gray and green eyes, pulled me into an uncomfortably familiar embrace. A fifty-year-old ladies' man who had five children by five different women, he was a creole cliché. Slick hair and vanilla skin with not one wrinkle to show his age, he had an easy accent that made you want to hear him speak. The joke was that you couldn't look into his eyes. Then you'd be the next baby mama, sure enough.

"Oh!" I wiggled around in his arms as Xavier got a peek at my butt.

"Nice and thick," Uncle Cat said.

"Thanks. I'll take that as a compliment."

"Ain't no other way to take it where I'm from."

Uncle Cat and Xavier laughed after slapping five and I imagined that Xavier would one day be just like him. X didn't have any children yet, though. Not that any of us knew of.

Scarlet was holding onto Ian's arm in the hall-way outside the suite like they'd already walked down the aisle. She had on a cute little turquoise halter dress and hot pink patent pumps that made her look like she was sixteen. Ian was simple in blue jeans and a FAMU T-shirt.

"What happened to the suit?" I asked, hugging Scarlet and then Ian.

"I already asked," Krista said.

I expected the same annoyance from Scarlet, but she kind of bit her lip and shrank under Ian's arm. The best man, Ian's only cousin and child-hood bestie, was standing beside them with the matron of honor, one of Scarlet's cousins who was a triplet and no less beautiful than Scarlet.

"Don't get on me, Rach," Ian said. "It's been a long, crazy day."

"We had to pick up my parents," Scarlet added apologetically.

"From the airport?" I probed. "You should've said something. We have people here to do that. Thought I told you."

"No . . . from Atlanta," Ian said and I could hear the anger in his voice now.

"Atlanta?"

"They missed their flight this morning, and they couldn't get on another one," he said.

"There's some kind of conference here this weekend," Scarlet added.

"We were on our way to the airport when they called, so we all decided to just drive," Ian said. "Seven whole hours."

"Well, where are they now?" Krista asked.

"Mom has a headache and Dad's returning calls from the practice." Scarlet looked like she was hiding behind Ian. Suddenly, all of her Black Power militancy was gone. She was a little girl. I had a feeling that she wanted us to handle everything.

I reached for Ian's hand. "It'll be fine."

I could feel Krista frowning beside me. "Are they coming down to the rehearsal?" She looked at her watch. "It's in an hour."

"Don't know. My mother has these migraines."

I could imagine how this was going to go over with Mrs. Dupree. This would be the story for years.

"We can fix it," I said. "Krista, send one of the staffers to their room to get a time and explain that they must at least come down to watch the rehearsal."

"Gotcha, boss lady."

"And take Ian's room key," I added. "Go up to his room and get his brown tweed Brooks Brothers jacket. That'll look great with what he's wearing."

"Done." Krista reached for the plastic room key card in Ian's hand.

"How do you know whether I have that jacket?" Ian asked, smiling because he did.

"You don't travel without that jacket, Mr. Dupree," I said.

"You swear you know me."

"I know you better than you know," I said and immediately regretted the intimacy in my voice.

Scarlet tightened her grip and looked like she was about to say something but felt she shouldn't.

Once Krista came back with the jacket, I escorted Scarlet and Ian into the reception, where Uncle Cat led a hysterical toast to the weekend by telling a story about the first time Ian fell in love.

"He came to his Uncle Cat, and I told de boy, love come Sunday, leave pain on Monday!"

We laughed at his frankness, but Krista, I noticed, was laughing the hardest. She was also gazing, in the style of a zombie, into Uncle Cat's eyes. I watched her tickle the inside of her elbow as he spoke.

"You OK?" I murmured, nudging her.

She smiled and straightened her arms.

Uncle Cat went on to welcome everyone to his hometown and share that New Orleans isn't Vegas, so "there's no 'what happens in New Orleans stays in New Orleans' rule." He said that no one in New Orleans should be sober enough to know or care what you're doing in New Orleans, so the only rule is to have a good time. "And be careful in the Quarter," he concluded. "For sure, whatever a man be seeking in the Quarter goin' crawl behind, follow him home at night. Wake wit' him in de mornin'. And I'm not talking no living desires neither. You can find anything in the Quarter. Your worst nightmare. Your best dream!"

Everyone was quiet, trying to decipher the weight of the mysterious message. Suddenly, though we knew better, we all imagined voodoo priestesses and witches' cauldrons mounted on every street corner in the Quarter.

"You stop it, now," Mrs. Dupree said, pulling Uncle Cat's arm. "You scaring these people half to death. Ain't nothing like that going on. This is a wedding. My son's wedding!" She smiled and turned to Ian. "I'm so proud of you!"

"Thanks, Mama," Ian said, kissing his mother on the cheek.

"My pride and joy," she beamed, hugging him.

As Mrs. Dupree loved on Ian, Krista announced that the wedding party needed to move to the hotel's atrium to rehearse for the ceremony and that the other guests were free to continue to party in the suite.

One of Mrs. Dupree's sisters started taking pictures of the Duprees and insisted that Scarlet get into some of the shots. Mrs. Dupree was still frowning, though, and kept her eyes sharp on Scarlet.

"Gwendolin, you get into the picture with Scarlet and Ian," the sister ordered. "I want one of just the three of you."

"Yeah!" Scarlet forced in her cheerleader voice, but I could tell she'd sensed Mrs. Dupree's stare. Everyone had. For some reason, Scarlet tried to trade places with Ian and stand next to Mrs. Dupree in the picture, but she looked at Scarlet like she was a dead squirrel and I literally felt the chill in the room. Ian wiped his forehead and smiled at his mother. There was nothing he could do but pray that she'd warm up to whatever was keeping her on ice.

Before her sister could snap the photo, Mrs. Dupree pointed to me and said, "You come on, Rachel! You get in the photo!"

"I can't; I'm working," I said.

"Nonsense," she argued. "I want a picture with you. Come on!" She called like I was her own child.

And I moved.

"Cheese!" we said as the cameras flashed. I was standing on the end beside Mrs. Dupree, who was beside Ian and Scarlet.

"Cheese!" again.

Mrs. Dupree rubbed my shoulder. "OK, now," she started, stepping backward and pushing Ian and me together, "let's get a picture of these two." She inched behind Ian and took Scarlet's hand.

"Mama, what are you doing?" Ian asked, seeing the repositioning come together.

"I want a picture of the two of you!" she replied. "You and Rachel." She pulled Scarlet. "Come on, sweetie!" she said like Scarlet was some hurt fawn.

The cameras started flashing again.

"Just perfect," Mrs. Dupree said, gripping Scarlet's arm. "Perfect."

"OK, we don't have long in here," Krista said, calming the wedding party down after the group trek to the atrium. "There's actually a ceremony in here tonight, so we're just going to walk through things one time and then we're out of here."

She had one of the staffers seat us in line order in the little white chairs in the front of the atrium as she went through the fine points of the ceremony on her iPad with Scarlet.

Mrs. Dupree kept asking about Scarlet's parents every thirty seconds or so, her voice getting more haughty, suggesting that if they didn't make it to the rehearsal maybe they didn't care about the wedding. "I wouldn't have missed this rehearsal for the world," she said at one point. "Even if I was dead, I would've paid the good Lord to resurrect me, so I could get back here to be with my baby."

Ian got up and pulled her into the back corner to talk to her. Some of Scarlet's other relatives had been listening to Mrs. Dupree's various comments and they were looking restless.

When Mr. and Mrs. Bloom finally did walk into the atrium, looking cool and nonchalant, everyone got quiet.

"Mami! Papi!" Scarlet ran to hug them like she hadn't seen them in years.

"Finally," Mrs. Dupree said, escaping Ian's hold in the corner. She straightened her jacket and headed to greet them, walking with her head high like she was some kind of New Orleans dignitary.

Mr. Dupree and Ian hurried behind her, looking less like anxious greeters and more like well-practiced buffers.

"Gwennie is about to show her ass," Uncle Cat said under his breath. "Sure as the sky is blue."

"Well, it's nice to finally meet you two," Mrs. Dupree said, loudly enough so we could hear in the front of the atrium. "It's not every day that two kids get married when their parents don't know each other—haven't met. Not where I'm from."

Krista ushered the parents to the front row.

Mr. and Mrs. Bloom were more beautiful than I remembered. I saw them at one of Ian's lectures at the public library when Scarlet and Ian first started dating. They looked like each other's patients—perfectly sculpted everything from head to toe. Mrs. Bloom's cream-colored skin looked like she sat in a vat of olive oil all day. She was dainty.

Looked like she was always wearing St. John. It was hard to imagine that someone so lovely could survive medical school and work with a scalpel everyday but easy to imagine she was Scarlet's mother. She looked just twenty-four hours older than Scarlet, but everything perfect in her face had been given to her daughter. The only thing she hadn't bequeathed was her color. That came from Scarlet's father. He was a muscular miracle in sepia. The kind of fine-ass older man that made girls more than half his age look at him and say, "He could get it . . . today."

This beauty meant nothing to Mrs. Dupree. It only gave her more reason to act upon her suspicions about Scarlet's parents and why she hadn't met them. For this, their punishment was incessant over-talking and grandstanding as Mrs. Dupree let them know that this was her town, her wedding, and her show. Even if they wanted to say something, they couldn't. Her tone said, "Pay attention before you get bitten."

Krista led the wedding party to the back of the atrium and got us in order, leaving Ian and his parents and Mrs. Bloom in the front. I was the last bridesmaid to walk down the aisle, with Scarlet's cousin. The matron of honor was behind me and then there was Scarlet.

"Now remember, bridesmaids and groomsmen, I don't want you to do a two-step tomorrow. You're walking to 'Ave Maria,' so just go slow and at your own pace," Krista said to us. "Let everyone get a look at you, take pictures, smile. Be natural."

"Don't be nervous, Star," Mr. Bloom said to Scarlet. Ian had told me that her parents wanted to name her Starlet, but there was a typo on her birth certificate and when they saw it, they liked Scarlet more.

I turned around and Mr. Bloom was gently massaging Scarlet's hand linked over his arm. She looked pale. Had the fearful look most brides had on their actual wedding day.

The line started moving forward after Krista cued the music.

Ian was already standing up front.

Mr. and Mrs. Dupree were seated in the front row in front of him.

Mrs. Bloom was seated in the second seat in the front row on the other side.

This order was so etched into my brain, it was like brushing my teeth.

"Ave Maria" continued to play and the line moved farther along. Jennifer and two of the triplets in front of me turned around playfully to wave goodbye to Scarlet before they left.

"Es mala suerte," Mrs. Bloom said, getting up from her seat right when I was about to step over the threshold. "Ella no puede pasar por el pasillo."

"What?" Mrs. Dupree shot up from the other side of the aisle.

"Mama!" Ian warned.

"What, she doesn't speak English?" Mrs. Dupree said. "No wonder she's so quiet."

"Of course she speaks English, Gwennie," Mr. Dupree said. "You just talk too damn much."

"It's bad luck," Mrs. Bloom said, translating her words, though her English was just as melodic and romantic as her Spanish. "She can't walk down the aisle. It's bad luck."

My first thoughts went to me. I assumed she was talking about me, since I was next. Oh my God!

Did she know what I was thinking about? Did she know about my feelings for Ian?

"Star," Mrs. Bloom said. "Estrella, siéntese!"

"What is she saying? This is just plain rude!" Mrs. Dupree fired off. "You know those women at my nail salon, they always speak in another language so they can—"

"Ain't nobody talking about you, Gwennie. Shut up," Mr. Dupree ordered.

"She wants me to sit down," Scarlet said. "It's bad luck for me to walk down the aisle before my wedding day."

"Of course," Krista said. "We're going to have your cousin, the matron of honor, walk down for you. I just wanted you in the back so you can see how the room will look when you walk in."

"Oh no, that's bad luck, too," Mrs. Dupree said.

"Mama!" Ian tried.

"I'm serious," she went on. "You can't have a married woman pretend to be a new bride. Down here that's almost like cheating on your husband."

"I ain't heard that before," Mr. Dupree said.

"Well, you *ain't* been in no wedding but your own neither, so unless someone else in here knows about New Orleans wedding traditions, I suggest we find someone else, who isn't married, to walk down the aisle for whatever her name is."

"Mama, stop it! Her name is Scarlet," Ian said.

"I'm sorry, son, but people keep calling her all types of things and stuff and I just met her, so I'm trying to keep up."

"That's fine, Mrs. Dupree," Krista said. She turned to the bridesmaids standing up front to pick someone to stand in and walk down the aisle for Scarlet.

"No need to send someone from the front. Just

let Rachel do it. Rachel can walk down the aisle!"
Mrs. Dupree said with mock randomness in her
tone.

"Me? No. I—I can't." I shook my head. (No way!)

"Yes, you can!" Mrs. Dupree pushed.

"But I'm—I—"

"Nonsense. Let's do this. You girls already said
we don't have a lot of time in here." Mrs. Dupree
took over. She went and stood next to Krista in the
aisle, grabbed the iPad, ordered Scarlet to come
and sit with her mother, and rushed my escort, the
matron of honor, and the best man down the aisle
with no music.

"I really don't think I'm the right person for
this." I tried to back out of the situation again just
before Mr. Bloom took my arm.

"Oh, aren't you the most beautiful bride," Mrs.
Dupree said. "Isn't she beautiful, Ian? The perfect
bride." She looked at Mrs. Bloom and explained
quickly and nonchalantly, "They're best friends. I
always expected them to get married. All of this
other stuff is really a surprise to me."

"Let's hurry up and get this over with," Krista
said.

"No, wait. I need a picture!" Mrs. Dupree started
snapping pictures.

There was a look of terror growing on Scarlet's
face.

Krista cued the music anyway. It was just instrumental, but Mrs. Dupree started singing the words,
serenading me as if I was the bride.

"Here comes the bride, all dressed in white. . . ."

Mr. Bloom started walking.

I was holding back, though, nearly pulling him
back to the start.

"Sweetly, serenely in the soft glowing light," Mrs. Dupree sang on, clicking pictures with her phone simultaneously.

Ian was in his own world, smiling at me like Mrs. Dupree was. He couldn't see Scarlet about to run down the aisle and snatch me off of her father's arm.

"Lovely to see, marching to thee, sweet love united for eternity . . ."

"No!" Scarlet hollered after Mr. Bloom got me to take three steps down the aisle.

Everyone turned to her.

"No!" she repeated.

"No to what, baby?" Mrs. Dupree asked.

"I don't want Rachel to walk down the aisle. I want to do it." Scarlet got up and started walking to the back of the atrium with her arms folded over her chest. She was turning back into the girl who'd fallen apart at the dress studio.

"But it's tradition—" Mrs. Dupree said.

"You can't," Mrs. Bloom said.

"I don't care, Mami," Scarlet said. "Esto no es correcto!"

"What?" Mrs. Dupree looked at Ian. "See, this is what I'm talking about. They don't like black people. They up in here speaking in different languages and stuff."

"Mama, calm down!" Ian said.

"I don't want to walk down the aisle," I said.

"Well, it's too late now. We've already started. It's bad luck to start and stop," Mrs. Dupree said.

"Estrella, siéntese," Mrs. Bloom ordered, seemingly annoyed.

"But I don't want her to walk down the aisle. I want to do it!"

"It'll be your turn tomorrow," Mrs. Dupree said. "Let's go. We're running out of time."

"Siéntese!" Mrs. Bloom stood and pointed at Scarlet.

Scarlet huffed and puffed and went back to her seat.

Mrs. Dupree went on singing and clicking her camera.

When Mr. Bloom and I got to the front of the church, Krista, who looked like there was a big red balloon about to burst in her head, showed him how to hand Scarlet off to Ian and showed him to his seat beside his wife.

Ian smiled and took my hand without Krista telling him what to do. I grinned back at him.

"Look at ya'll. Like you meant to be together. Get in closer for a picture!" Mrs. Dupree was laying it on so thick, Mrs. Bloom was finally catching on to her act.

Mrs. Bloom said something in Spanish to her husband, but Mrs. Dupree pretended not to hear her. She went on with her speech.

"Guess this is the last time you two will be together," she said.

"Mom, Rachel and I will always be friends," Ian said, looking into my eyes. "Best friends."

"Let's finish," Mrs. Bloom said.

"Are you rushing this rehearsal?" Mrs. Dupree turned to Mrs. Bloom with knives in her eyes.

"They said there's another event in here," Mrs. Bloom said.

"I can stay in here as long as I please. My son, Dr. Ian Dupree, a professor at a top university, is getting married tomorrow—and I don't know why, but he's marrying someone who I ain't never met and who ain't got half of what he has."

"Mama, stop it!" Ian said. "That's not right. Take that back."

"Take it back? I meant every word. That wasn't to hurt anyone's feelings. Those are the facts."

"My family has money," Mrs. Bloom said. "We can afford to take care of our daughter."

"Well, I hope you can do that for the rest of her life because Miss Star don't have no good plans but mooching off my son. Watch. She gonna get pregnant and lay her ass up for the rest of her life. I know the type."

"Now, hold on. You can't talk about my daughter like that," Mr. Bloom jumped in.

"You don't need to be jumping up in my wife's face like that!" Mr. Dupree got up and went to defend Mrs. Dupree.

It was about to turn into a full-scale circus.

All the while, Ian was still holding my hand. I looked at his hand. It looked just like it had when we were in Social Circle. I held on tighter and he looked at me for a second. It was like we went away together and came right back. I needed to talk to him. I needed to say what I'd been feeling.

"Can we talk later about—" I tried to whisper, but then the fighting with the parents got louder.

"You don't even know my daughter to talk about her like that," Mrs. Bloom said.

"Maybe that's the problem," Mrs. Dupree said.

The entire wedding party looked on with their mouths open.

"Esta mujer es un imbécil!" Mrs. Bloom shouted.

"Imbecile?!?" Mrs. Dupree said. "I got your imbecile!" She was about to take off her shoe, but Mr. Dupree stopped her.

"Ian, stop them!" Scarlet yelled at Ian.

Ian let go of my hand. "Mama, stop it. What are you doing? You're ruining everything. Everyone stop!" His voice shot through the atrium and everyone stopped talking. "Now, listen. We're going to get through this rehearsal like adults."

"But I—" Mrs. Dupree tried to jump in.

"Mama, sit down!"

Mrs. Dupree sat with her husband and Ian pointed to Krista to begin again.

She moved me into my place with the bridesmaids and summarized what would happen with Scarlet and Ian during the ceremony. To avoid having another war break out, she and Uncle Cat demonstrated how the wedding party would leave the atrium after the ceremony was over.

Every face in every seat at the dinner in the Belle Suite after the rehearsal was streaked with "salt." The whimsical, antique charm in the design of the room that was set up to seat twenty-two guests along either side of a long, Tudor-style dinner table was in direct contrast with the inhabitants. After what happened at the rehearsal, folks were picking sides, frowning, and sucking their teeth. While the dinner was supposed to be used to unify us, everyone there seemed so far apart, avoiding eye contact and rolling their eyes way far back in their heads. Things were just that tense.

Ironically, the only smiling face was that of Mrs. Dupree. She seemed to be getting what she'd wanted: the upper hand.

Scarlet's parents completely stopped speaking in English. They'd refused the food Mr. Dupree had paid for and were going to sit at the table plateless until Krista insisted they put in special orders with the chef.

Sitting between his mother and Scarlet, Ian looked like he was slowly suffocating. I knew I was running out of time, so I tried to make eye contact with him, hoping maybe I could speak to him, but he hardly looked in my direction. Just down and across the table. He'd smile flatly at someone. Accept a hug and a well wish.

The awful air latched onto the champagne toasts. As Krista selected people around the room to share a few words and well wishes with the couple, each speech seemed to focus only on one person. Mrs. Dupree's speech was about how much she loved Ian. The matron of honor's speech was about how much she loved Scarlet. After a while, it seemed like they were in a competition to see which one in the pair was the best. Scarlet's mother sounded like she'd started speaking in tongues in Spanish again when Uncle Cat alluded to Scarlet as having been "lucky" to have met a man as intelligent and strong minded as his nephew. Mr. Dupree looked like he was about to walk out when Scarlet's father seemed to suggest that he'd kill Ian if he cheated on his sweet, demure little flower of a daughter.

"This is falling apart. I need to say something to get these people together," Krista whispered in my ear, holding the microphone she'd been giving to people behind her back.

"What?" I waved at Ian again, trying to get his eyes so I could ask him to come meet me outside, but he looked right past me.

"I have no idea what to say," Krista said.

"I'll say something." I reached for the microphone; if I wanted to get Ian's attention I had to do it right away.

"I don't think that's a good idea. Not after what just happened in the—"

I don't know what came over me, but I snatched the microphone.

"Hello everyone!" I started. I didn't know what I was about to say, but I was tired of being quiet. I looked at Ian.

He was smiling at me in his way.

Scarlet was right there on his arm. She'd produced a half-decent smile that looked a lot like a friendly grimace in case she was caught on camera. She looked so nervous. Had the tense air that I'd seen on so many brides I'd ushered into their new lives. I knew that this was also my job with her, but I couldn't think about her at that moment. I was two people—Ian's best friend, who was in love with him, and the wedding planner. In that moment, I could only satisfy the needs of one of those titles.

"What do we know about love? We know that it's hard to maintain. It's hard to control. It's hard to stop. It's hard to understand," I said. "A wise man once told me that none of that matters one bit when you find love. And perhaps that's the reason love is so sacred to us: it's hard to find. But when you do find it, you hold onto it. You nurture it. You choose it every day. Abide by it. Invest in it. Protect it with all your heart. Ian, this is how I've felt since the first day I met you." I looked right into Ian's eyes and locked in, ignoring all the interrogating looks around the room. "You're more than just my best friend. You're my heart. The love I found when I wasn't even looking." Ian swallowed deeply and his Adam's apple seemed to stall as it rolled back into position. "And it's not always easy to love you. But I do. I choose to love you every day. Even when I don't know it, my heart chooses to love you all on its own. And I hope you'll choose me, too." Krista had made her way to the other side of the room and was standing behind Ian rubbing her right ear, which was our internal distress signal for STOP!, but I couldn't. I had more to say. "Life is about choices. The choices we make and the risks we take." I started hearing people mumbling and looked over at Mrs. Dupree, who was frozen in a state of amazement. Suddenly, I realized what I was saying. What I was doing?

Krista's attempt to stop me nonchalantly was out the window. She was cutting herself off at the neck to get me to wrap it up before a riot broke out and Scarlet stabbed me in the eye.

I looked back at Ian. He'd put his arm around Scarlet and was giving me a serviceable smile that openly detailed his desire for me to stop whatever I was doing.

"I know this sounds weird to everyone," I said. "But I just wanted to let you know, Ian, that you're my best friend and I do love you. And because of that, I love Scarlet. And the three of us can have love now." (Awkward? Yes!)

Uncle Cat started clapping and chuckling a little to suggest that his understanding of my statement was a little more intimate than I could've intended.

"And . . . we can choose . . . this . . ." I kept speaking, but all of my words after that were low and off-mic. Krista had found the receiver and unplugged the microphone adapter.

When it had become obvious that no one in the room knew what to do next and no one was going to clap for my speech on their own, Krista stood up at the receiver and started one of those slow "you made your first and only home run" claps that brings everyone to tears at the end of baseball movies.

First only Scarlet's parents joined in—and I think it was because they wanted to go upstairs. Next was Mrs. Dupree and her flashing camera. Then everyone else slowly caught on.

"Some speech, Rach," Xavier said, after having walked over to me when people started getting up to head upstairs to get dressed for the evening's festivities.

"Thank you," I said.

"Great speech, Rachel," Jennifer said, coming over to get the scoop and be beside Xavier.

He kissed me on the cheek and walked away without hardly looking at her.

"Very—personal," Jennifer went on. "It reminded me of this one time at—"

Ian's father had pulled Ian and Scarlet into the corner with Pastor Thomas. Ian kept looking over at me and I wanted to wave for him to come and talk to me, but Jennifer was all in my face talking about love and how it can make people feel confused sometimes.

"Jennifer," I called to stop her from chattering. "I am not confused."

"You're not? But your speech—"

"You read into it what you wanted to hear," I said.

"Well, I heard that you are a little infatuated

with my friend's future husband—as in tomorrow," Jennifer snarled in a whisper.

"That's what you heard?"

"Isn't that what you meant?"

"I meant what I meant to say," I answered.

"So, Rachel," the matron of honor jumped in, stopping what could've turned ugly—unlike Jennifer, she was clearly already drunk, "you coming out with us later? Bachelorette party! Whooooaaa!"

More people were beginning to leave the room.

Pastor Thomas had taken Ian and Scarlet out into the hallway.

Krista was helping the staff get things in order in the room. In the morning, it would serve as a holding room for VIP guests before the wedding.

"It's going to be a blast. We have six strippers riding with us on the party bus. It's about to be dicks and tricks all night!" She gave icy Jennifer a high five.

"Wow—'dicks and tricks'?" I said. "You guys sure Scarlet is going to like that? Doesn't exactly sound like her speed."

"Speed?" she said, laughing. "Oh, you obviously have a lot more to learn. Scar—she's the one who requested the busload of strippers. So, are you down, Rachel?"

"You know, I wish I could, but I have so much work to do tonight."

"Owwww," she sighed in fake sadness. Jennifer just rolled her eyes. There was no way they wanted me to come along for the party.

"Yeah, sorry. Krista and I have so many things to get squared away by sunup. I can't leave her on her own."

When my interrogators left to go up to their

rooms to get ready to party, I ran outside to see if I could find Ian, but he was gone.

"This is it, Kris. It's over. I've lost." I was sitting on the second queen-sized bed in Krista's hotel room. I'd lied to the interrogators; Krista didn't need my help. We did have a few last-minute things to handle, but Krista was capable of folding the twenty-two silk handkerchiefs we'd had embroidered with Swarovski crystals in the pattern of my company logo on one end and the Dupree family crest on the other as gifts for the wedding party.

"You can't lose what's meant for you," Krista said, tossing a folded handkerchief into the basket on the floor between the beds.

"Guess I was wrong, then. Guess Ian isn't meant for me," I said, tossing another handkerchief into the basket. "It was my last chance at fate. Maybe my real fate is to be alone—always planning a wedding . . . never a bride."

"Rachel, you'll find someone. I don't care what that old myth says about wedding planners. The man—your dream man—is out there. He'll find you. You're a wonderful woman," Krista said, and I know she was only trying to comfort me; but due to the present circumstances, it sounded like a bunch of baloney people tell you when you're the last person to cross the finish line.

"There are only so many more times I can stomach hearing that from someone when I'm still single," I said. "If I'm such a wonderful woman, why aren't I getting married? Why hasn't my dream man come? If I'm so wonderful, why am I all alone? Sitting here in a hotel room talking to you?"

"I didn't think I was such bad company," Krista said sarcastically.

"If I'm so freaking wonderful why won't the entire universe get behind and support me, even fucking conspire for once in my whole damn life to give me the one thing I want? The one thing I ask for? True love?" I said and tossed the handkerchief I was folding onto the bed beside Krista.

The hotel-room phone rang loudly and boldly on the nightstand. And it wasn't odd for it to ring. The hotel staff was always calling our rooms the night before weddings with final questions and suggestions. Still, for some reason, Krista and I looked at it as if we'd never seen a phone before. Neither one of us moved until the third ring.

"It's probably just the manager," Krista said, rolling over on her bed to get the phone. "Some of Scarlet's relatives are coming in tonight from Miami. I wanted to make sure they were escorted to dinner." She picked up the receiver. "Hello?" She nodded. "Yeah. It's me." She looked at me like it was President Obama on the other line. "No problem. She's right here. Hold on."

"What? Who is it?" I whispered.

She took the phone from her ear and held her hand over the receiver. "It's Ian. He wants to talk to you."

"What?" I mouthed.

Krista held the phone out to me as I returned her wide-eyed stare.

"Hello?" I kicked up my voice a few notches, trying not to sound as depressed and dramatic as I had seconds earlier.

"Hey, Rach. What's up? You're not answering your phone."

"It's on," I said, walking over to my purse. "Did you call? Need anything?" I pulled the phone from my purse and saw that it was on silent. I'd turned the ringer off at the rehearsal dinner. I had two missed calls and three texts from Ian.

Krista followed me around the room, trying to lean her head into the phone to hear what Ian was saying.

"I want to see you. Tonight. Before I go out with the guys."

"Tonight?" I repeated, making faces at Krista.

"Yeah, I just want to talk about some stuff that's been on my mind. Some things about us."

"Us?"

Krista mimicked my wide mouth.

"Yeah. Can you meet meet me?"

"Meet you?" I asked.

"Yeah. At the Pier."

"Meet you at the Pier?"

"Yeah. At 9:00 PM."

"At 9:00 PM?"

"Work?"

"Works." If I'd had any urine in my bladder it would've trickled down my leg and hit the floor. I handed Krista the phone and stepped back from her, covering my mouth. I couldn't believe what I'd just heard.

"What was that?" Krista asked after hanging up the phone.

"He wants to talk to me."

"About what? How did he sound?"

"I don't know. It sounded important," I said. "It sounds like he wants to talk about us."

"Really?"

"Well, that's what he said. He wants to talk about us. Something he's been thinking about." I looked up at the ceiling. "Oh my God! Thank you, Jesus! Thank you, Jesus! Finally you conspire to make things go my way."

"You're going to meet him at the Pier?" Krista asked.

"Yes. He wants to see me before he goes out with the guys."

"Wow. That's serious."

"I know! I know! This is it, Krista. I can feel it. He's going to ask me to help him call off the wedding. He's going to say he wants to be with me."

"Slow it down a little, Rachel. Don't you think you're—"

I cut Krista off. "No. See, you don't understand. You don't know our history. This is just how it goes. How it's always been. We get each other out of trouble. That's why Ian's coming to me. I'm sure. There's no way he can stop this on his own. He needs me."

"Well, I can't tell you what you already know," Krista pointed out. "But I can say this: take your time. Remember what Journey told you—you can't go telling Ian how you feel about him until you're sure how he feels about you. You have to listen. You have to wait. Wait until you're sure."

The pier was alive at sunset. A crowd of tourists had gathered around a small street corner band. They were dancing and marching, tossing dollars into the open instrument cases as the music took hold of their souls, blessing them with freedom for a little while. The best of New Orleans was always in the street. Most people called it a party town, but that wasn't what it was about. It was a place to be yourself. To forget your trouble and pain. To be a toddler again. A human spirit in a wasting vessel unfettered by what was expected and accepted. The tools to get you there were dance and liquor and music and magic.

I walked around the crowd looking for Ian, but I couldn't find him.

I kept passing the same homeless lady rattling coins in the same old tin cup.

"Hey! You're here."

I turned to see Ian about to tap me on the shoulder.

"Of course. I came right away," I said.

"I'm sorry if I disturbed you guys. I was just thinking about some things and I wanted to see you. Kind of like to talk to you."

"It's no problem. You're fine. Krista's quite capable of handling everything else."

"I know. That's why I was wondering why you didn't go out with the other girls."

"Not exactly my cup of tea. And I'm sure Scarlet wasn't too upset I stayed behind. She probably didn't want me peeking over her shoulder all night."

"True. Well, the invitation is still open. You can come kick it with me and the fellas if you want."

"Really?" I squinted my eyes at him and laughed.

"OK, maybe not," Ian admitted.

"Yeah, my presence alone would kind of ruin the entire concept of it being a bachelor party. For some reason the men find it hard to objectify women when women they know are around."

Ian took my hand and we walked to the back of the crowd where there were a few benches and it was less noisy.

"So this is it. My last night of freedom," Ian said, pointing out a bench for us to sit on. "Tomorrow, I'll be someone's husband."

"Woo-hoo. " I shook an imaginary pompon in my hand and sat down beside him.

"And it's funny because with all this future talk going on, all I can think about is my past."

"What about it?"

"Just old times. About us."

"What?" I asked. "What about us?"

"I don't know. My mom was kind of getting into my head at the rehearsal. All that talk about you and me making the perfect couple."

"She was just saying that to be mean to Scarlet."

"I know, but that didn't make it false," Ian said. "You ever wonder why we didn't ever get together?"

"Yeah. All the time."

"We're just alike—you and me. When I'm with you, it's like I'm all alone."

"Um . . . is that supposed to be a compliment?" I asked, rolling my eyes.

"Yes, crazy. I mean, like I don't have to work to be around you. I'm just chilling. I know what you need. You know what I need. There's no mystery."

"Yeah. That's how I feel, too."

"Shit can get difficult with Scarlet sometimes. She's so young acting. It's like we don't connect. I love her, but sometimes I feel like she might wear me out before I can wear her down. I don't have to worry about that with you. You're my equal," he said and all I could think of was what Journey had said online about the right time. "Rachel, there's something I want to say to you. And I don't know how. Really how to find the right words."

"Don't marry her, Ian."

"What?"

"Don't marry Scarlet. I know what you're about to say and I want to say that I feel the same way. I love you, too. You're the man of my dreams. The man who loves music and art. The man who respects the spirit world. And I don't want to lose you. I don't want you to marry Scarlet tomorrow. Because I love you and I want you to marry me. "

"Rachel, I—" Ian tried.

"No, wait. You keep saying something's missing between you and Scarlet. That you're missing something. You're right. She's not your equal. Scarlet is just some schoolgirl. A pretty face who knows big words. She's fake. A phony. All those lies about going to the Congo. It wasn't even real. I checked into it. She was lying. She's not right for you. I am. It's me. I'm the one for you. I'm what you've been missing."

"Rachel, stop! I—I wasn't going to say that to you," Ian said, getting up from the bench. "I was going to—how could you say those things about Scarlet? You looked into the program? You did that without telling me?"

"I was trying to protect you." I got up and stood in front of him.

"Rachel, I wasn't going to say that I didn't want to marry Scarlet. I do want to marry Scarlet. I was going to tell you how important you are to me. And that I want you to be by my side as my friend for the rest of my life. That I wanted you to know that things won't change between us."

"You weren't—"

"I'm in love with Scarlet. Even with her faults," he said. "She loves me more than anything. And I'm going to marry that woman tomorrow. And you know what? I'm thinking after listening to everything you just said, maybe you shouldn't be there."

"What? Ian, I was just saying how I felt—"

"Yeah. That's what I'm afraid of. If you felt all this time that Scarlet was lying to me—and you had proof—why would you keep it from me? Why wouldn't you have told me sooner? You wait until the day before my wedding to break this shit out to me? You're not my fucking friend. I can't have you at my wedding."

"Whoooa! Calm down, Ian. You're going a little too far." I tried to take his hand, but he snatched it away.

"No, you went too far this time." He started walking away.

"But, Ian, you have to listen to me," I tried, grabbing him, but he pulled away angrily

"No, Rachel. You listen to me. I can't do this, stand in between you and my future wife and try to pick sides. I'm not that kind of man. If I marry Scarlet, I have to pick her side. And after hearing what you just said, I know you don't support her, so you don't support us. My mind is made up."

"Ian, don't do this. Don't walk away. I didn't mean to—I was just trying to—follow my heart."

6

"What She's Been Missing"

#Wheredobrokenheartsgo? Ian left me standing alone at the Pier. I watched his back for so long, praying he'd turn around and say he was just kidding or he'd changed his mind.

But he never stopped. He never turned around. And soon he was gone.

My heart was suffering. It sank into my toes and I felt every ounce of blood in my body pump toward my eyes to accommodate the outpouring of sad tears that fell once I couldn't see him anymore. What had I done? How had I misread someone I knew better than anyone else in the world? And the price I was about to pay was so high. I couldn't show my face again. Not anywhere.

I started wiping my tears and turned around, feeling like someone was watching me. Like some-

one saw everything. The band was still there playing their upbeat music. The crowd was getting bigger and ready for the night party. Everyone was
smiling. Dancing. Having the time of their lives.
To them, this was paradise. To me, it was hell.

"Baybee, yah lost?" the old homeless woman
with the cup asked. She'd replaced it with a bottle
of gin I supposed she'd purchased with her earn-
ings.

"No. I know where I'm at," I managed.

"Hum . . . Yah take dis. Sip some." She handed
me her bottle. "Yah lak like yah need it more den
ole mi."

"No. I'm fine," I started and tried to give the
bottle back, but she wouldn't take it.

"Drink, baybee. Yah can bury yah trouble 'til
morning," she said. "Chase it away a lil' while longer."

I took a deep breath and snapped my head
back. I chugged the gin with my eyes closed.

"Das right, baybee. Wash it all away!" She rubbed
my back. "See if Monsieur Gin gon be de marshal
on yah trouble."

I took another chug and finished off the bottle.
The gin pushed the rest of the tears out of my eyes
and I wrapped my arm around the woman to keep
my balance.

"Easy nah, baybee," she said and so fast her voice
started to sound like lyrics over the street music.

I felt like my legs were dancing and I didn't
know if my feet were taking me to the center of the
crowd or the back. I needed to sit down. And fast.
But my legs were moving. The music got louder
and glimpses of the old woman and the bottle
came in and out of view.

"You looking for a good time, sugar?" a fat white

lady in cowgirl chaps and no underwear asked beneath a sign that read LAISSER LES BONS TEMPS ROULER.

"Huh?" I focused my vision and looked around. I was far from the crowd and the band. The old woman and the bottle were nowhere. I remembered giving her twenty dollars.

"A good time? You need a good time?" The woman pointed at the sign. "I think you do! You look like you do."

"I just need to sit down," I said. "Figure this thing out. Why he left me. Why he doesn't love me. I thought I had it all planned." I was leaning into the woman. Breathing all the dirty gin in her face.

"Yeah, this is the place for you, sugar. Go in and talk to the pastor. He'll set you right."

"Oh, this is a church?" I started crying again. I whispered into the chubby naked club promoter's ear, "I have sinned. I have coveted my neighbor's husband. Well, they're not married yet, but he won't marry me. He won't. No one will. You understand now?"

"Sure as hell don't, sugar," she said. "But that ain't my job. See the pastor at the bar. No charge for you tonight." She opened the door and the next thing I remember I was sitting at the bar and crying into a bottle of bourbon as I told some black man with one dreadlock hanging from the top of his head, a bull ring in his nose, and a priest's collar around his neck all about Ian and my troubles.

"He was my best friend! My best friend. And I betrayed him!"

"I don't know, sweetie," he said, flicking his bar towel over his shoulder. "I kind of feel like you betrayed yourself long before you betrayed him. And maybe you betrayed him because you've been betraying yourself for so long."

The bourbon kept me from understanding anything he was saying. I just wanted forgiveness. For a miracle. For me not to have to walk back into my life and live it without Ian.

"What?"

He took the bottle from me and poured another glass. "You're looking for love. That's why you're acting like you're acting. How you're acting. You just want what he has."

"I do! You're right. I want love. I want someone to love me!" I looked at an older, gray-haired woman with crossed eyes sitting next to me at the bar smoking a sweet-smelling thin cigarette and told her a little bit about Ian as we passed the cigarette back and forth. My mind started floating away with the puffs of smoke.

"So you have to get what he has," pastor/priest said, shaking his little dreadlock in a way that made me laugh.

"I can't! I can't just get love," I slurred. "If it was that easy, we'd all have it!" I raised my hands and nearly fell out of my seat.

"Whoa!" the woman with the cigarette said, pulling me back to the bar. "Well, you're in the right place. This is New Orleans. We can all have whatever we want here."

The pastor/priest traded sharp eyes with the woman. He started wiping the bar again. Shaking his head.

"What do you mean?" I asked.

"I know where you can go to make your trouble go away," the woman said.

"Go away?" I looked up into the ceiling like I was watching my problems rise with the smoke in the bar.

"Go anywhere you want. You pay and it'll happen," the woman said.

"Pay who?"

"Don't tell her," pastor/priest jumped in. "She's in no condition to deal with—"

"No! I want to know! I need to know," I said. "I want to fix everything. Make it go away." I remembered Ian's back to me. His words.

"Well, if you tell her, I don't want no part of it." Pastor/priest walked to the other end of the bar.

"What's wrong with him?" I asked.

"He's not from here. He don't understand the ways of the people here. I was raised in the Quarter. Been running in this swamp since those old bells used to ring in the graveyard. People like him don't know those times. They only know what they see on TV. What they hear." Her voice was so mysteriously seductive. Wickedly inviting.

"Tell me how I can make my problems go away. What I have to do."

"You go see Tante Heru in the back of the Quarter. In her old shack. You tell her what you want. You make an offering. She'll see that it happens."

"What? Tan-what?" I laughed. "You trying to send me to some psychic? A fortune teller with a crystal ball? I don't believe in that stuff."

"She ain't no fortune teller. And she ain't no psychic. She's a roots woman. Been working 'round here longer than time. She born in Treme—in Place Congo—right in the dirt. She has the power of the ancestors in her pot. She can make any magic she wants to." She blew a puff of smoke in my face.

"You go on and see her, sweetheart. She'll make you all right." She poured me another glass of bourbon and the next thing I remember, before I blacked out, was being carried through the bar— the pastor/priest and his bullring under one arm and the naked fat woman in the chaps under the other.

"Take her to Tante Heru!" the cross-eyed woman yelled and cackled all at once. I was sure she was a nightmare and I'd wake up in my loft in Atlanta. Maybe everything was a nightmare.

I felt like I was sleeping in a plastic bag and had just taken my last breath. There was no air. And something heavy was pushing into my chest. No. My face. All over my face. Like a warm pillow or balloon. One of those flat plastic water bottles Grammy Annie-Lou used to have hanging over the bathroom door. If I didn't fight back, this thing would suffocate me.

I jerked forward and realized that I must've been lying flat on my back because I couldn't move my legs. I tried to push back with my arms, but they were being held in place. I tried to open my eyes, but the warm covering that I now thought was flesh—that belonged to the hands holding me down—were completely blocking my view.

"Let she go now, Kete," an aged and mysterious voice said. "She go die if you don't."

"I will, Tante Heru, if she stop fighting me so." This second voice was closer to me. Right near my ear.

"Baybee, you gon' haf stop ye fight, hear ya ma?" A soft, shaky hand was at my head. "Rest easy

now. Relax, baybee. Ya wit ya Tante Heru now. Ya
come look fa mi? Ya fine mi."

I just stopped moving with that soft, shaky hand
on my head. Then the hands over my arms slack-
ened a little and the darkness around me disappeared as the covering over my face lifted. I peeked
at two huge brown breasts that parted down the
middle like ass cheeks and looked something like
two smoked turkey butts. The farther they got
from my face, the bigger they got. A dingy white
peasant blouse that looked like it was worn more
to showcase the ample breasts than to clothe them
was a second thought right at the nipples. A face
that was young and cute, fat and simple with
brown freckles over the top of the nose sat on the
neck above the breasts. She had stringy black hair
and baby blue feathers in her ears. She smiled.

"*C'est ça*, baybee, rit. Nah, relax nah," I heard,
and remembered the hand at my head.

I rolled my eyes to the top of my head. "Tante
Heru?"

"Good, so wi know who I is."

From upside down and flat on the table, I saw a
whole head of bushy white hair that extended on
the chin and over the top lip of a blue black face
that looked so ancient I was almost sure I was
dead. Nothing like her could still be alive. Her eyes
were almost gray. Almost. So many colors that it was
clear whatever color they originally had been had
long ago been washed away with time.

"Let she go now." She poked at the young woman
with the feather earrings. "She be right now. Right,
baybee?" She looked back at me.

The woman let go and I sat up on what was just
a long oak table with four uneven legs. Candle wax

in all colors was smeared beneath me. It was hard, though, and looked like it had been there for some time. In fact, everything around me seemed old and hard and that it had been there for some time. There was a wall lined with shelves filled with glass containers and old coffee cans, jars, and some books. Dust was on every shelf. On everything. An old woodburning stove with two boiling pots that looked more like something out of a movie about New Orleans than something you'd actually see there were on the lit eyes. The only window in the room, a thirsty square that was kissed with years of dirt and grime, was cracked behind the stove. A single lightbulb with a string hung above me, but it wasn't on and giving light. The light in the room came from the candles on the other table beside me.

"There," Tante Heru said, after watching me gather my surroundings. "Now ya is good. Now ya kin talk to ya Tante Heru."

"Talk?" I repeated.

"Wha ya want? Why ya come to dis place?"

"I love him. But he doesn't love me," I said. "He's marrying someone else!"

"Ya wan Tante Heru to stop de wedding?" Tante Heru pointed her wrinkled and knotted index finger to something on one of the shelves and Kete ran to get it.

"No," I said. "Not that."

Kete stopped.

"Wha ya wan?"

"I want love. Real love. I want someone who wants to marry me. Not the man who wants to marry her," I said. "I want what I've been missing: the man of my dreams."

Tante Heru pointed in a whole different direction at a potted plant that was sitting on the windowsill behind the sink.

Kete went to the plant and there was noise that sounded like a garbage can falling over outside the window. Kete quickly opened what was left of a raggedy and stained old curtain over the broken window and cursed in French at whatever made the noise.

"What is it?" I asked.

"I didn't see," Kete said. "Probably just some schoolkids. They be trying to spy on Tante Heru." She said something in French and took a few sprigs from the plant. Handed them to Tante Heru.

"Ya come to auntie in pain, baybee," Tante Heru said, tossing the sprigs into one of the pots on the stove. "Ya come fa ya love. I kin give it to ya."

"Give it to me? From that pot?"

Kete put her hand out to me. "Fifty dollars. We take cash or charge. No checks."

I almost laughed. But they both looked so serious.

"You're saying you can give me true love for fifty dollars?"

"You choose from three wishes. One ta make 'im come in de morning, two ta make 'im appear jes when ya need 'im, three ta make 'im go away," Tante Heru said.

"Why would I want him to go away if he's my true love?"

"Baybee, true love nah always wha ya reckon it be," she said. "Sometimes wha da trut is can take ya breath. Right?"

I looked around the room.

"Whatever," I said, reaching into my pocket for a credit card. "If it works, it works. If not . . ."

Kete took the card and scanned it through a little machine tucked on the side of one of the shelves.

Tante Heru was standing over the boiling water chanting in some language that didn't sound like French.

When the credit card cleared and Kete brought it back to me, Tante Heru, with her face sweaty with the steam from the pot, came back to me.

"Speak ya love, baybee. Speak it loud," she ordered.

"Speak my what?" I asked.

"Tell her what kind of man you want," Kete explained.

As the water began to boil over uncontrollably onto the stove, Kete and Tante Heru joined hands and started chanting again.

I started quoting the lyrics from India.Arie's "Ready for Love."

The curtains blew into the room like there was a hurricane outside and the floorboards began to shake. The candles blew out one by one and Tante Heru and Kete started chanting even louder. Kete grabbed my hand and something like an electric current went right through me.

The dull light flickered and then went out. We were in total darkness.

Kete stopped chanting, but using a streak of light sneaking in through a hole in the curtain over the window, I could see Tante Heru with her eyes rolled back in her head. She seemed like she was in a trance. She kept repeating the same word: "Yemaya. Yemaya. Yemaya. Yemaya."

The water from the pot was spilling onto the floor.

"Yemaya. Yemaya. Yemaya. Yemaya!" she shouted and then she opened her eyes. And I know I was completely drunk and struggling to see in the darkness, but I swear they were black. Fully black and shining in the dark. I nearly fell off of the table.

The water stopped boiling without anyone touching the flame. The light came back on. The floorboards stopped shaking. The curtain fell flat with no breeze.

"He come in de mornin'. Come rit ta ya. Wan he leave, ya decide whan he go. Den ya say whan he go fi good. But only fa good, baybee. Only use de third wish fa good. Ya must be sure."

7

"Joy Cometh in the Morning"

#thehangover . . . The bourbon in my belly pulled me from a heavy sleep that didn't want to give me up. I'd never be able to fully recall how I'd gotten back to the hotel from Tante Heru's—along with how I'd gotten upstairs, disrobed, and made my way to the bed—but the second my head hit the pillow would never leave me. It was like falling onto a happy Care Bear cloud I really needed. Really loved. Cool and forgiving. Welcoming like the back of the blue Care Bear; maybe the yellow one. I kissed the pillow a few times—I knew this because there were perfect puckers all over the pillowcase the next morning—and tumbled like Alice down the rabbit hole into the kind of hard, wicked sleep only liquor after a broken heart can give you. There was no chance I'd be able to recall what I dreamed. When I closed my eyes, there was just blackness spiraling everywhere in more blackness and I'm sure it stayed that way until the bourbon was tired of being inside of me.

I tried to open my eyes, but sleep had caked them closed, like they did when I was younger and got a really bad cold. My head was so viciously heavy I felt the weight of everything I ever knew. And one side of my body was rigid and cold. But still, when bourbon called my name in boils in my stomach, I had to answer, and in one second I overcame every ailment that had me jailed in my hotel-room bed and staggered blindly to the bathroom and got on my hands and knees in front of the toilet.

Everything came out of me. As my father used to say, "There just ain't no better way to put that." I was retching and convulsing, twisting around on the floor. Bourbon was determined to teach me a lesson. My heart was palpitating faster than I could breathe and I was so hot I didn't care if my face touched the cool water in the latrine.

I just wanted the bourbon out of me. And from the looks of things, it seemed like the bourbon wanted the same. Maybe it was going on down into the sewer to start another party someplace else.

Lying there on the floor, I looked into the dark room to see that it wasn't even 6:00 AM on the clock yet. Night was still outside the window and I could actually hear people still partying in the street outside the hotel.

When I thought maybe I'd emptied out the last of the last inside of me, I looked at the ceiling, cursing whatever made me think I could drink an entire bottle of any liquor. And then, like any good

Southern girl, I prayed to God to make it stop. Promised I'd never do it again. I was a good person. Really. Just make it stop. I called on Jehovah and every name I ever heard Grammy Annie-Lou call the Interceder when she got the Holy Ghost in church. Sure, God likely didn't care about drunk middle-aged women passed out on bathroom floors, but wasn't he the God of small things, too?

I crawled out of the bathroom and managed to pull the phone down from the nightstand to call room service for more towels. Before I could hang up good, there was a knock at the door.

"Hold on," I said, pushing myself up from the floor. "I didn't expect you to get here so soon." I toddled around, turned on the light, and grabbed my bathrobe. "OK," I said, halfway in my robe as I opened the door. I reached out to grab the towels, and they were there, but it wasn't a maid holding them. "Xav?" I grabbed the collar of my robe to be sure nothing was slipping out. "What are you doing here?"

"Morning jog!" He stepped back so I could see his sweat suit and sneakers. "I figured I should be lean and mean up there on the altar today."

"Whatever." I remembered Ian's snarl at the pier and reached for the towels, but the bourbon took my hands farther than I meant for them to go and I lost my balance.

"Easy, girl!" Xavier helped me regain my footing. "Yeah, I saw you come in last night and I figured you'd be needing these towels. Got you some water, too." He held the towels up to show me a bottle of water hidden beneath the pile.

"Oh no, you saw me? Did anybody—"

"No one else saw. Don't worry."

"Whatever, Xav." I reached for the towels again and snatched them. "Look, thanks for the towels."

"And the water!" Xavier held up the water bottle.

"And the water."

"Can't forget to hydrate. Big day ahead of us. Wouldn't want you to faint at the wed—"

"Good-bye," I said in a way that could easily be translated to "fuck off." I closed the door with Xavier on the other side and leaned up against it with the towels and water in my arms. "Fuck! Fuck! Fuck!" I banged my head back against the door at the mess I'd made with Ian.

"He told me," I heard.

"What?" I dropped the towels and water.

"He told me what happened at the pier."

"What?" I opened the door again. "He told you what I— What did he say?"

Xavier widened his eyes on the threshold, begging to enter the room

"Whatever." I poked my head out of the doorway and looked up and down the hallway before pulling him into my room. "Oh my God. What did he tell you?"

"Just that you tried to break up the wedding. Stop him from marrying the woman of his dreams."

"She's not the— He said all that?"

"Oh, and that he doesn't want you to come to the wedding."

"Has he told anyone else?"

"I don't think so. Definitely not Scarlet. Look, it's not as bad as you think," Xavier said rather unconvincingly.

"I knew I shouldn't have done it. Fucking Journey! Feelings! Fuck all that shit!" I was circling the room, toddling and stumbling, looking for nothing but my right mind.

"Whoa, hold up now!" Xavier had picked up the things I'd dumped on the floor and arranged them on the nightstand. "Calm down. You're getting all worked up. Let's get you back in bed."

"Bed?" I resisted Xavier's arms pulling me to the bed, but I was still a little dizzy and drained.

He took one of the towels and went into the bathroom.

"What are you doing in there?" I tried to get up to see what was going on, but Xavier came back out with a wet towel in his hand and forced me back down. He sat on the edge of the bed beside me, plumped the pillow beneath my head, and pulled the blanket up over my chest.

"I can't believe I did this," I said. "Ian's going to hate me forever."

"Not forever. He doesn't have the heart to hate anyone forever."

Xavier helped me to a sip of water from the bottle and slid the wet towel onto my forehead. The coolness immediately made a clanking in my brain subside.

"He gets emotional sometimes, but it'll pass. You know our boy," Xavier added.

"No. I've never seen him so angry. He was serious. He doesn't want to see me again," I said.

"Come on, he didn't mean that. He can't get through today without you. You know that. You're his best friend," Xavier said so softly I almost forgot who he was.

"But he said he didn't want me to—"

Xavier placed his index finger over my lips. "You get better. I'll talk to him. He listens to me."

"I don't know. I'm just so embarrassed," I said when he moved his finger. "I can't go through this alone. Even if no one else knows, I'll feel like they all do. They're all laughing at me. After that crazy toast? Uggh!"

"No one will be laughing at you, Rachel," Xavier said. "Because I'll be with you."

"With me?"

"Maybe you could be my date."

"Be your date?"

Xavier winced and one of his dimples puckered in his cheek.

"I could be *your* date? But why would we—?"

"I just thought it would make things easier. But if you don't want to, I understand."

"I don't care," I said. "Ian isn't going to let me come to the wedding anyway. It doesn't matter."

"Let me be the judge of that." Xavier winked at me and got up from the bed. "I'll go talk to him now." He started backing away from the bed slowly, but he stopped and stared into my face.

"What?" I asked, afraid I'd left some residual vomit on my chin. "Do I have something on my face?" I tried to swipe at my chin, but he stopped me.

"No, stop moving," Xavier said. "I was just looking at you lying there. No makeup on. Hair all over the place. A little crust on the side of your mouth." He laughed a little and I tried to wipe my mouth, but he stopped me again. "No, don't do that," he said. "Stay just the way you are." He started backing up again and made it to the door. "Beautiful." His eyes left me and went to the window where the blinds were half drawn. I turned, too, to see the sun full in the sky. "Good morning, Rachel," I heard Xavier say. I turned back to the door, but he was gone.

I looked back at the sun in the window and remembered a whisper in my ear.

"Tante Heru?" I said. "No. He can't be."

Uncle Cat answered Krista's hotel-room door like it was his. He was wearing a hotel embroidered robe and a smooth, old-player grin that nearly invited me in. Only a smoky cigar hanging from his mouth would make the ridiculous spectacle complete.

"That isn't room service, is it?" Krista called helplessly from inside, probably sensing that her cover had been blown.

"Service, it be not, baybee," Uncle Cat said. "You have a visitor."

Krista pushed her head underneath Uncle Cat's arm holding the door open.

"Oh shit," she said. "I can explain. See, he was trying to—"

"No need, Krista," I stopped her. "That's not why I'm here." I looked at Uncle Cat. "Can I have a moment with her?"

"Right by me, baybee," he said. "Cat only knows one kind of laydee business anyway."

"Sure. Fine," I said.

Uncle Cat went back into the room and Krista took his place in her smaller hotel embroidered robe.

"Really?" I held my hand up to her in disappointment.

"It's not how it looks."

"You looked into his eyes, didn't you?"

"Yeah." She looked off all dreamy eyed. "It was like looking at an emerald forest. He had me." She looked back at me. "Took me! And I liked it."

"He's fifty-six. He has six kids. Six kids!"

"Lord, I know why now! Whew! That man!" She fanned herself.

"You know what, whatever! I just came here to tell you what happened last night," I said before telling Krista about the fight with Ian at the pier, the priest with the bull ring in his nose and Tante Heru. I explained that Xavier was going to talk to Ian for me, too. That I really didn't want to miss the wedding.

"You sure you can do this? I mean, after all that's happened?" Krista asked.

"If he'll let me, I have to. I owe him that much. If I'm not there, people will ask questions—it'll be—"

"I get it," Krista stopped me. "I just don't want anything else to happen."

"I'm fine," I said. "Look, I'm about to go call Xavier and if everything is cool, I'll meet you down in the ballroom? Say fifteen minutes?"

"Baybee!" Uncle Cat called from inside the room. "Come over to me. I have something to show you."

"Make that thirty minutes," Krista purred to me after hearing his call.

"I can't," I said. "Grandpa R. Kelly? Really?"

"I'll get rid of him." Krista said. "In about thirty minutes."

About an hour later, Krista showed up in the ballroom with her shirt misbuttoned. I couldn't believe Ian agreed to allow me to come to the wedding, but Xavier was right—it was hard for him to hold any kind of grudge. Also, as Xavier explained, my not being there would actually make this harder for him—then he'd have to tell Scarlet what happened and that would present a whole new set of problems. I just had to lay low and keep a smile on my face.

Krista surprised me and had gone through a final check with most of the vendors before she'd hooked up with Uncle Cat last night, so we just did a walk-through once they started arriving, connected with the hotel staff, and made sure every beautiful blush bow from Scarlet's dream was tied.

"You sure you're up to this?" Krista asked me again after we'd gone through the song list with the DJ and I was about to go up to my room to get dressed for the ceremony. "I really can handle this on my own. And about the ceremony, I can just tell everyone you're sick."

"No," I said. "Time to put on my big-girl panties; gotta reap what I sow. Ian made his decision and I have to live with it. I'm just lucky he didn't completely cut me off."

Testing his speakers, the DJ began to play Celine Dion's "Because You Loved Me."

"God, I hate this song," Krista said, playfully covering her ears.

"It's Ian's favorite."

"Really? Mr. African American History likes Celine Dion?"

"We sang it together one time at a karaoke bar on spring break," I said. "It's been our special song ever since."

"Oh," Krista said, but she seemed distracted looking down at the song list.

"What?"

"Just that—I don't know if you noticed, but, well, that's the song they chose for their first dance. That's their song," Krista said.

All I could do was close my eyes and breathe deeply.

"I'm so sorry, Rachel," Krista said. "Just the way you two were . . . no one would've thought he'd . . . choose her. . . . I'm so sorry."

"You know what? No more sorries. Promise that. Forever."

Krista slid her arm around my waist and gave me a half hug that said, "I'm sorry."

I could hear Celine's voice bellowing through the hallway behind me after I walked out of the ballroom to head back to my room.

Weddings, from beginning to end, have a rhythm, a beat that takes off on the morning of the ceremony, climaxes at the altar, and subsides somewhere at the reception when the couple has their first dance or tastes that first piece of wedding cake. And the rhythm can be anything. Jazz, hip-hop, salsa, blues, rock and roll, classical, even country. It depends on the couple, the place, the time of day, how the sun shines, if raindrops fall. Whatever it is, I can feel it hours before the couple takes to the altar to say "I do." In my feet as I run around making adjustments; all around me, as I talk to the soon-to-be-newlyweds. And it's so beautiful to experience. To sense the beginning, middle, and ending of this short song in the entire opus of their lives together. And knowing I'm a part of getting that song just right—like a classical conductor on her stand directing with the baton—is one of the biggest joys of what I do.

Standing in my hotel room, looking at my bridesmaid dress, steamed and lovely, hanging on the
back of the bathroom door, I tried so hard to hear
the rhythm of Ian's wedding. All day, I'd gone
about business as usual. Clipboard in my hand, I
pretended everything was as fine as it could be. As
fine as the world might have it after I'd taken the
chance to gain something and nearly lost everything. All I heard was a dull, drab stream of white
noise—whatever that sounds like. Nothing. I wondered if everyone else could hear it, too. If I'd put
it there. If me chasing my needs had robbed Ian of
the music of his big day.

I put the orange dress on with my bottom lip
hanging so low from my face, I nearly got it caught
in the zipper. In the mirror, I looked more like I
was going to Ian's funeral than his wedding. Maybe
Xavier was wrong. Maybe I should've gotten my
silly ass right on that first flight back to Atlanta. I
was no good to Ian like this. I was no good to anyone at all. (Violins, please.)

I slid on my shoes, grabbed my clutch, and
promised myself I'd stop at the hotel bar for a shot
before I went to the bridal suite to get in line with
the other bridesmaids. I remembered my toilet-
bowl promise of hours earlier to stop drinking, but
this was a special case. In fact, maybe I needed to
stop at the gift shop for a flask.

Xavier was standing at the door when I opened it.

"I didn't think you could get any more beautiful," he said, looking so effortlessly debonair in his
suit I wanted to slug him in the stomach for every
girl's heart he'd ever broken. "But here you are."

"Thank you," I said tightly. I'd thought about
Tante Heru and her promise to send me true, per-

fect love—the man of my dreams; all that I've been missing—at sunup. What a waste of fifty dollars. A belly full of bourbon, eyes filled with tears, and a broken heart, I had wanted to believe in her and her little accent. That it could be that easy. Speak to the universe of love, shake a chicken foot at it, and voilà! But no! Xavier was no Mr. Right. Not even Mr. Right Now. More like Mr. All Wrong. And I could tell by how good he was looking in his suit. As Uncle Cat said, "Men like me are too pretty to fall in love."

" 'Thank you,' " Xavier mocked me, making my voice sound like a robot's. "Come on! I go to talk to my boy and get you back in the wedding and that's all a brother gets? I thought we were allies!"

"Fine, Xav. Well, thank you for helping me out earlier," I said as kindly as I could. I actually felt a little bad that my voice sounded so glum. "Look, I'm sorry. I'm just a little confused. This is the second time I'm opening my door and you're standing here. I'm just wondering what you want."

"I want to make sure you're OK."

"Please. I doubt Mr. All About Me cares about how I'm doing."

" 'All About Me' was just a little name some girls on campus gave me. I had nothing to do with it," he replied and it was such a lie we both laughed.

"Xav, you had that shit sewn into your sheets," I pointed out.

"Someone gave those to me."

"It's tattooed on your back!"

"Damn! You got me!" he said, looking like he'd just lost a bet.

I giggled at his breakdown and he pinched my cheek.

"Made you laugh," he said gently.

"Yeah, you did."

"I really did want to make sure you're OK. I can't have you up in the wedding crying like we're at a funeral."

"How's Ian?"

"He's fine. The brothers have his back." Xavier popped his collar a little. "And now I believe one of those brothers would like to escort you to the bridal suite." He held out his elbow for me to latch on.

"Escort me?"

"Yes, Mi Lady," he said in an English accent. "Shall we?"

"You're too much," I answered, holding on to him.

Krista had just finished prepping the brides-maids when Xavier and I got to the suite. She was walking out with empty bottles of wine in her arms.

"Guess I didn't need to stop at the bar," I said.

"It's like a sorority house in there," Krista said. "Those chicks are wild."

"Let me take those." Xavier took the bottles from Krista's arms.

"You should've let the hotel staff pick these up," I said.

"I was afraid one of the girls would knock a bottle over and crack her head open."

"They're that bad? Probably a runover from last night. Look, go and order two carafes of coffee. We can't have them wobbling down the aisles," I ordered.

"I already did that, boss lady."

"Hum . . ." I nodded at Krista. "And where's your bride?"

"Hair and makeup. She'll be down in five minutes." Krista poked out her hip and crossed her arms dramatically. "Anything else?"

"No. Looks like you're on a roll. I'm scared of you."

Xavier pushed the suite door open with his free arm.

"I'm gonna walk her downstairs to get rid of these bottles," he said as if it was his duty in some way to inform me of where he was going. "See you later."

"Thanks again," I said more softly this time. I really had appreciated his help. He'd kept me laughing the entire way to the suite.

I stepped into the doorway and he started backing away in front of Krista, who was behind him staring at me all bug eyed and suggestive. I broke her nosy stare by looking away and frowning.

"Focus," I said before turning into the suite. "Focus."

The only thing missing from the bridal suite was a kegger and go-go dancers. I'd seen wedding parties cut the fool before, but those were usually the groomsmen. Krista wasn't lying. These ladies were having a good old time. When I walked in, one of the bouquets was in the air. The matron of honor was dancing on top of a chair and another bottle of wine was being uncorked. Then I remembered whose company I was in—married, engaged, and spoken-for women. Really, they weren't too different from groomsmen. Weddings were more of a social event for them. An opportunity to cut loose and take shots, all in the name of love.

"I'll take that," I said, snatching the wine bottle and taking a few sips before heading over to the sink to empty it out. The wedding was starting in an hour.

"Awww! Don't be a hater," Jennifer shouted so loudly I was sure the hotel staff would be coming to the suite any minute.

"Oh, I hate to be a party pooper, but it's almost showtime, ladies," I said after a collective groan.

"Was that Xavier outside?" the married triplet asked with her head half in and out of the suite door.

"Let me look," the engaged triplet said, running up behind her sister. "I know that sweet ass any-where." She was too late. "Damn, he's gone," she added.

"That man is a fucking orgy in a body, bitch," Jennifer said, sounding more like a street walker than a med-school grad. "He can get it anyway . . . and anyday."

Engaged triplet came over and gave Jennifer a fist pump.

"What? Aren't you about to get married?" I asked, feeling like I was back at FAMU in the dorm with some girls swooning over Xavier.

" 'About to' is the key, Rachel—as in, I'm not married right now." She gave her married sister a high-five and they giggled like hyenas.

"Well, I'm definitely not married," the triplet whose boyfriend was the DJ said. "And I went and knocked on Xavier's door last night . . . no dice."

"Really?" Jennifer asked.

The women huddled around for the 411.

"I told him that I was too drunk to go to my

room—that my boyfriend would be mad that I was
so jacked up. I needed to get myself together."

"What did he do?" Jennifer pushed.

"Girl, he gave me a cup of water and some Ex-
cedrin," she said. "I opened my legs wide enough
so he could see my neon thong. That fool put a
towel over my legs and walked out. Said he was
going for his morning jog. It was dark as fuck outside."

The room erupted in mocking laughter.

"I don't get it," she went on. "I didn't think he'd
turn me down."

I was on her side. I couldn't believe it. She was
trim, tall, light skinned, had big breasts. His type. I
was wondering if she was really talking about
Xavier.

"I heard he was a big player in college," someone said.

"I know. I was counting on that when I went to
his room." She turned to me. "Was he? Is it true
what they say? That he gave half the women at
FAMU their first orgasm?"

"Well . . . kinda," I said. "I'm not sure that's
something to be proud—"

"Oh God! I love him," she said. "He's the one!
The total package: fine, filthy rich, and a good
fuck! What more could a girl want? I'm about to
break up with Austin and marry him!"

We laughed at her revelation. She was clearly
joking in the way brothers do when they say they'll
marry a stripper. The sincerity in her voice was
priceless. Still, I was more shocked that Xavier had
turned her down.

"You'll have to get him to look at your neon
thong first," Jennifer said.

The door opened again just as I was regretting pouring that wine down the drain. In order to enjoy this kind of crazy talk, I needed another drink to get on their level.

"Dear Lord, she's beautiful!" Jennifer pointed at the door with one hand and covered her mouth with the other like she was about to cry.

I turned to catch Scarlet gliding into the room in her rose-colored dress. The dress was breathtaking on Scarlet. The neckline dipped down her chest and she was all neck and brown skin beneath a soft rose lace fringe. She looked like the angels of little girls' dreams. Happy and soft. Pink. Krista was carrying the train behind her.

Everyone rushed over to kiss her and get a hug, but Krista held them back.

"No touching the bride," she said. "And please don't make her cry."

"Ohh!" they sighed, giving her air hugs.

And it was too late. Scarlet was already tearing up.

Krista let one of the hotel waitresses in with a platter holding sippy cups of black coffee—my way of avoiding potential spills. She started handing them out to distract the party from going all gushy over the bride. My girl Krista had learned so much from me. Made me proud to watch her work.

"Rachel! You're here!" Scarlet whined in the way only the bride can on her special day.

"Of course I am," I said and to my ears my voice sounded so detached. Like everything that had happened last night at the pier was being translated from those four words. "Why . . . why would you think I'd be anywhere else?"

"It was the craziest thing," she started, wiping away one of the joyful tears from the corner of her eye with the blue handkerchief Krista had given her. "Last night I had this nightmare that you and Ian got into a big fight and you stormed off and left. And you wouldn't come to the wedding. It was awful. Ian was so sad." She started crying a little harder and the handkerchief was being blackened with her eyeliner. "I didn't know what to do. I just wanted everything to be perfect for him. It was a disaster."

"Now, now. No sense getting worked up over a dream," I said, trying to comfort Scarlet and stop the tears.

"But it was so real," she said crying into a new blue handkerchief Krista had handed her. "I just want to say that I'm so happy you were kind enough to participate in my wedding. I know things between us haven't been the best, but Ian loves you, so I love you. And I wouldn't want our wedding to be any other way. I wouldn't want to do it without you here."

Scarlet reached out to embrace me and I felt guilt shoot so fast up my spine that I nearly fell on top of her. Her love for Ian was all in her face. The music, anything I needed to know about this wedding, could be heard in her voice. It was soft, serene, hopeful. Celine. The song was for them.

"I'll be right back," I said.

"What? Where are you going?" Krista said. "I'm about to start getting folks lined up. We start in twenty minutes."

"I just . . . I left something in my room. I'll be one minute."

I dashed out of the room before anyone else could disagree. I had to go. I couldn't let things move on this way.

* * *

"I'm sorry," I said to Ian's back. I'd excused myself through the groom's suite with a pretend message from Krista. Xavier tried to stop me, but I
assured him that it was official wedding business
only.

Ian was standing in the bathroom alone with
the door open, frozen, looking at himself in the
mirror. I closed the door behind me.

"Don't do this—I can't turn you down again—"

"No, that's not it." I stopped him and stood in
the mirror beside him. "I'm not here for that."

"Good, because I don't think I can—" He held
onto the edge of the sink. He looked more nervous than he had the night he was supposed to
propose to Scarlet. His eyes were withdrawn.

"I came down here because I wanted to say
that— Wait, are you OK?"

"Just my nerves. Just nervous." He pulled at his
collar. "I think my collar is too tight."

"Cold feet," I said.

He looked at my reflection. "You think so?"

"It's your wedding day," I said. "Of course it's
cold feet."

"How's Scarlet?"

"Beautiful. Happy."

"Really?" His eyes softened the way they usually
did when he saw her.

"She loves you, Ian," I said. "And you love her.
And I'm just so— I came here to tell you that I'm
so happy you didn't lock me out today. That you
let me be here for you. Like you've always been
there for me."

"I was really mad at you last night. You put me in

a bad position. If it wasn't for X, I don't think I could've—"

"I know. I know. I don't know what was wrong with me. I think I was just confused. Jealous. I don't know . . . but whatever it was, afterward I did a lot of soul searching—and drinking—and I know my place now," I said. "And it's here with you . . . as your friend. You remember senior year at FAMU? The muscly Omega at the hotel?"

Ian cracked a half smile. "You called me at 3:00 AM. Tyson was about to catch your ass cheating."

"I was terrified. I thought I was about to lose everything . . . and I eventually did."

"Yeah. After they fought, the Omega told Tyson everything and he broke up with you the next day."

"But I didn't have to face it that night. Because you saved me," I added.

"I parked my pickup at the window behind that beaten-down duplex and told you to jump."

"And I was so scared. But you held out your arms, and I jumped."

"You always make it sound so dramatic. The flat bed was like five feet down." He turned to me with a full smile.

"It could've been a two-foot jump from the window—I was so shaken up, I would not have done it," I said, "if it wasn't for you being there for me."

"So?" he pushed. "Why are you bringing up that old story?"

"Because you were there to support me. And that's what I want to do for you right now. Just be there for you."

"What you did was real fucked up," Ian said sternly.

"I'm sorry! I'm so, so, so, so sorry. Please for—"

"But I still love you," he said, before hugging me. He looked into my eyes and kissed me on the forehead. "It's my wedding day, Rach," he said grinning.

I wiped a tear from his eye.

"Yes, it is," I agreed, not bothering to catch my own tears.

There was a knock on the door and Ian's father called to us, "Time to get going. Folks are lining up out here."

"You ready?" I asked Ian.

"I was born ready, baby!" He did a boxer's two-step and stretched his neck from side to side.

"All right, go ahead with your bad self!"

I rushed downstairs just in time to get in line to walk down the aisle.

Krista, in her headset and holding dutifully to her iPad, grabbed my hand and said in my ear, "You can do this."

I crossed the threshold and held my breath, insisting that I wouldn't cry, I wouldn't breathe until it was over and Ian and Scarlet had said, "I do."

I took slow steps, arm-in-arm with my escort, facing the flashing lights from cameras at every angle.

Ian was up ahead, standing like the man I'd always known, but more mature, seeming to be off on his own.

I wasn't going to look into his eyes, but I did. Halfway down the aisle, I looked into his eyes and he was looking back at me and crying. But the tears weren't for me. Before I knew it, I was standing in front and facing the back of the room.

The chords for the bride began to play. Everyone stood.

Scarlet entered in rose on her father's arm.

The air I'd been holding in my lungs escaped without me being prepared to hold back. My tears began to fall.

This was it.

Everything was about to change forever.

Through my tears, I said good-bye to Ian.

When he stepped forward to take Scarlet's hand from her father's arm, I saw Xavier smiling at me.

"I'm here," he mouthed.

"Ladies and gentlemen!" The DJ's shout piped through the ballroom after the wedding party had been welcomed into the reception and only Ian and Scarlet were left waiting on the other side of the grand entrance. "I give you Mr. and Mrs. Ian Ward Dupree!"

We'd formed a man-made tunnel in the middle of the ballroom, bridesmaids on one side, grooms-men on the other, and waved our hands over their heads as they danced along the line to one of Ian's old favorite rap songs.

Ian twirled Scarlet around in her rose gown. Their eyes linked and it seemed as if we weren't all standing there. Like they were alone. Somewhere more beautiful. We backed away and found our seats at the head of the dance floor as Celine Dion's soft serenade sprang through the speakers for their first dance.

Ian led Scarlet to the perfect spot beneath the biggest twinkling chandelier and held her so softly in his arms. Celine sang, "Because you loved me."

Anything I thought I would feel at that moment was gone as Scarlet began to cry. Ian whispered something in her ear. They laughed. He leaned down and nestled his head into the space between her shoulder and neck. I knew he was crying, too.

A lump grew in my throat. And not because I was jealous. It was because I finally knew for sure that this was the right thing. With my eyes, I saw what they felt in their hearts for one another. I was a witness. I'd been made a witness.

When the song was over, the DJ called everyone to the dance floor to join the couple. The other bridesmaids found their men. Someone even came and claimed one of the flower girls. Uncle Cat went and grabbed Krista.

I looked down the table at Xavier talking to one of Scarlet's cousins. She was twirling her hair and batting her eyes so hard it looked like her fake eyelashes would fall off and land in his drink.

"Another victim," I said to myself. "Oh well, guess I'm on my own." I'd predicted this.

One of the waitresses came by and offered me a scallop wrapped in bacon. I couldn't resist. I took two . . . really three . . . popped them into my mouth like cherry bombs and washed them down with the last sip of wine in my glass.

I looked from the glass and Xavier was no longer down at the other end of the table. Fake lashes was standing alone, looking like a stepchild.

"You can't go eating all the product!" I heard beside me.

I laughed. I knew it was Xavier.

"I ordered those scallops just for me," I said to him. "It's the best appetizer."

"Pork and seafood? Can't be wrong," he said.

I looked up at him standing beside my seat.

He held out his hand.

"A dance?"

I looked around as if there were options. "Sure. Why not?"

Xavier easily maneuvered us through the packed crowd. While it usually took a little time for people to get going on the dance floor at a reception, it seemed liked everyone there was just waiting to dance. There had been an open bar during cocktail hour, but something told me that this dance mob was more about where we were and who was present than the free alcohol. While many of Scarlet's relatives were still sitting, all of the Duprees were linked arm in arm.

Xavier picked a spot near the back of the dance floor where the younger couples were grinning at one another and whispering plans for the after party. We were far enough from Ian and Scarlet, but I still felt pangs of humiliation tickling up my back. Although only Xavier, Ian, and Krista knew what had happened at the pier, to me the feeling in the room wavered from full acknowledgment of my silly disclosure to indifference that I was even there.

Xavier held me tighter, like Ian would if I was dancing with him and Ian was reading my mind. I let out the kind of breath that left me knowing I was going to feel better about what happened someday.

"Thank you for looking out for me, X."

"What? I get a sincere thank-you?"

"No, really. I know I've been a little hard on you. But I appreciate what you did."

"Just looking out for my friends."

"Friends?"

"Sure. We go way back. Once a Rattler always a Rattler."

"Yeah. But I haven't heard from you since we were Rattlers on the Yard," I said.

"I figured you weren't interested in hearing from me. All busy with your big-city Atlanta life. Making moves. Shaking and breaking." He did a little shuffle and bent me backward into a dramatic dance competition dip that made everyone around us laugh.

"What about you? What have you been up to?"

"A little bit of this. A little bit of that."

"Yeah, I bet." Some slow O'Jays song I couldn't remember the title to came on and Xavier slid his arms around my waist. It was a "move," but I didn't stop him. "God! I love this song," I said as Xavier sang the words into my neck.

We danced to three more songs just like that.

I'd taken a few more deep breaths and had forgotten where I was. Beads of sweat trickled from the nape of my neck and down my back.

A song was ending. I felt Xavier clasp his hands on my waist. The beat kicked up and some Zydeco song started playing. The few people who'd sat down rushed back to the dance floor.

"Want to go for a walk?" Xavier asked me. "It's hot as shit in here."

Outside of a line of glass doors was a half-moon-shaped terrace with white lightbulbs strung up overhead in random, romantic lines that would look like stars when the sun had fully set. The terrace was high up enough from the street that we couldn't see what was going on or hear any noise other than the steady pulse of the Zydeco rhythms coming from inside the ballroom. Two of the young couples from the dance floor were already hugged up in one of the corners looking like they were avoiding their parents.

"Look at them?" Xavier said, nodding over his shoulder at the foursome, "The game never changes."

"Yeah, I guess," I said, looking back into the room and wishing we'd stayed inside somehow. It was hot in there, but it was no competition for the heat outdoors, even though the sun was going down. I reasoned that at least there weren't as many people outside.

Xavier had walked to the edge of the terrace. He was holding two full flutes of champagne he'd grabbed from one of the waitresses on the way out- side.

"So, what's really going on with you in Chicago? You dodged the question in there—the very elu- sive Mr. Xavier Hamilton." I came up behind him.

He handed me one of the flutes.

"That's Hamilton the third!" he pointed out and we laughed. "Not much. Just trying to live in my father's footsteps without scaring my own shadow. No easy feat for a brother."

"Business good?"

"It's great. Everything is great. But sometimes, you know, I wonder if this is what I really want."

"Money? Success?" I joked.

"Well, money and success are nothing if it's not what you want to do. This is my father's empire. I want my own."

"And what does Xavier Hamilton the third's em- pire look like?"

"Hum . . ." Xavier scratched his forehead.

"Come on, you can tell me. I can keep a secret," I pushed.

"Promise you won't laugh?"

"Never! Well, maybe I will . . . if it's funny."

Xavier playfully looked away and shut his eyes like he was expecting a slap in the face after he let the words come from his mouth. "I want to open an art gallery." He peeked at me through one eye.

"Art?" I laughed before I could stop myself—it wasn't that opening an art gallery was so absurd, more that it was Xavier who'd mentioned doing it.

"Why is that funny?" Xavier asked, chuckling, too.

"Art? Come on! You don't exactly strike me as an art lover. Unless you count that Lil' Kim poster you had over your bed in college."

"For your information, Ms. Rachel, I'm an avid collector."

"Of Lil' Kim posters?"

"Of art! Fine art. Paintings. Sculptures. Sketches."

"Really?"

"I took this art history course senior year and I've been collecting ever since. I have two Kara Walker silhouettes."

"Walker? I love her. I have a print of one of her silhouettes over my couch."

"She's awesome. A little dark, but rather magical," he said. "I also have a Bearden. An Alexander."

"Larry Alexander? I love his work, too. I have one in my office. Well . . . it's a print." I shrugged.

"Lately, I've been getting into some of the newer guys in Chicago. I back a few."

"You're a benefactor?" I was almost sure I wasn't speaking to the same person I'd known at FAMU.

"Whoa! Nothing as big as a benefactor," Xavier said. "I just make sure cats are eating. Might pay rent. Let someone stay at one of my lofts downtown."

"That's amazing. I never would've thought . . ."

Xavier smiled at me so openly that I just stopped talking.

"So a gallery is the next step?" I said.

"Been thinking about it. The Chicago scene is so swamped, though. Got my eyes on ATL. Know anything about the art scene there?"

"Ashamed to say I don't. For me, art is one of those things I always wished I knew more about but didn't. Guess I've been waiting to meet someone to teach me more about it."

"Maybe we could find out more about it together." His voice went deep. His eyes were as soft as his smile. Xavier was flirting with me.

"We?" I'd known him too long to pretend I wasn't clear on where he was going. I laughed and scrunched up my face. I wasn't about to be another name on X's list.

"I mean . . . like I could come visit and you could show me around. Help me get my feet wet. What? I meant that strictly in a professional way. However you took it in your dirty little mind is on you." He placed his empty champagne flute on a little table beside the ledge. Straightened and crossed his arms over his chest, and then I wasn't sure if I'd read him correctly. My champagne flute was almost empty, too. Was the alcohol making me see what I wanted to see? What did I want to see?

The foursome must've gotten tired of the heat. They went inside, and through the open door there was the sound of Mr. Dupree's band playing.

"I just wouldn't think you'd need me to show you around. I'm sure one of your many FAMU concubines would love to hear you're coming to town," I said to Xavier. "Hell, half of them flocked to GA after graduation."

"Rattlers are everywhere," Xavier said, nodding. "But maybe I don't want just anyone's company." His voice slowed and he moved in closer to me. This time, it was obvious that he was flirting and he wasn't bothering to cover anything up. He took my empty champagne glass and slid it onto the table close enough to kiss his. The moon was out now and daylight was swallowed whole. The white lights overhead were so bright. "Maybe I want yours." He looked back into my eyes and just the two of us breathing seemed to collapse every inch of air between us. We were drawing closer.

The moonlight in his eyes. The throbbing of the band from inside the ballroom beneath our feet. The champagne tickling my heart. I closed my eyes. I breathed him in like all those other girls. I waited, too. Waited for his lips to touch mine.

But then . . .

"Come inside, Rach!" Krista's voice cut in all away. So quickly, we turned from whatever was happening to her standing halfway out the doors we'd exited. "They're about to cut the cake."

Xavier grabbed my hand proudly under Krista's stare and we walked inside without saying a word to her.

8

Aliens in ATL

#*Shesaidhe'dcomeinthemorning. But I wasn't ready for what he had in store.*

I thought I'd crumble watching Ian cut his wedding cake and feed the moist white insides to the woman he wouldn't leave for me. After everything that had happened, after everything that I did and he'd said to me, it didn't make any sense that I'd still be standing, another smiling and hopeful face in pictures from the wedding reception right there behind Scarlet and her girls. But I was. Still, a close look at those pictures would show that I was too busy looking across the room at Xavier behind Ian and his boys to think of losing my footing and crumbling over Ian. Xavier's coming so close to kissing me was like handing a baby a new toy. From across the room I saw him in a new way. And damn, he looked good.

He had my attention. I was thinking of him incessantly after the wedding. And while my mind told me that I was probably just masking the pain of the disaster with Ian at the pier with the promise of Xavier's kiss, the pounding in my heart was much louder. Being a hopeless romantic, my heart was filled with an acute case of the "what if's." What if I'd stumbled upon my "and I wasn't even looking for him" fairy-tale man? What if he could be mine? What if he was what I'd been missing?

"Dammmnnnn," Journey said, looking at me on the computer. She and I had matching wineglasses and our favorite bottle of pink Moscato. "I'm just saying, I expected fireworks in New Orleans, but dammmmnnnnn, you traded in your best friend for his best friend?"

"Xavier is not Ian's best friend. Well, he was his best friend in undergrad, but they don't really get with each other like that anymore. You know, life."

"Does Ian know about this budding love affair?" Journey asked.

"No," I said. "We haven't really spoken since I saw him walking out of the reception with Scarlet in New Orleans. The office sent them flowers when they got back from the honeymoon and I know Scarlet was e-mailing Krista about some loose ends. But Ian hasn't called me . . . so. I guess he wants it this way. It's been almost a month now."

"And you don't think Xavier has said anything to Ian?" She sipped her wine.

Journey and I shared a toast at the start of the conversation. She was in Dublin. Dame had taken the kids on a walk. They'd be there for a few

months as Dame taped his scenes for a movie he
was starring in with Colin Farrell. She'd been trav-
eling and constantly on the go for the last few
weeks, so I had to get her caught up on everything
that had happened in New Orleans. About the
pier. Oh my God. Tante Heru. She laughed about
that and said she was sending the "Holy Ghost
Drop Squad" from her father's church in Alabama
to pick me up for talking to a roots woman. I told
her about the romantic scene outside the reception with Xavier.

Xavier and I had been regular phone buddies
since we left New Orleans. In fact, he'd called me
every night. Sometimes twice in one night. Sometimes three times in a day. He wanted to know
what I was eating. Maybe have me text him pictures of me brushing my teeth in the morning, my
office, the red truck parked in Bird's garage. We'd
talk for hours. Like boyfriend and girlfriend in a
long-distance relationship. He made me laugh like
we were still in college. He was so funny and so
smart, I was almost embarrassed that I didn't know
these things about him. Xavier could tell a joke
one minute and make me cry the next. He'd finished the Ironman Triathlon twice in Hawaii. Had
traveled to every continent. Taught himself Man-
darin. He donated half of his salary each year to
scholarships for first-generation college students
enrolled in the business school at FAMU. He was
the first man I'd met in a long time who made me
feel like I needed to do better. Hearing all these
new things in late-night chats over the phone, I
guessed that previously my young mind had just
been happy believing what every other girl had to
say about Xavier. But then he'd openly admitted

that those girls weren't making it all up. It had taken him a lot of time and a lot of heartbreak to get to where he was right then. One night while we were Skyping at 3:00 AM, he yawned after reading Rumi's "The Springtime of Lovers Has Come" and said, so eloquently, "Sometimes a man's got to get to his future to know how important it is."

"You know I have to tell you that this is probably nothing, right?" Journey looked nervous, playing with the stem of her glass. "But, you know, you're probably kind of—"

"I know," I interrupted her. "I'm substituting my feelings for Ian with this thing with Xavier, so I don't have to think about what happened with Ian."

"Good shit, Rach. What do you need me for?" Journey said and I laughed. "You've got it all figured out."

"You'd think I would, after all this drama, but I don't know, Journey. There's something about him. Xavier. A clean slate. I mean, we have a past, but where we are right now is so new. Just cute." I laughed. Looked down at the wine in my glass. It was so sweet. That's why I like cheap wine. Cheap and sweet. "I hope I'm not just spinning my wheels with him."

"What is he saying? Like what kind of stuff is he saying to you?"

"Girl, what isn't he saying?" I grinned. "It's like he knows me. Like he knows just what I want. Just what to say at any moment."

"And you think it's the roots woman."

"I didn't say that."

"Well, I know you."

"OK. But what about me says I'd believe anything some bearded roots woman in the French Quarter would promise for fifty dollars?"

"You want love," Journey said. "You believe in love. I never told you this before, but you were the first person I thought really believed in me and Dame—in our love. You were so ready to accept it. I never felt like you were working with us just because it was your job. You stand for what you do. For love. And that's all I've ever wanted for you. For you to find it. And I know you desperately want the same. That's reason enough to believe the bearded roots woman."

"He is some kind of miracle, though," I said. "Guess I'll just have to wait and see where it goes— if it goes anywhere. Who knows: this could all amount to a series of phone conversations that lead nowhere." I tried to play it down a little. "X seems to have slowed down with the ladies, but I'm sure he's still out there playing."

"Don't let him decide if it's going to be all about you. You hold the power," Journey instructed. "You decide if you want to be down with him. I'm just requesting one thing."

"What?"

"Figure out the deal with Ian before you move onto something else. I could be wrong, but something tells me that some of this is just in your mind. We believe what we want to believe for whatever reasons. We keep secrets from others and sometimes ourselves."

"But Ian married someone else," I said. "Who cares?"

"You'll care, if it's not resolved," Journey said. "Because if it has to resolve itself, it's going to be a motherfucker."

I closed the laptop and went to bed drunk and thinking about Ian and Xavier. I'm not stupid. I've been in and out of my feelings enough to know when I'm lying to myself. I've made bad choices. But they were because I didn't want to hide my feelings. I didn't know which one was better—bad choices or hidden feelings—but I knew Journey was right. Whichever one it was, I had to figure it all out before I could move forward.

My phone rattled on the nightstand and I read a text from Xavier:

> **I know I've called you three times today, so I'll text you instead of picking up the phone and bothering you. ☺ I'm lying here on the couch and I just finished watching *Love & Basketball* and I was thinking about you. I wish you were with me right now. I wish I'd taken that kiss. Can you send me one right now?**

It took me ten tries and a walk to my purse to get my lip gloss to get the picture of the perfect pucker on my phone and text it to Xavier.

He responded with a picture of his lips.

I went to sleep with the phone on the pillow beside me.

"Oh my God, look at you two! Is that the Mediterranean behind you again? You guys spent your entire honeymoon in the water." I was sitting in the conference room with one of my former clients, Bisa Ojaku, looking at pictures from her honeymoon in Cannes. Her wedding to an Ara-

bian prince was my last wedding of 2010 and, like
most of my brides, Bisa was still a little attached to
me. I hadn't seen her since the wedding six months
ago because Prince Ayat insisted that she move to
Dubai with him right after the wedding; still, Bisa
e-mailed Krista and me updates of her marital bliss
every week. She'd called the office a few days ago
saying that she was in town visiting and asked
Krista if it would be OK for her to stop by to show
us her wedding album.

"Yes, the Mediterranean was so beautiful," Bisa
said, sliding her hand over the water in the picture
like she was imagining that she was still there. In
the shot, she and Prince Ayat were embraced at
the helm of a yacht with the sun setting behind
them. "We didn't want to leave Cannes. As soon as
we got back to Dubai, Ayat bought a yacht. Can
you believe it? All those years living in Dubai and
that man didn't own a yacht." Bisa had been as single as a drop of water in the Arabian Desert until her
fortieth birthday, when she met Ayat on a sleepover
camping expedition in the Arabian Desert. She was
a retired porn star. She was sure she'd never find a
man who could accept her past and envision her
in his future. But her prince, and I mean he really
is a prince, came to pick her up on his camel in the
middle of the night. Prince Ayat was filthy, stinking
rich, and too old and tired to care about Bisa's
past. He just wanted good company and great conversation for the rest of his life. Basically, someone
to spend his money with him. And he loved black
women. There was one catch, though—Bisa had to
move from Atlanta to Dubai right after the wedding. A friend had told her about my company
and she called me two weeks before she and

Prince Ayat would be in Atlanta to say their vows. It was a rush, but he'd paid handsomely for the rush. We rebuilt a desert camp with real camels, hookahs, and tents on the turf at the Georgia Dome.

"Must be nice to go yacht shopping, Princess!" I joked with Bisa.

She laughed and kissed Prince Ayat's image in the picture. She seemed so happy. Still had the sparkle in her eye of a new bride. Some people say there's a difference between a young woman and a more mature woman getting married. I never noticed. The heart was the same. Both Bisa and Ayat had seen it all and done it all, but their love was baby new. Fine newborn-baby new. Looking at them made me think of Xavier and his late-night sweet nothings. Bisa turned the album to a picture on the last page; it was of Ayat and her standing on the strand in Cannes hand in hand. She fingered the link between them.

"My prince charming. He found me! It's a miracle. A real fairy tale." Bisa smiled and did a little dance in her seat before closing the book.

"So how's Dubai?" I asked.

"It like a big resort. Beautiful every day. It's still taking me time to get used to some of the customs, but Ayat and I hardly get out of the house right about now"—Bisa winked suggestively and we laughed—"so I'm cool. Lord knows that man is a freak. What's up with you? You know Ayat has a few friends who love the sisters, too. You should come visit."

"I'll visit, but I don't know about needing a date. I'm kind of—"

"Wait a minute," Bisa started, "I knew there was something different about you."

"What?"

"Your eyes . . . your smile . . . your clothes . . ." She sat back and looked at me from head to toe with a sistergirl glance. "Uhhmmm hum."

"What?" I laughed, knowing what she was getting at.

"You been getting some!"

"No—not exactly."

"You're in love?"

"No—not exactly."

"Well, both must be on the way. Because you have that glow, honey bunny. You look exactly how I did before I moved to the other side of the world to be with a man who'd never had macaroni and cheese." Bisa pinched my knee. "So what's your boo's name?"

"Xavier."

"Hum . . . sounds smart. Successful. Freaky."

"Well, I wouldn't know all that yet," I said. "He lives in Chicago."

"That's right up the street. You better get on a plane. Bring that thang to him. Young girls like us don't have a lot of time to debate over such minor details as air mileage."

"I know, but I'm trying to take it slower," I said. "Don't want to crowd him. He's kind of one of those 'reformed player' types."

"Look, Ms. Rachel Winslow—never underestimate a man's potential to adapt. I never would've thought Ayat would really have married me—a Muslim man with a former adult actress? Crazy! But men know what they like. And when they find it, they pursue it," Bisa said.

"I guess I'll have to wait on him to get on a plane to Atlanta, then!"

"I know that's right!" Bisa laughed and we slapped hands dramatically. "So, how'd you meet this man who has you glowing?"

"It's the funniest thing—but you have to promise not to laugh at me—"

"I'll probably laugh, but tell me anyway," Bisa joked.

"We've known each other for years. Went to college together. I hadn't seen him since. But a few weeks ago, a friend of ours got married, and Xavier was there and I was there, and I went to see this roots woman—"

"A roots woman?" Bisa coiled up.

"Tante Heru. We were in New Orleans. It's a long story," I explained struggling to sound nonchalant. "Anyway, I was feeling really down and I asked Tante Heru to send me the man of my dreams." As I repeated the rest of the story about Tante Heru in the Quarter, it was like I was seeing it all again. I remembered parts I hadn't been able to recall. Being lifted from the floor of the bar. Hands all around me. Tante Heru chanting over my forehead. Her laugh. Her gray beard. Her promise about sunrise. Xavier at the door of my hotel room the next morning. "I asked her . . . I asked Tante Heru for—" I stopped. I was feeling dizzy. Like I was back in Tante Heru's shack. I could smell her all around the room.

"For what? What did you ask her for?" Bisa had big fish eyes.

"Lovvveee," I said. "A man who loves music, a man who loves art. Who respects the spirit world and thinks with his heart."

"Oh girl, I love that song! India.Arie! And that's my favorite part," Bisa said and then she started singing, "A man who loves music, a man who loves art—"

And then I joined in, "Respects the spirit world and thinks with his heart." It sounded like an incantation. The lights in the conference room began to flicker. I looked over at Bisa to be sure I wasn't still off in my thoughts and imagining what I was seeing.

The exposed insides of Bisa's mouth confirmed the paranormal potential of the event.

"It's nothing!" Bisa said.

"Yeah. Just a coincidence! These lights flicker in here all the time." (Lie!)

"Really?"

"No . . . but let's pretend they do. I'm sure it's nothing. That's the thing about those crackpot roots women: they get you going and then you're convinced their little spells are working, but it's just your imagination. Right?"

"You seem pretty convinced about this guy," Bisa said. "And he seems pretty convinced about you. Maybe it is working."

"Maybe I just want it to work. And what's happened since is just my imagination."

"Could be."

"Well, there's one test. When I was leaving, Tante Heru said she'd grant me two more of loves wishes whenever I wanted them. The second wish is that I can wish that my true love be by my side whenever I want him."

"Well, wish Xavier here! Wish him by your side."

"But I don't even know if it's him—if Xavier is my true love," I pointed out. "And I don't even know if it's working." I laughed. "And I don't even know why we're talking about this!"

"The only way to know is to try. Put it to the test. Wish."

"Wish what?"

"Whatever you want!" Bisa threw up her hands. "Whatever you want right now. Look, if this guy is your true love and you wish for your true love to appear, then he'll show up. Then you'll know."

"That's ridiculous. You sound like you're in some teen movie."

"We could stand to be teenagers again sometimes," Bisa said. "And I think it's ridiculous not to make the wish."

I exhaled and rolled my eyes. "Fine, Bisa. I'll do it! But only because it's you and you're one of my favorite clients!"

"*The* favorite!"

"*One* of the favorites."

"Whatever!" Bisa took my hand and put it over her photo album like it was some sort of love Bible. She closed her eyes.

"What are you doing?" I laughed a little.

"Shhhh." She gripped my hand tighter. "I am waiting for your wish." She peeked out of one eye at me staring at her. "Close your eyes and wish."

"Why?"

"Just do it!"

"OK!" I closed my eyes. "So what am I supposed to say?"

"How am I supposed to know? Just ask for your wish!"

"OK . . . well, I ask that the man of my dreams appears right now!" I opened my eyes but Bisa's were still closed. I waited a second, but she sat there. The lights started flickering again, but this time it wasn't coming from the ones overhead in the conference room. It seemed like it was something in the hallway. Maybe the fire lights. I turned and looked at the doorway, and there standing in the frame was Xavier. Red roses were at his chest.

I got up. Slid my hand from Bisa's and ran to him. I had to feel him to know he was really standing there before I could believe it and say it aloud.

"It's you!" I felt myself being held in his arms. The cool, wet touch of the flowers in his hands now on my back.

"Yeah, baby, it's me. Three weeks was too long. I couldn't stay away a minute longer." He kissed me and I felt like I was up off the ground. "Had to see you."

"No shit!" Bisa said. "No fucking shit!"

"What?" Xavier was laughing.

"Oh, I'm sorry, X." I peeled only halfway from his hold to turn back into the room to face Bisa. "Let me introduce you to my client."

She was standing up with the photo book in her arms, looking at Xavier like he was Moses walking on water.

"This is Bisa Ojaku—one of my favorite clients," I said. "And Bisa, this is Xavier." I patted Xavier on his chest and looked into his eyes. "My very good friend."

Bisa shook Xavier's hand and grinned at me knowingly.

"I hope I didn't disturb anything," Xavier said to me. "Krista wanted to come back here and get you, but I wanted to surprise you on my own."

"I think you've succeeded," Bisa joked.

"We're fine," I said. "We were just looking over Bisa's wedding pictures."

"Yes, and I was just leaving," Bisa said excusing herself out the door.

After Bisa was gone, Xavier pulled me back into his arms.

"Now, I was hoping you were free for the rest of the day, Rach," he said. "Was hoping to sweep you off your feet."

"Sweep me off my feet?"

"If you'll let me."

Xavier had his bags in the reception area with Krista. Under her watchful eye, we picked them up and walked out of the office and into a romance.

Twenty years from then, if things worked out between us, I kept thinking that I'd have to lie to our children and say that we left the office and went to a café to listen to some jazz or walk through a park where Xavier picked daisies for me.

Unfortunately, it went nothing like that.

When we went to my place to drop off Xavier's bags, I went to make dinner reservations and he decided to get in the shower to wash away the musk of his flight.

Somehow (and I mean for that to sound ridiculous), while passing each other in the hallway, I got a look at Xavier's arms. Wet. Big and brown. Made for holding things. His skin made me beg to touch it. I had to know what else he was hiding under my white towel.

Now, I'm not the kind of girl who sleeps around. I left that in my twenties with a bad case of gonorrhea I got from a guy I met at my church. But I hadn't had a gentleman caller in months— and not one before that drought looked quite as good as Xavier.

I guessed my interest was in my eyes, because in the middle of the hallway where I was passing while on my cell phone and he was heading to the living room to get his bag, he leaned up against the wall and grinned so I could see his white teeth.

"What?" he posed with his hand holding his towel in place at his hip rather indifferently.

"That's just a lot." I looked at his chest. Two solid pectorals with licorice-colored nipples still wet from the shower led to a staircase of abs that led down to a solid V-shaped pelvis. "I guess you just like to be in the gym, like, all day."

"Not really. I just try to stay healthy."

"You look healthy."

"You wanna touch?"

Sure we could've gone on with this exchange, but the wonderful thing about being in my thirties, I was learning, was that it was hard to keep me away from physical action with a man I really wanted. And I really wanted him.

I jumped on Xavier with everything I'd heard about his bedroom acrobatics in my ear. But this was no college boy anymore. He was a grown man. And he handled me that way. Handled me with my back against the wall in the hallway, and then in the bedroom, and then on the floor beside the bed after I tried to get away. I wasn't a smoker, but I would've liked a hit of something after that. I wasn't thinking about going to a café or walking through the park to pick daisies. Right then, I was cool with staying in my place forever.

We laid on the cold floor, naked and thirsty, for thirty minutes, linking fingers and laughing.

"You must think I'm a slut. A straight-up freak ho!" I said, trying to gauge his reaction to my action. He may have played the game, but I'd started it. And sometimes that perception dictated how a man treated a woman, moving forward.

"Nah. That just lets me know that you know what you want out of life." Xavier reached up to the bed and pulled the covers down over us.

"Cool . . . wait a minute . . . isn't that André 3000?" I said, trying to remember where I'd heard that line. "That's from 'Where are My Panties.' "

"Damn! You got me!" Xavier laughed.

"Trying to run lines on me up in here," I said, laughing with him.

"I'm sorry. I just figured Dre said it better than I ever could. I judge women based on how they chase their dreams, not how quickly they sleep with me. I didn't mean to offend you."

"I'm more offended that you obviously didn't think I would know that song!"

"I didn't peg you for an OutKast fan," Xavier said.

"Um . . . you're in Atlanta. . . . It's my hometown."

"No, your hometown is out in the country. Ya'll probably listened to people yodeling. Probably didn't have radios."

"OK . . . you got jokes. So, what, you're some kind of OutKast head or something?" I asked.

"I like them. My musical taste is very diverse, though."

"Who's your favorite artist?" I asked.

"That's hard. I like so many."

"Name one that might surprise me."

"Meshell Ndegeocello," he replied.

"No!" I sat up and looked at him. "She's one of my favorites. I love her work. She's totally my lesbian crush."

"Lesbian?" Ian frowned comically. "You get down with that?"

"I don't like girls. I just really like her lyrics. She has this way of communicating her feelings. You know? I know all of her songs."

"So you say . . ." Xavier said dubiously. "I guess I'll have to test that statement. See how real you are about your lesbian lover's music."

"Go ahead. Try me." I scrunched up my face to accept his challenge.

"Name this tune: 'I'm sorry I left you no home, but your words they shattered my bones.'"

"That's super easy!" I said. "That's from 'Shirk'! *Devil's Halo!*"

"And . . . she's wrong!"

"Hell no!" I laughed.

"Well, right song, but wrong album. 'Shirk' is on my favorite Meshell Ndegeocello album—"

"*The World Has Made Me the Man of My Dreams!*" I cut him off.

"Gold star, boo!"

"Boo?"

We looked at each other.

"So who else do you like?" I asked.

"That might surprise you? Hum . . . India.Arie," Xavier said and then he started singing, "I am not my hair. I am not this—"

"Please stop!" I covered my ears. "India is probably somewhere screaming!"

"What, a brother can't get in touch with his feminine side?" Xavier said and he kept singing horribly.

We went on playing like this for hours. Until the sun went down. Dinnertime passed and only growls in our stomachs forced us to get up from the floor.

This easy conversation. This easy connection. I was immediately taken away. I kept looking at him in disbelief that he was with me. But then I was so happy that he was. After two days in the house, eating everything in my refrigerator and two pizzas Goldie delivered (Goldie was not happy to see Xavier), Xavier insisted that we go somewhere.

I was in the shower having withdrawals. I felt like if we went out into the world everyone might notice that I was living in a little fantasy and maybe the fantasy would shatter. I was also worried about how we might operate together. Ian still didn't know about Xavier and I didn't know how to tell him—not that I needed to tell him anything. There was also still the lingering question I'd been considering when Xavier was asleep with me in my bed—why was he so into me? He knew what had happened between me and Ian at the wedding in New Orleans. Why wouldn't that turn him off? Was he just jonesing for me because he knew how much I'd wanted Ian? Was he jealous?

The new events manager at the Atlanta Botanical Garden had been trying to get me to come see the summer bloom for weeks in hopes of talking me into perhaps booking my client's summer wedding there the next year. I asked Xavier if he wanted to visit the garden with me, sure he'd say he wasn't interested—it wasn't the most masculine place. He surprised me by saying he often went on walks in the Chicago Botanic Garden to clear his head and would like to see if Atlanta would top it. I swear, everything about that man was mounting up to be a surprise. A beautiful surprise.

* * *

"It's the *Punica granatum.*" Leek, a slender, soft-shouldered man in peach pants and a cream shirt with a peach collar, walked Xavier and me through a spinning maze of flowers that overpowered our senses with colors and sweet scents. We waited until sundown when they served wine and played jazz for couples walking through the gardens. The June heat was making Atlanta melt, and while the moon in the sky made little difference in the humidity, it was far more romantic than the sun. There were a few more couples with wineglasses walking through the maze ahead of us.

Like them, Xavier and I held hands and sipped wine. He grabbed my butt a few times when Leek wasn't looking.

"Taste it," Leek said, pointing to the red flower he'd identified as the *Punica granatum.*

"Eat the flower?" Xavier asked.

"Yes. Everything in here is edible. The *Punica granatum* is a dwarf pomegranate. You can eat the little orange bulbs." Leek pointed to a round growth that looked like fruit hanging from the flower. "Please."

"Go ahead, Xavier. Eat it," I pushed.

"Um . . . no, Eve. Last time I checked, a man shouldn't eat red things offered to him by a woman in a garden."

"Well, maybe she could eat it first," Leek said. "Maybe you could feed it to her."

Xavier looked at me and picked the tiny pomegranate. "Sounds like a plan."

Everything slowed down. Stopped moving. I just saw Xavier and the red fruit.

He held it up to my mouth and set it on my tongue slowly, locked in a stare.

"How does it taste, Ms. Winslow?" Leek asked, coming into our world with us.

"Like something in Eden," I answered. "Perfect."

"This is the *Dendrobium spectabile*," Leek said, pointing to an orchid in the Orchid Display House that looked just as alien as it did beautiful. He turned to me. "It's one of the most deliciously unique orchids that grows year round, here in the garden."

"Lovely," I said.

"Look at it closely." Leek stepped back so Xavier and I could see. "It is an exotic flower that shows something different to every eye."

We leaned in.

The *Dendrobium spectabile* was maroon and lily white in the center with yellow tails that looked like flames poking out around the edges.

"Tell me what you see," Leek said. "Get in closer."

Xavier and I leaned our heads from side to side.

"Hum," we said together, then we started laughing. Maybe giggling. There was only one thing to see. A woman's vulva.

"Whoa!" Xavier said. "It's a pus—"

"You better not!" I laughed.

"Ahh," Leek started. "I see the flower has shown you two the same thing. That's a good sign."

"There's nothing else it could be," Xavier said.

"I've heard many others," Leek revealed.

"Like?" I asked.

"A dragon. A heartbeat. Curls of pasta." Leek started walking to the next flower bed. "Funny how beautiful things in nature's garden speak to us. Maybe what we see is more about who we are on the inside than what it is on the outside."

Later that night at dinner, I finally got the nerve

to ask Xavier what I'd been thinking about since he'd arrived in Atlanta: why was he so interested in me? And why now? He didn't even blink before answering.

"You're dope. Period. Everything about you."

I'm sure I was blushing, but I pointed out that his compliments, kind as they were, didn't fully answer the questions. "Ian told you I was in love with him. He's one of your best friends. Doesn't it break some kind of 'man law' to date me? Or is this just a sex thing?"

"You think I packed my bags to come down here for a sex thing?" He laughed.

I didn't move.

He sobered up. Put down the drink he was holding and reached out for my hand. "I am not afraid of who you loved. I'm more interested in the fact that you loved. And, to be honest, how you loved—"

"You mean that I tried to break up his wedding? My best friend's wedding!"

"Yeah, crazy," he said, nodding. "But also honest. And courageous. That shit is such a turn-on."

I recoiled.

"Calm down," he said. "I don't mean that in a sexual way. Rachel, most women today don't really know how to love—not with their whole selves. They love because they want a ring. A husband. A nice house. Kids. Someone to go to church and sit up in a pew with. They love because they're supposed to. Not because it's urgent."

"And you know about loving urgently? Mr. All About Me?"

"I'm learning." He looked at me sharply.

"This is crazy."

"Precisely."

"What do you want from me?"

"I want you to love me that way."

"Is this some kind of competition?" I asked. "Who will *she* love more? I'm not trying to get involved in a pissing contest."

"There is no competition," Xavier said confidently. "I knew I won when you opened your hotel-room door that morning. You wanted to let me in. Admit it."

The music in the restaurant stopped suddenly. We looked around. The piano player was getting up from his bench.

"Tell the truth." Xavier turned back around and nudged me in the stomach playfully.

"You're a player, X. Maybe I kind of thought you were fine, but it wasn't like that. I was dealing with a lot. I think I wanted a shoulder to lean on."

"I'll be your shoulder to lean on," he said. "And my playing days are behind me. I'm an old veteran now. And, by the way, I could turn all those question on you."

"What?"

"You said you were in love with Ian. He's your best friend. Is this just a sex thing?" He cupped his pecks like a girl whose bra had been snatched away. "Are you using me for my body?"

"You're a mess!" I said. "I don't really know what's going on. I admit that I love Ian—that I was in love with him when I said what I said, but you . . . you came in and . . . I probably shouldn't be saying all of this."

"No. You probably should."

"I really like you. It's confusing the shit out of

me, but you just . . . it's like you're whispering in my ear," I said with the candle on the table between us flickering in Xavier's eyes.

"Damn, girl"—Xavier leaned into the table toward me—"you just made me hard as hell!"

We both laughed so hard, we nearly knocked the drinks off the table.

"You're a mess," I joked. "But I mean what I said. You've got me feeling a whole lot of things. I'm just wondering what Ian will say."

"Say?"

"Yeah. About us . . . hanging out. I haven't spoken to him since the wedding. It's been over a month."

"I spoke to him yesterday," Xavier said, taking a sip of water.

"What? You didn't tell me that. He knows you're here?"

"Of course." He looked at me, surprised. "What, you thought me being here was some secret?" He chuckled. "I don't get down like that. I don't creep."

"What did he say?" I was just stunned. My heart started beating faster. Suddenly the month I hadn't spoken to Ian felt like years, and miles, and landfills of distance. I imagined him living his life with Scarlet. Eating at the table I was sitting at with Xavier. Not thinking about me. Not missing me. He hadn't even called.

"Not much. He was shopping with his wife." (Wife? Why had Xavier said that like I didn't know Scarlet? Suddenly, she was to be referred to as "wife"?)

"That's cool," I said, taking a sip from my water then, too.

"Are you OK?" Xavier asked.
"I'm fine."

I've always been happy that I can't sing or dance or play the guitar or do a handstand. Those are all talents people like me are better off without. Like, if I could do a handstand or play guitar, I'd be doing it all day and every day. God forbid I had the skill to do both at the same time. I'd be in Vegas right now performing in Cirque du Soleil. If I could sing, anytime anyone needed a singer—say, at an open mic or funeral—I'd graciously decline all offers to bless the mic, but then, I'd hit the audience off with a wicked medley of "Amazing Grace," "God Bless the Child," and "Natural Woman." I'd then fall out on the stage and arrange for random people in the audience to carry me out.

After hanging out with Xavier for two whole months, him out of my sight only four times when he went home to Chicago to meet with his restaurant managers, I was thinking I should probably add "having a man" to that list of gifts I shouldn't have. We showed out all over Atlanta through the heat of the summer. Every Saturday, we packed a real picnic basket along with a plaid blanket and sat in the park, where we sipped wine from real glasses and Xavier fed me cucumber sandwiches. We'd take pictures, smiling and poking out our tongues to catch the perfect French kiss on camera. We'd lean into each other over flowers at sidewalk tables in front of Buckhead cafés. Xavier would hold my hand on top of the table and kiss it while looking into my eyes. It was wonderful for us, wrapped up in our own world where perfect ro-

mance was acceptable and I knew he wouldn't let
go of my hand if I reached for his. But everyone
else around us looked nauseated by the total and
careless exploitation of intimacy. Single women
looked at us as though they would put arsenic in
our glasses if we looked away. Single men looked at
us like Xavier must be whipped or I must have the
best vagina in the world. (I agreed on both
points.) The only people who seemed excited to
see us coming, walking beneath my parasol at the
shops in midtown or hugging up on line at the
amusement park, were old couples. They'd smile
and ask how long we'd been dating. Xavier would
proudly announce that we'd been "courting" for
two months. I was loving that about him—how he
seemed so unafraid of being with me. So damn
sure. I was used to men playing all kinds of silly
games, but he came right in with his heart open.

This allowed me to open myself to him. I didn't
even realize that I'd been closed, but after years of
dealing with those other kinds of men, I had invisible barriers up that I was beginning to realize may
have kept me from finding out what I'd been missing. I'd learned not to say how I felt about someone. Not to ask for what I wanted. Not to hold
hands in the park. How to accept a man letting go
of my hand, by pretending it was OK, that I didn't
need it. But Xavier gave me what I needed and I
gave him what he needed.

What was interesting about having him in my
space, so close and for so long, basically playing
house, was learning about Xavier. His needs.
Like how he hated cheap toothpaste. When we
went grocery shopping he'd go to the natural
foods aisle and get this organic blueberry tooth-

paste that tasted like softened chalk . . . with blueberries. He hated the sun in his eyes in the morning when he was half asleep. Claimed it messed up his "circadian rhythm." (I had to look that up.) He started turning the blinds up to the ceiling, so when we woke up, the small glints of light would shine on the ceiling and not in our eyes.

Xavier liked going to happy hour and trying new restaurants. And after being in Atlanta only a few weeks, he knew a whole lot of insiders, many of them our former FAMU classmates who'd made it big time in the city, and had a list of investors and artists who wanted to help him with his gallery. He decided that he wanted the mission behind the gallery to focus on the early twenties set. Project X would expose abstract works created by minority artists to their peers. He was so excited about it. One day, he picked me up at the office and took me to a 3,000-square-foot, raw loft space in an artist community right near the Atlanta University Center that housed Spelman, Morehouse, and Clark, and told me he'd purchased it outright for Project X. "I'm not the kind of man who drags his feet when he sees something he wants," he said, holding me in his arms in the middle of the loft.

"Guess you'll be here for a while," I said.

While Xavier kept encouraging me to reach out to Ian, I didn't speak to Ian for the first few weeks while Xavier was there. I just didn't know what to say, and I wasn't sure how I'd feel. But when a reminder for his approaching birthday popped up on my phone in August, I sent him a birthday card. I didn't write anything personal on it. I just signed my name and put it in the mail.

Two days later, I got a text from him:

FROM: IAN DUPREE
TIME: 10:23am
It's Wednesday. I want to see you.
Meet me at Fado for lunch.

At noon, I found Ian sitting in our back booth
across the table from Shane.

"There she is!" Shane said, getting up and clearly
unaware of the predicament between Ian and me.
Or was there a predicament? Maybe there was nothing. Maybe we were both just busy. I mean, when I
got his text, I was at the office and I called Xavier
to tell him I was meeting Ian for lunch. Xavier was
cool. He told me to say hello and invite him and
Scarlet over for dinner.

"Hey . . ." Ian said, looking at me like I was partially a stranger and partially a family member. He
got up and hugged me like there was an invisible
person between us.

After asking me where I'd been through the summer, Shane hustled to the bar to get the pitcher of
beer Ian had ordered.

"You look good," Ian offered.

"Thank you. You, too." There was really no reason for this exchange. We both looked exactly the
same. It was just something pleasant to say.

"Thank you."

"So—" we started at the same time after an awkward pause.

"I'm sorry," I said. "You go first."

"How's business? I was reading in the newspaper
that you're planning Alarm Clock's wedding?" he
asked. A gossip reporter for the *Atlanta Journal-*

Constitution had gotten ahold of my client list for the next two years and wrote a story about local celebrities getting married.

"Yeah. It was supposed to be last week, but his manager booked a bunch of shows this month, so we moved it to the spring—if we can make it to the spring. I get paid either way, so I'm not tripping."

"Yeah. I read that. It also said something about A. J. Holmes from CNN?"

"Yep. He's jumping the broom next week. The great thing about moving Alarm Clock's wedding was that I got to make A. J. and Dawn my summer couple. They're so cute."

Shane poured two beers from the pitcher and took our orders.

"Sounds like you're having a lot of fun," Ian said to me after Shane was gone again, with a tone that could be taken many ways.

"Yeah, I am." My answer sounded like it was meant to be taken many ways, as well—I hadn't intended that. "What about you?"

"I'm good. Scarlet is finally getting back to normal. For a while there, she was going a little 'black Martha Stewart' on me."

"Well, it takes awhile to decompress after a wedding."

"Yeah . . . decompress. I'm sure that's what it is."

After a little alcohol and food, it didn't take long for Ian and me to go back to who we were. We were all politics and disagreement. The first pitcher of beer was followed by a second and then a long sigh where we just smiled at each other. I realized how much I had missed my friend and wondered what I'd been afraid of.

Then he brought it up: "So how's Xavier?"

"Good," I said like I was on an interview. "He's at my place working. He Skypes his business meetings. Welcome to 2011!"

"Fancy. So—how did you two get together?"

"Wow! I didn't expect you to ask me that."

"Why? I mean, I'm cool with it and stuff. You and I are just friends. I just want you to be happy."

"Really? I thought it would be awkward . . . since . . . you know . . . what happened."

"You thought I'd be mad?" Ian asked.

"No. It's not like you tried to get with me." Right then, just right then, I remembered everything Ian had ever done in my life that could be confused with him trying to get with me: the foot massages, posting up at my place, making me tea, coming to the rescue, holding my hand, kissing me on the lips. Maybe he hadn't tried, but looking at him, I was thinking he sure made it easy for me to get it twisted.

"Sometimes, I regret that I didn't."

"What?"

"Joking!" Ian laughed. "That's the old beer bitch talking! I'm happy for you, Rach! If you think Xavier is the right man for you, go for it. I'm sure Mr. All About Me will make a great husband."

"Husband? And what is that supposed to mean, '*If* I think'?"

"My boy don't have the best track record," Ian pointed out.

"He's different now."

"I'm sure he is. Listen, I'm cool. In fact, why don't you two come by and visit Scarlet and me sometime? It'll be great."

"You think so?"

"Yup."

Ian and I toasted to the promise and agreed that we'd try our best to keep our Wednesday lunch dates alive. The next week, I had to call off lunch, though. Xavier wanted me to join him at a meeting regarding this woman's paintings. Ian texted me two times during the meeting.

On a humid summer night, in a plantation house in the North Georgia Mountains, Mrs. Dawn George became Mrs. Alexander Justin Holmes. At first, they were a little let down that I'd wanted them to move up the date from New Year's, but when I told them how colorful and vibrant and full of life the mountains that cradled the plantation would be in August, they perked up. And it was the best decision possible. Dawn's twins were all over the property, chasing lightning bugs and picking the flowers we used to decorate the bridal suite.

Neither one of them cried when they said their vows. They held hands with the twins in front of one of the lakes on the property and spoke like they were lying in bed together, promising that their love would never end.

There were only sixty guests. No one from entertainment. Only one professional photographer taking black and whites. It was quiet and beautiful.

At the wedding reception, under a tent beside a field of strawberries, R. J., Dawn's son, led the Soul Train line and asked Krista to dance with him—I think he was in love.

Xavier surprised me and showed up right before it was over to drive me home. I'd ridden up with Krista and was planning on coming back that night, but he said he missed me too much to wait for me to return.

After Dawn threw her bouquet, she and A. J. said good night to their guests so they could enjoy their wedding night alone in a cottage at the back of the plantation. Xavier and I ended up being the last two people on the dance floor. My feet were hurting, so I took off my shoes and danced to Anita Baker singing about being caught up in the rapture of love. It was so appropriate, because I was caught up in the rapture of him . . . until he let me go and we did a two-step that led to him stepping on my pinky toe.

"Ouch!" I hollered.

Xavier had to carry me to the car and we argued about his sloppy misstep all the way back into the city. I was calling him Vanilla Ice and joked that I might have to cut him for messing with my pinky toe.

When we got back to my place, he insisted on carrying me into the building like I was a little baby.

"Baby hurt her pinky toe?" he teased with one arm behind my back and the other under my knees. "Daddy has something for that."

"Stop it!" I said, laughing hysterically. "You sound like a total pervert! And you're the one who's responsible. How are you going to be the one to fix it?"

We'd been in the car for an hour, so my toe was fine, of course, but I was playing it up for the attention.

Jeremy met us at the door looking worried about Xavier carrying me. "Will you need a wheelchair, Ms. Winslow?"

"I'm fine, Jeremy."

"Nah, man, call 9-1-1! She hurt her pinky toe!" Xavier interjected playfully. "We might have an amputation on our hands."

"Whatever!" I plucked Xavier in the forehead. "Will you put me down now?"

"With a toe injury like that?" Xavier joked. "I most certainly cannot."

Jeremy had already pulled out his phone, but then he figured out the joke and was laughing, too. He opened the elevator door and Xavier stepped on with me still in his arms and giggling. Jeremy was about to come into the elevator with us, but Xavier stopped him.

"I'll take it from here, man," Xavier said.

"It's no problem, sir. I always escort Ms. Winslow to her floor. It's our—"

"I'm her escort now," Xavier said strongly.

"But I'm supposed to—"

"It's fine, Jeremy," I said. "I'll be fine."

Jeremy nodded and stepped back from the doorway.

When the door finally closed, Xavier let me down and pulled me into his arms. As the elevator started climbing from floor to floor, he kissed my ears and neck. Massaged my lower back.

"I know a special cure for stubbed toes," he whispered in my ear.

"What?"

"I can show you better than I can tell you." He lifted me up and wrapped my legs around his waist, staggering from one side of the elevator to the next, where my back was against the wall. One of his arms was under my legs and he was thrusting his hand into my underwear. The other arm managed his belt strap as he loosened it. "You're all mine," he said breathlessly.

"Oh shit," I cried, feeling Xavier tear away the seat of my underwear. I closed my eyes and bit into his neck.

His kiss and touch were so engulfing I hadn't felt that the elevator had stopped and had no idea how long my neighbor, Mrs. Jackson, who happened to be the oldest woman in the building, had been watching us going at it in the corner, with Xavier's pants falling down to his ankles.

Luckily, my phone started ringing and I opened my eyes to see her standing in the open doorway, holding her trash.

"Shit!" I wiggled out of Xavier's arms and stood up.

Xavier snapped around to see what I was looking at, but he forgot to pull up his pants and Mrs. Jackson got a big eyeful of his whole anatomy.

"Oh!" she said and her voice was more pleasantly surprised than angered.

Xavier apologized and pulled up his pants.

We ran down the hallway to my door, laughing like we were teenagers who'd been caught making out by one of our schoolteachers.

Fully embarrassed, I kept turning around to the elevator. Mrs. Jackson was just standing there in awe, looking like she hoped Xavier's pants would fall again.

The phone was still ringing when Xavier and I were in my place and pulling off clothes in a race to the bed.

I'd forgotten about my stubbed toe and flashes of his hand in my panties in the elevator had me ready to tear off his underwear.

"What's that ringing?" Xavier asked as I pushed him into the bed, ready to show off my skills.

"It's just my phone." I hopped onto his waist and started kissing his chest, moving my hands up and down the muscles in his stomach.

"Ohh," he moaned, but I could feel that he was distracted. The phone was still ringing. "Maybe you should get it. Maybe it's your grandmother."

"She wouldn't call me so late." I flipped my hair forward over my face and ran it down the center of his chest.

"Maybe it's an emergency."

"It's not!"

The phone finally stopped again. I tried to focus Xavier by placing his hands on my hips. I ground seductively on top of him and twisted my feet in between his legs.

"I guess your toe is feeling better," he said playfully.

"Yes, Daddy. All better." I went down to kiss him, but then the ringing started again.

"Maybe you should check it out." Xavier moved his hands to my shoulders to stop me.

I climbed off of him and fumbled around in the bedroom to find my purse and get the phone. I was so frustrated that I didn't even look at the name on the screen.

"Hello?"

"What are you doing?" The voice on the other end of the phone sounded more frustrated than mine.

I looked at Xavier and he held up his hands.

"I'm— What do you want?"

"What do you mean, what do I want? I've texted you three times." It was Ian.

"I was out. I didn't see the texts."

"I wanted to know if you asked X about coming over for dinner tomorrow," he said. "And then I got so scared when you didn't respond . . . I don't know . . . I just rushed over."

"Rushed over?"

"Everything OK?" Xavier asked.

I covered the phone with my hand. "It's fine." I backed out of the room and went to the window in the living room. "Rushed over where?" I looked outside into the lot and there, right beside my car, was Ian's.

"I'm outside," he said.

"Why?"

"I was afraid. I thought something happened to you. I just wanted to make sure you were OK."

"I'm fine."

"Well, you didn't answer my texts. You always answer my texts. What did Xavier say about dinner at my place? I want to see you."

"Ian," I whispered, looking over my back to make sure Xavier hadn't come out of the bedroom and could hear me. "It's almost 1:00 AM. Can't we discuss this in the morning? I'm going to bed."

"What? You have a curfew now?" He laughed.

"No. I'm just busy," I said.

"Well, are you busy or are you going to bed?" He laughed uneasily this time.

"That's none of your business."

There was a long pause.

"Oh, is Xavier there or something?" Ian asked.

"Where else would he be?"

"I didn't know you two were like—you know— like that at 1:00 AM and stuff," Ian said. "Excuse me."

"I didn't say we were any kind of way. I'm just saying it's late. I'll call you tomorrow."

I hung up the phone and looked out the window for a minute. Ian just sat there.

"Rachel? I got the Band-Aids out of the medicine cabinet," Xavier called from inside the bedroom.

"I'm coming," I answered.

Ian was still sitting in his car when I turned from the window to go into the bedroom.

"Who was it?" Xavier asked.

"My grandmother," I said.

"Everything OK?"

"Yeah. She was just checking in on me."

"This late?" Xavier pointed at the clock.

"She's called me a few times today and I didn't answer. I think she was worried."

9

What He's Been Missing

#friendsandlovers . . . Xavier was all over me in the hallway outside Ian's place. Xavier couldn't keep his hands off me. I was wearing brand-new Blahnik's and had been complaining about my toes hurting when we walked into the building. Xavier said he had a cure for my pain. Something to distract me. I was never one for sexual public displays, but there was something about his hand grabbing my whole left ass cheek in one tight grip that made me weak in every area of my body. I felt like I belonged to someone—like I belonged to him. I was giggling. Grinning. Blushing.

"Calm down, baby," I said, giggling into Xavier's ear as he pushed me up against the wall beside Ian's door. I licked his ear and knocked on the door lazily.

"I can't help myself, baby. You got me all tied to you. Can't let you go," Xavier said hungrily.

"Well, you're gonna have to let me go. If you don't stop, there won't be any of me left!"

"I doubt that!" Xavier squeezed both of my ass cheeks with both hands and we laughed before kissing harder and nearly forgetting we were waiting outside Ian's door.

"Um . . . you guys coming in?" I heard before we snapped our necks to see Ian standing in the doorway in a red apron.

"Is this dude wearing a fucking apron?" Xavier said to me with his eyes on Ian.

"I think so."

"Fuck you. It was a wedding gift. We got a matching set and we're trying to make use of it," Ian said, defending his outfit as Xavier and I struggled to keep our laughs in. "I'm secure enough in my manhood to wear an apron. Wait." He paused. "Why am I explaining myself to you two? Get in here. You're letting out all my air-conditioning!"

I broke from Xavier's hold and eased into the apartment after kissing Ian on the cheek.

"And you're complaining about air-conditioning? Yeah, you're married now!" Xavier laughed and gave Ian a hug.

"What's that I smell?" I said. "I'm starving."

"I don't know. Something Scarlet has going on in the kitchen," Ian said.

"But you have an apron on," I pointed out, standing in the foyer with Ian and Xavier.

"I only agreed to put on the apron. My job is to pour the wine."

Ian's apartment was like a small house inside of an apartment building. Two floors, three bedrooms, a formal dining room, and library. A front and back balcony. To the left of the foyer was the

living room, with leather couches and three flat
screens Ian commonly kept on each major news
station. To the right was the dramatic formal dining room Mrs. Dupree had decorated with her
mother's china cabinet and eight-person dinner
table. I'd spent so much time in the apartment
when Ian had first moved in, the neighbors thought
I was going to live there, too, and started calling me
Mrs. Dupree. I laughed it off, but it was kind of
cool helping him get settled in, pick out drapes,
and paint. For the first time, I'd felt what it must
be like to move in with a man—to find a place
naked and make it a home.

"Welcome!" Scarlet called happily from the
kitchen. "Come in! Make yourselves at home."

Ian and Xavier went into the living room, joking
as Xavier continued to give Ian a hard time about
the red apron. I knew it would be off by the time I
saw Ian again. No man could handle that amount
of teasing—not even a newlywed.

Only because people always expect women to
help other women in the kitchen, I decided to go
see Scarlet. There were still gift boxes and moving
boxes lining the walls in the hallway and dining
room. A brand-new set of beautiful, gold-rimmed
china sat in a formal layout on Grandma Dupree's
dining-room table. The knife they'd cut their cake
with was in the china cabinet.

"Hi, Scarlet," I said, reaching out to hug Scarlet
in the kitchen.

She was in her red apron, rushing around like
she was hosting a dinner party for fifty. Flour. Sugar.
Cooking books. Bags from the grocery store. Everything was everywhere.

"You need any help?"

"Rachel!" Scarlet leaned into my hug but kept her oven-mitten-clad hands to her sides. "I'm fine. Almost done. Just some final touches."

A full soul-food spread was forming on the counter.

"Wow, girl! I see you're in here throwing down. I didn't know you could cook."

"I can't. But there's nothing a cookbook can't handle. A man's got to eat. Right?" Scarlet reached into the oven and pulled out a tray of fresh biscuits. I leaned in to catch the scent and noticed that they were shaped into little hearts.

"Cute," I said. "Heart-shaped biscuits."

"I got the cutest cupcake-shape-maker kit with one of my wedding gifts," she said. "I use them on everything: turn sandwich bread into stars, biscuits into hearts, cheese into rainbows."

She smiled and slid the biscuits onto the counter with the rest of the spread—macaroni and cheese, fried chicken, collard greens, and sweet potatoes. Suddenly, I saw all of the "black Martha Stewart" changes in Scarlet that Ian had brought up at lunch. Listening to her move around the kitchen talking about recipes and what she was going to do with all those wedding gifts, I wondered where the woman with the black and purple fascinator was.

"Wow! You're very busy," I said. "I wonder what Ian is going to do when you leave for Congo. Probably lose like fifteen pounds."

"Oh, he'll be fine. I'm not going."

"What?"

"I called it off," Scarlet said passively. "A woman's place is at home with her husband."

"But you were so excited," I pushed. "What are you going to do?"

"Stay at home."

"What?"

"Yeah. Stay at home. Do some modeling. Volunteer at the center downtown."

"Does Ian know about this?" I asked.

"Well, we haven't talked about it just yet, but I know he'll be thrilled," Scarlet gushed. "We're getting pregnant soon, too. I'll have to be at home for that. What? Do you think it will upset him?"

"Oh, no," I said, helping Scarlet begin to carry the food trays into the dining room. "I just thought he assumed you'd stay in school—since that's what you'd talked about before. I'm sure you're right."

Scarlet danced in and out of the kitchen like she'd just brokered the deal of a lifetime. I followed her lead in silence, wondering what exactly was going on in her head.

The night before the visit, for the first time ever, I'd lied to Journey about the reason I wasn't so sure I wanted to do the double dinner date at Ian's house. It wasn't because my love with Xavier was so new like I'd said to her. It was because a part of me was afraid to see Scarlet moving around Ian's house as "Scarlet the wife" who would be here forever and not "Scarlet the girlfriend" whose presence I simply had to tolerate. Mrs. Scarlet Dupree. The lady of the house I'd decorated. The house where I'd once been called Mrs. Dupree.

"Damn, Mrs. Dupree! You have a full spread up in here for your man," Xavier said, standing in the dining room beside Ian, who was filling the formally set glasses with red wine.

"Stop cursing in these people's house," I said.

" 'Damn' is not a curse," Xavier said.

"Yes, it is."

"No, it's not! Tell her, Ian."

"I don't give a damn!" Ian joked and we all laughed.

"Well, I do," I said. "As Grammy Annie-Lou always says—"

"If the baby Jesus wouldn't say it, you shouldn't either," Ian cut in, trading a smile with me.

"Oh, I'm sorry, baby," Xavier said, flinging me into his arms. "I'm sorry to you and the baby Jesus. And Grammy Grams. Can big daddy make it up to you?" He kissed me hard with his eyes closed, but I had mine open and on Ian, who seemed to be struggling with a lump in his throat. Scarlet whistled as she worked around the table, making everything perfect.

"Oh, I'm out of wine," Ian said abruptly. "Rach, can you come with me into the kitchen to get some more?"

"I can get it, baby," Scarlet offered.

"No, I can do it," he said. "Rachel, come with me." He nearly pulled me over, yanking me out of Xavier's hold, and I stumbled to catch up to him.

Once we got into the kitchen, Ian said, "I see you two are snuggly in there." He peered into a cabinet that hardly looked like it was for storing red wine.

"Snuggly? Please. That's how you describe a blanket. We're sizzling!" I laughed and opened the cabinet where I'd started stashing Ian's wine months ago. I handed him a bottle of Malbec.

"Thank you." He sounded annoyed. "Scarlet's been moving things around in here."

"No, that's where the wine has always been."

"Whatever." Ian got the bottle opener from a drawer and wrestled with the cork a bit. "Sizzling, huh?" He pulled the cork out. "Guess you two are having sex then?"

"I hope so!" I laughed because the slight concern I heard in Ian's voice had to be a joke. "We're both grown and I ain't no virgin. Someone better be fucking." I laughed again, but I was alone. "Damn, why are you so stone-faced?"

"I don't know. I'm concerned, I guess. You know how X can be. Hit and quit. That's his style," Ian said. "I just don't want you to get hurt."

"X won't hurt me," I said. "He's different now. Trust me."

"I trust you. And I trust X to be who he is."

"Well, trust me when I say who he is now."

"Hum." Ian shrugged.

"What's wrong?" I said. "You make it seem like you're not happy for me."

"I just didn't think you'd like someone like him."

"Like what?"

"All over you," Ian said. "You know how he was out there—grabbing on you. It's so unnecessary. Didn't think you were into that."

"Every woman likes to be grabbed sometimes, Ian," I said, turning to go back into the dining room.

Ian and Xavier went through every undergrad story over dinner. I playfully complained and pushed for them to stop. Scarlet looked like she was daydreaming the whole time, but kept a Stepford smile splashed on her face.

Xavier's hand was on my knee under the table. Ian's arm was draped over Scarlet's shoulders across from us. The scene was so interestingly adult it felt like we were on the set of the Cosby Show and

Judith Jamison or Sammy Davis, Junior, would walk into the room at any time and get the party started. I pretended the hand on my knee had a wedding band on it that matched the one I pretended I had on my ring finger. All the gifts against the wall were mine and this was how I'd spent every Saturday night for the last year and how I'd spend them for the rest of my life. No more NyQuil or nights alone. I leaned over and kissed Xavier on the cheek as he teased Ian about being dropped from the pledge line for Kappa his sophomore year.

"This fool had the nerve to tell the big brothers that there were too many typos in the pledge book," Xavier said, laughing and pushing a last bit of food around on his plate. "We're lined up against the wall in the middle of the night in some Kappa's room and Ian wants to talk about the proper use of a semicolon."

I laughed. That was classic Ian. I didn't think he really wanted to pledge anyway. He'd just gone along with it because Xavier wanted both of them to be Kappa men. In the end, neither of them made it.

"Well, I'd rather get dropped for complaining about punctuation than getting caught smashing the chapter president's girlfriend," Ian said.

"That was a rumor!" Xavier looked at me for approval.

"A rumor? The shit was on video," Ian replied. "You and Missy Hoover going at it in her dorm room with our big brother's pledge jacket hanging over the bedpost!"

"What?!" I slapped Xavier's arm. "That's gross."

"You really did that?" Scarlet asked.

"I was lost," Xavier said with a mix of humor and solemnity in his voice. "I was confused. A young boy out there in the streets looking for love in the arms of any sweet lady he could find."

"So it's not just because you were a womanizer?" Scarlet asked, and Ian and I laughed. "What? That's what you all say about him."

"Maybe I was," Xavier said. "But now I'm not. Now, I'm home. I found myself one sweet lady!" Xavier kissed me on the cheek and mimicked Ian's position across from us by placing his arm over my shoulders.

"Speaking of going home, when are you going back to Chicago?" Ian asked. "I'm sure you have a lot going on back there. People must miss you."

"I have a lot going on here, too," Xavier said. "In fact, I've been thinking about making this here thing permanent. Send home for my things and stay here for the rest of my life." Xavier locked eyes with me, but I could see Ian staring with his mouth open on the other side of the table.

"So soon? After a month? You're deciding to move here? Why?" Ian asked.

Xavier turned back to him hesitantly. "I just told you why. I've found what I've been missing. No need to go back to searching."

"Ian, stop being so nosy," Scarlet said. "They're in love."

"Love?" Ian laughed.

"Why is that so funny to you?" I asked nonchalantly.

"Well, come on, guys—'love'?"

"Yeah, I still don't get why that would be so funny," I said.

"OK." Ian rested both of his elbows on the table

like a Vegas gambler and looked from Xavier to me. "Then, is it love? Are you two saying this is a love thing?" he pushed.

I felt Xavier stiffen, and then something in me sagged and flew out the window. My world where I was Ian's equal, sporting a set of matching wedding bands under the table, was pulverized by one rushed question. It was just too soon for that kind of interrogation. And Ian knew that.

Quickly, I was furious with my best friend. I wanted him pulverized, too. Alienated. To have his hope laid out on the table and dissected like a bio-lab frog.

Xavier was about to say something, but I cut him off.

I dug my elbows into the table to play, too. I leaned toward Ian and Scarlet and smiled.

"Scar, I totally forgot to ask you," I started, smiling and laughing a little to make my coming attack appear to be friendly fire. "Did Ian ever tell you what happened the day you two got engaged?"

"No?" Scarlet looked over at Ian nervously. "Something happened? What?"

"Oh, nothing bad," I tried to calm her. "Just our Ian being Ian. It's actually rather hilarious. I'm surprised he didn't tell you." I dared not look in Ian's direction.

"What happened, babe?" Scarlet deferred to Ian like a good wife.

"Nothing," Ian said dryly. "It's nothing worth sharing right now."

"Good," Xavier jumped in, "because I'm ready for dessert." He looked at Scarlet. "Ian told me you made strawberry pound cake?!"

"Yes," Scarlet answered with a half smile, showing that she wasn't sure where to set her attention.

"Girl, you may be a new bride, but you cook like it's your diamond anniversary. This food was excellent!" Xavier was trying to shift the focus from Ian and me. He'd been stuck in the middle of one of our random fights before and probably knew the tension well enough.

The only thought I had right then was that I wasn't sure where the tension was coming from nor what I was fighting for, but I wasn't backing down.

Ian and I stayed in an intense stare.

"Guess I'll get dessert," Scarlet said, pushing back from the table to get up. She collected two of the empty dishes and went into the kitchen.

Xavier's hands fell to his sides and he exhaled deeply to exaggerate the condition of his full stomach.

"I can't even breathe, man," Xavier said. "Haven't had home cooking like that in a minute."

"I cooked dinner last night," I pointed out.

"Come on," Xavier said. "Spaghetti and eggplant doesn't exactly compare to what went down here."

I rolled my eyes.

"Don't be like that, Rach." Xavier put his hand back on my knee. "I'm not saying anything was wrong with your food. It was excellent. You know you're my favorite cook ever."

Ian rolled his eyes.

An awkward instrumental that sounded like a little high school orchestra trapped inside a cell phone clanged through the silence at the table. It was a familiar pulsing that pulled my eyes to Xavier's pocket between us.

Xavier tried to talk over it, saying something about getting Knicks floor tickets if he was in New York in the New Year, but the little orchestra in his phone kept playing.

"It's probably just work," he finally said.

"You can get it, man," Ian said. "We're all professionals here. We can stand to hear a little bit of your Chicago-style wheeling and dealing. Right, Rach?"

"Nah. I don't want to interrupt your dinner. I'll send it to voice mail," Xavier said, reaching into his pocket.

"No, I insist," Ian said. "Don't miss a call on my account." He looked at Xavier the way a father looks at his son before sending him off on some great mission that will decide for all around if he's a man or not, and I knew that Ian was working to prove something to me or Xavier or both of us.

Xavier, of course, didn't send the call to voice mail. He looked at the phone and put it to his ear.

"Hello? Yeah, hey, what's up?" He struggled to sound blasé, to lace his greeting without care, but through such detachment in his voice, an actual attachment to whomever was on the other side of the call was apparent from the first syllable.

I moved my knee away from him. Nothing was fair right then.

"I'm great. I've been fine," Xavier said after pausing to let the person speak. He playfully mocked interest to Ian and me to get us to smile.

Ian laughed just enough to let me know that his missile was landing.

"Just having dinner with some friends," Xavier went on with his call.

KABOOM! *Friends.* I heard Ian repeat this a million times even though he hadn't said a word.

I wondered where on the wall of gift boxes he and Scarlet had stashed the cake plate I'd sent them. I wanted it back.

"Cool, then. I'll give you a call back later," Xavier said. He paused a little and then closed with, "Yeah. Great."

By the time Scarlet came back into the dining room juggling four gold-rimmed saucers with pillows of pink cake perfectly placed in the center, her first dinner party had turned into the ground situation in Hiroshima just hours after the A-bomb. I was furious. Xavier was embarrassed. Ian was awaiting an attack. All elbows were on the table.

The little saucers went around. And we ate. We stuffed the sweet little cakes into our mouths and wrestled with the notion of the ongoing war as the strawberries provided an interesting distraction for our taste buds. They were so good at such a bad time.

The only neutral nation at the table, Swiss Scarlet, kept the conversation going by sharing every little step she'd put into making the cake. The organic strawberries. Expensive flour. Cane sugar. She'd followed the recipe exactly. And "anyone could be a cook if they just followed instructions."

"Good thing you like to cook," I said, seeing the perfect new weapon to draw. "Since you won't be going back to school, you can be our Ian's own little chef!"

"What?" Ian looked at me like I'd said the most ridiculous thing. "Scarlet's going back to school. She's starting her graduate program in the fall." He turned to her.

"I was telling Rachel in the kitchen that I was thinking about not going back to school right now . . . that maybe since we'd just gotten married I could stay home and focus on the house. You know?"

"No, Scarlet, I don't," Ian said. "And why would you share something like that with Rachel before you—"

"Oh no!" I cut Ian off. "You know what, I'm sorry. Scarlet did say it was a secret. I was confused. I couldn't remember if that was the secret or the baby! Wait, whoops!" I laughed like a confused little old lady and dabbed the corners of my mouth with my napkin. TAKE THAT! JAB! KABOOM!

"Whoa!" Xavier dropped his fork.

"Baby?" Ian turned his whole body to Scarlet.

"No—I'm not pregnant," Scarlet said. "I was just telling Rachel that I—well, we—so, I—and a baby— we said we'd have one someday!" She was so tongue-tied her face was turning red.

I actually felt bad that she'd come into contact with combat, but her ally was too close to the fire for her to miss all the shots.

"I was just talking," she said.

"Just talking? You don't just talk to people about things like that," Ian said. "You come to me first. I'm your husband. You make decisions with me— not Rachel."

Scarlet's eyes went wet with humiliation and then everyone at the table felt sudden shame.

"You ready to go?" Xavier announced.

"Yes," I answered.

Xavier started to get up and I tried to move with him, but he stopped me.

"I'll go get the car. You can wait up here," he instructed.

"I'm fine," I said.

"Rach, you were complaining about your shoes walking to the door earlier. I'll get the car and pick you up right downstairs."

"But I can walk."

"Listen to your man!" Xavier said. He looked at Ian. "See what us brothers have to deal with?"

Xavier said good-bye to Ian and Scarlet and left to get the car.

Ian started helping Scarlet carrying plates and such into the kitchen and, needing air or just a way out of the debacle, I got my purse and went out to stand on the front balcony so I could see Xavier when he pulled up.

Ian only lived on the second floor, but the view of twinkling lights that dotted the midtown skyline made it seem like I was up in the sky with the stars. On so many nights, Ian and I had sat out there and talked about our dreams. Where we were going and what we wanted. So many nights, I'd told him about the love I was looking for. How I felt like I couldn't live, that I wouldn't live until I'd found it.

It was getting cool. But I let the breeze blow pocks all over my shoulders.

The glass door slid open and I knew it was Ian stepping outside. I could feel his energy. As tight as mine. For what? He was quiet.

"You don't want me to be happy," I said, still looking at the lights. "I don't know why. You know how much this means to me."

"It just isn't right, Rach," Ian said. "It's not for you. It's just a feeling I have. This isn't right for you."

"Yeah, well, feelings are like assholes," I said. "Everyone has one." I stepped closer to the ledge. "And what was that shit in there? You invited me here to try to ruin things with X? You know we're just getting started."

"Starting what?"

"Starting us. Starting something. Starting what you have," I said.

"Well, don't rush. It's not all it's cracked up to be."

I looked at Ian and we were talking in silence. He meant to tell me something about Scarlet that he couldn't share because we were still on two sides of a battlefield. Maybe it was about the secrets in the kitchen. Maybe it was about the geometrically shaped food.

Whispers from beneath the balcony injected noise into the exchange.

"I'm sorry. I just got away so I could call you back," we heard. "I'll be home real soon to check on you."

We knew the voice. It was just low enough to be a secret, but still familiar enough that we didn't need to rush to the balcony's edge to see who it was. The door that led to the parking lot where I'd parked was on the first floor right beneath Ian's balcony.

"I'm just in Atlanta visiting my boy from college. My old roommate. Yeah, the one who got married," the whispering beneath us continued. I closed my eyes and pretended I couldn't hear this. I didn't want to hear this. Because hearing meant knowing and I couldn't unknow this once I'd heard it. The talking stopped and I looked at Ian before we both looked out over the parking lot to see Xavier walking toward my car with his phone in his hand.

I balled up my fists and wanted to swing at the wind. To throw my shoes into the night and hit everyone in the head. Every man I'd ever loved. Or pretended to love. Or just thought I'd loved. But my shoes were $800 and I'd only worn them once so I kept them on. I pushed Ian out of my way and went through the doors in a hurry to get my purse and get out of there.

"Wait, Rach!" Ian tried to grab my arm.

"Night, Scarlet. Thanks for everything," I said sharply to Scarlet, who was still picking up in the dining room. I grabbed my purse from the couch and raced out the door with Ian behind me.

"Rach, wait!" He grabbed my arm just before I made it onto the first landing in the stairwell.

"What? You happy now?" I asked.

"No, I'm not happy at all."

"What? Wasn't that the point of everything you did in there?"

"I don't know what's going on with me, but seeing you here tonight—with him—I can't just let you be with him." Ian was rubbing his forehead like his head was about to explode. "I can't be happy without you. But I can't be with you."

"What are you talking about?"

"Sometimes I don't think I made the right decision, Rachel," Ian said quietly.

"About what?"

"That night at the pier in New Orleans. What you said to me," Ian said. "Sometimes I don't think I made the right decision—marrying Scarlet. Maybe my mother was right. Maybe I was supposed to be with—"

"Don't! Don't you dare do that!" I cut Ian off. It was just too much. I felt like everyone was playing with my mind. With my heart. "Don't put that on me! You save that shit and you wrap it up and you throw it someplace far away because you don't ever need to bring it up again. You married Scarlet and that's it."

"But I—"

"And you know what? I'm not even surprised that you're so petty about this. Claiming you want to be with me now that you see me with someone else? That's so classic, Ian! All about you. Can't get from inside that head of yours for five minutes to see that it's my time. You have to take the spotlight. Self-absorbed bastard." I shook away from him. "Enjoy your cake."

I didn't say anything in the car ride home. I was too afraid I'd explode and every tear I hadn't ever cried would come rushing out of me and wash Xavier clear out of Georgia and straight into the Atlantic Ocean. There was no need to tell him what I'd heard from the balcony. We both knew what the call was at the table. But the way things are, the way we all have to behave so pleasantly without accusing one another of anything that might make the other person accuse you of being suspicious or jealous, trying to ratchet up some fake anger to send a red herring up into the sky— I just couldn't do it. Not anymore. If I opened my mouth, it would be with the truth. And we both knew the truth, so what was the sense in saying anything? Saying something would mean I wanted an explanation. Maybe an apology. I was sick of explanations. I was sick of apologies. I was so very sick of believing I'd ever meet anyone who didn't offer me a combination of the two the moment I opened up my whole heart. I just wanted to go to bed.

I threw one pillow at Xavier and slammed my bedroom door.

He knocked before I could get to the bed.

"I'm going to bed," I said.

"Just let me explain."

I went and sat on the edge of the bed. I hadn't turned on the light, so the room was still dark.

He tried again: "I just want to say I'm sorry."

"You think I'm gullible."

"Rach, I'm—"

"You think my life is so empty that I'll just be your fool. Come along for a ride. Short. Fast. Give you what you want. All while I think I'm getting what I want. When, you know, we both know you'll be gone before that ever happens."

"She's my ex-girlfriend. We—"

"I don't want to know! I don't give a fuck who she is. Who you were."

"I have to, Rachel. I have to tell, because—"

"Because what?" I stopped him. "Because you don't want me to hate you? You don't want me to think of you like every other woman does? To know who you are? To sleep with you again? Is that why?"

"No. I have to tell you the truth, because I don't want to lie to you anymore." His voice was cracking. He stopped and I heard a plop against the door that sounded like him leaning up against it. "Because I can't lose you."

"Maybe you never had me to lose."

We were quiet for a minute and then I saw a little black rectangle slide through the small space beneath the door.

"Look at the floor near the door," Xavier said. "It's my cellphone. My code is 1905. Her name is Anabell."

"What do I need that for? You think this is high school? You think I'm about to call some woman about you? Please!"

"If you look at my text messages, you'll see that we stopped seeing each other a month before Ian's wedding. She had a real bad time with it. Went to therapy. I even went with her. Thought it would help, but it only got worse. Then I didn't know how to say good-bye. Now I'm just afraid I'll hurt her too much if I tell her the truth."

"What truth?"

"That I'm in love with someone else."

"Well, that love should've made you tell me what was up a long time before your cell phone went off at the wrong time."

"Rachel, you have to believe me," Xavier said. "I thought I'd be able to get back to Chicago, sit her down somewhere, and tell her the truth. I just couldn't do it over the phone. And I didn't want to bring you any drama if I didn't have to. I didn't want our start to be dirty with one of my endings. I wanted us to just be happy."

"Too late," I said, getting up from my corner on the bed.

"I'm really trying to change. Please don't hold this against me."

I got into the bed. I could smell him everywhere.

I looked at the cell phone on the floor.

"Just read the texts," Xavier said. "Call her if you want. I don't care anymore."

Donnica was standing on Peachtree in front of the office when I pulled up. She was wearing teal suede platform stilettos, an orange miniskirt, and a matching fur jacket. A tumbleweed puff of a dog was trapped in her embrace. Cars in swiftly moving traffic tried to cross lanes to get to her curb to stare.

"I'm sorry I came by your office without no invitation—I know that's ghetto, but I had to!" She was sitting across from me in my office, crying and staining the dog's tan coat with indigo teardrops from her fake eyelashes.

"You're fine, darling," I said. "I can see you're upset."

"I ain't know what to do. Who else to talk to about this." She clenched the little dog tighter and he jumped, but she caught him before he could escape. "I'm just so motherfucking pissed off." Her sadness was punctuated by angry inflections in her voice each time she said a polysyllabic word. The dog jumped again.

"Hey, I'll hold the dog," I said, standing to reach for the dog. "You talk!" I said louder so Krista could hear me outside, "Krista, get Ms. Grant some water!" I looked back at Donnica.

She was blowing her nose on a Hermès pocket square.

"Talk," I said.

"I ain't about to marry Zacariah no more!" she said. "It's over!" She tugged the huge diamond ring off her finger and threw it at the door just in time to nearly hit Krista in the head. Luckily, it hit the wall and bounced to the floor. I looked at it and wondered why Donnica would wait until she was in my office to dispose of a two-million-dollar ring. Drama.

"OK . . ." Krista picked up the ring awkwardly and slid both the ring and the water onto the desk in front of Donnica. She tiptoed back out and shut the door halfway while looking at Donnica crossly the whole time.

"Why are you calling the wedding off?" I asked. "You two seemed quite happy last time I saw you."

"I know!" She started crying harder and one of her lashes came loose from the corner of her eye. "But it won't work! It doesn't matter how happy I am with Zacariah. He ain't fit for marriage. Come on! You know it. He been married twice. He cheated on his baby mama. He gonna cheat on me. And I ain't having that! No! I ain't having that!" She jumped out of the chair like Alarm Clock had just walked into the room.

"But you knew all that when you started dating him," I said, remembering that Donnica was the woman he'd cheated with.

Donnica kept talking like I hadn't said a word. The dog looked up at me and moaned.

"He ain't never been faithful to nobody," she said. "Why he gonna be faithful to me? It's just like my grandmamma said. 'Some men just ain't made to be married. They cold as ice. Brick.'" She walked to the window and pulled out a pack of cigarettes.

"No smoking in the office, please," I said.

She looked out the window like I hadn't said anything and threw the pack to the door just like she had the ring. She had some arm. The object did hit Krista this time. She appeared in the doorway in time for a tap on her forehead.

"OK . . ." she said, bending over to pick up the cigarettes. She rolled her eyes at me as Donnica sobbed into the glass. "Ian on line one," she said.

I waved my hand for her to take a message and looked back at Donnica. She was wiping her nose again and looking miserable. I never really considered that Donnica really loved Alarm Clock.

Through the corner of my eye, I could see Krista still staring at me. "He wants to know about lunch. Where do you want me to tell him to meet you?"

I kept my eyes on Donnica.

"Rachel!" Krista called. "Where do you want me to tell Ian to meet you?"

"Nowhere," I said soberly. "I need to call off lunch today. Tell him I'm meeting with a client."

"Really? You're canceling lunch?"

I kept stroking the little dog, watching Donnica cry.

"Maybe you should tell him," Krista added. "He sounds upset—"

"Just tell him what I said."

Krista turned on her heels to reluctantly excuse herself.

"He probably isn't the best fit for a husband," I said. "He has his old ways. He's not perfect. Not what you imagined he would be. But he's what you've been missing. What you've been waiting for."

Donnica turned to me with her face streaked into a Halloween costume. "He is! You're right!" she said.

"And, and, you can't let his past stop that love.

Not if you really want to be with him, and you know he loves you," I said and Donnica nodded. "And who knows, who really knows? Love changes people. Love changes things. You can't give up on love. Love hasn't given up on you!"

"You right!" Donnica was wiping her black tears, smearing the makeup into a new mask.

I didn't realize it, but I'd stood up while I was speaking. And I was holding the dog up to my chest.

"If there's anything I know about love, it's that it's worth taking a risk for. Even if you fail, you have to say you tried. If X says he wants to try, you have to give it a try!"

"Yes! Try!" Donnica shouted. "Wait." She gathered herself. "Who's X?"

"What?" I snapped out of my thoughts.

"X? You said X," she pointed out.

"Oh, that was nothing. Just pretend I said Alarm Clock—Zachariah—whatever."

Donnica sat back down and cleaned her markings with the Hermès cloth before I returned the dog. She picked up the ring and put it back on her finger.

"I don't know what I was thinking," she said. "I'm so glad I came—"

I saw shoes in the doorway. Before I could turn they'd rushed to stand behind Donnica.

"Ian?" I said. I turned to the doorway again and there was Krista with her hands up.

"I told him," Krista said. "I tried to stop him!" She backed away from the door.

"You're canceling lunch with me?" Ian charged.

"Yes, I told Krista to tell you over the phone."

"She did."

"So then why'd you come here?"

Donnica's eyes were bouncing between us. It was the quietest I'd ever seen her.

"You know why I came here. We need to talk."

"Well, we can't," I said. "I have a client!" I pointed at Donnica.

"I was just leaving," Donnica said. "I already texted Zach to tell him his Powerpuff girl is—"

"Your client is leaving!" Ian said.

"No, she's not!"

"Yes, I am!" Donnica got up and straightened her little orange skirt like she hadn't just had a breakdown. "I got to get home to Zach! We got us some making up to do." Donnica wiggled to the door. "Ms. Winslow, I'll see you next week." She looked at Ian sharply. "Don't be messing with my wedding planner." She readjusted the dog on her hip and walked out.

"There's nothing for us to talk about," I said, slamming my laptop closed and getting up from the desk.

"Yes, there is." Ian closed the door. "We need to talk about last night. About what you heard. About what we heard."

"I'm fine. I don't need to talk," I said. I picked up a file from my desk and tried to busy myself by arranging the papers. I couldn't look at Ian. I was embarrassed by what had happened at his house with Xavier. And totally confused by Ian's behavior before I left. "Look, everything is fine with X. We're going to work it out."

"Work it out? No, Rach—"

"No, what?"

"He's not good enough for you. He never was."

"Not good enough? You said you were happy

about us hooking up. That you could 'get behind that.' Remember that? Now you're flaking on your boy? On me?"

"He hasn't changed. You know that. He's still the same player from college."

"You don't know him," I charged.

"I know him well enough," Ian pointed out. "I know what I heard last night. And I know you."

"She's his ex-girlfriend."

"Well, if you're his new girlfriend, he doesn't need to talk to his ex-girlfriend."

"It's a long story," I said. "Stop it, Ian. Xavier explained everything. I have to believe him."

"He's playing you, Rachel. I can't believe you can't see it. It's all a show." Ian walked over to me and took the file from my hand. "Ever since we were in New Orleans for the wedding—when X saw you leave that witch doctor's house—he's been putting on this routine. Trying to pretend he's something he's not."

"Saw me? X saw me at Tante Heru's?" My mind went back to that night in the Quarter. Kete's breasts in my face. Tante Heru. The knocking at the window. "I was alone. He never said anything about seeing me."

"He came to my room and he told me he saw you down in the quarter at a roots woman's house."

"Why wouldn't he tell me?" I asked.

"I don't know. What happened there?"

I remembered everything I said to Tante Heru—my prayer said aloud to the spirits in the corners. In my mind, I looked around the room. Remembered it all. Was he there? In the window? Did he hear me? I was the fool. I was the Big Easy fool. If Xavier heard what I said at Tante Heru's, then he—the art, the music, the hugs, how he held me? Lies? I couldn't think of it.

"I have a client coming in soon," I said, wiping tears with my sleeve.

"No, you don't."

I looked at Ian. "Fine. Well, I just need you to leave."

Ian came in right up on me. I could smell his cologne. See the little hairs growing above his lip.

"You don't know what you need," he said.

"You don't either," I said.

Ian grabbed my shirt. There was this aggressive intensity and passionate determination in his eyes. "You told me you loved me," he said.

"Yeah, I did. That was then—in New Orleans."

"You told me you loved me before. Say it again," he demanded.

"No."

"Say it again."

"No. No, I won't."

"Well, I love you."

"Don't do that. Don't say that!"

"I love you. I love you, Rachel. I love you." Each time he said it, he grabbed me tighter. "I love you. I want to be with you."

"What?" I started struggling to get away from him. "This is fucking crazy. Get the fuck off of me."

Ian would not let me go.

He grabbed my arms and held me right in front of him.

"I love you," he said. "I love you. I love you."

I looked away.

"Look into my eyes." He shook me. "Look at me. I love you. And you love me, too."

I couldn't say anything.

"You love me, too."

"Ian, I'm—" I tried.

"You love me, too!" he shouted. He wrapped me in a passionate embrace. And then lowered his arms to my waist. "You love me, too. I love you." He started kissing me.

I wrapped my arms around his neck. I closed my eyes.

He lowered his arms again and wrapped them under my butt. He picked me up and sat me on the desk. Parted my legs and pushed his body between them.

It was hard for me to sit upright and not fall back onto the desk. He was moving so quickly.

"I love you, Rachel," he said into my ear. "I want this. I want you."

It was hard for me to breathe. To know what was happening. To realize what was happening. I wanted everything. But what? I always knew what I wanted. I always knew. But what now?

Ian started moving his hands up underneath my skirt from the hem.

Was this what I wanted? I let myself melt. Eased my legs in a little so he could get a good hold of my thigh.

"I love you," he said again, but this time I swear it sounded like Xavier in my ear.

Something shot up my back and around my neck like a whip.

My office door slammed open. I turned, thinking I'd been caught by Krista, but she wasn't there. It was Scarlet rushing in fast with Xavier behind her.

"See! See! See!" She pointed at Ian pushing away from me. "I told you something was up. I knew something was going on between these two. Ian, what the fuck?"

"Scarlet, I can explain," Ian said. He held his hands up like Scarlet had a gun.

Xavier pushed Scarlet to the side and was on his way to Ian. I jumped in between them.

"Stop it! Just stop," I said, but Xavier didn't look at me. He pushed me to the side and, without saying a word, cracked Ian right in the face. I hadn't ever been that close to someone who'd been hit that hard. Blood shot out of Ian's mouth before he hit the floor.

Xavier stood over him with his hands balled. "Get up, bitchass nigga. Get the fuck up, so I can whip your ass! Fucking fake-ass nigga. Get the fuck up!"

Ian was disoriented, but looking around.

Xavier was about to punch him again, but I grabbed his arms.

"No," I said. "Not here."

Scarlet was crying and shaking so badly. She pulled her ring off and threw it at Ian.

"Scarlet!" Ian cried, struggling to get up.

Xavier tried to get at him again, but I held his arms.

"I can't believe you did this to me," Scarlet cried. She ran out of the office.

Ian stumbled to his feet and looked at me. "I have to go," he said. He ran out of the office behind Scarlet, leaving the ring and a red stain on the floor.

"Look what you did," I said to Xavier.

"I'm sorry. I couldn't handle seeing him—"

"You're sorry? You're sorry? Did you just have the nerve to say you're sorry? Sorry about what?

About lying to me? About coming into my fucking office and turning it into a street corner? About spying on me in New Orleans?" I said. "Fuck you, Xavier. You can't say shit to me. You don't have shit to say to me. You hear me?"

"I wasn't spying on you," Xavier said.

"Then what were you doing? Hum? Tell me. Tell me what you were doing following me. You want to say something? Tell me what you have to say about that. About following me and claiming that you're someone that you're not. About lying to me all this time just because you knew what I was looking for. Just because you knew I wanted to be in love."

"That's not it."

"What is it? Are you about to tell me that Ian was lying?"

"No. I was there. I did hear what the woman said and . . . I wanted the same thing you wanted: real love."

"You call this shit real love?" I pointed to the blood on my floor. "Lying to me? Lying about who you are, what you like, what you want just so you can be what I'm looking for?"

"I didn't lie about any of those things. I am who I am. Maybe I'm just what you've been looking for."

"Yeah, maybe you're not," I corrected him with every ounce of bite I had in my words.

"Rachel, don't be like this." Xavier tried to grab me the way Ian had, but I wouldn't let him. "I—"

"Get the fuck out!"

"Rach—"

"Get the fuck out of my office before I call the police on your crazy ass," I said. "Get the fuck out."

"But—"

"I want you to go away. I want you to go far away."

The lights in my office shook a little and there was a sound like a boom of thunder outside, but it wasn't raining.

"Go," I said.

"This is what you want?"

"I want you to leave and never ever come back."

10

Birds of a Feather

#Winning? I knew it was Ian when I heard the dull ding the elevator made outside when it stopped on my floor. Jeremy called me, whispering from the lobby when Ian walked into the building. I guessed he was confused and thinking Xavier was still at my place.

I sat on the couch and let him use his key to come in.

He didn't say anything. Opened the door. Closed it behind him and then I heard the lock snap back into place.

He'd sent me a text a few hours after the incident in the office with Scarlet and Xavier. Scarlet had kicked him out. He wanted to talk.

He walked into the living room with a stuffed weekend duffel bag on one shoulder and his laptop bag on the other. A bag of what smelled like Chinese food was in his hand.

"Hey," he said so casually.

I returned the greeting and smiled.

I moved over on the couch to make some space for him.

"I brought some food." He held out the greasy brown paper bag.

"Already ate," I said. (I was lying, but my stomach already felt like I was about to throw up and it was empty.)

"Well, have you had a drink?" He nodded at my little bar in the back of the room. He put his bags down by the wall, right where Xavier's suitcase had been. And walked toward the bar. "Want some wine?"

"JD," I said. "No ice."

Ian clattered around at the bar longer than he needed. "I can't be here and not talk to you," he said still at the bar.

"What?"

"I came here because I want to talk."

"You haven't been here five minutes. Talk."

"You know what I mean. I don't want to not talk directly about what's going on because of what I told you in your office. I don't want to feel like you're judging everything I say. I just want to talk to you. To Rachel. The way I always do."

"You didn't mean what you said?" I asked.

"See, that's what I'm talking about. I can't speak openly with you if I have to be careful and be fake. I'm not used to that with you." Ian walked over to me and handed me what had to have been every last bit of the JD. He sat down next to me. He had a full glass of Scotch and no ice.

We gulped the drinks down like we were in a race.

"So you meant what you said in the office?"

Ian turned to me. "Every word."

"Then why did you marry Scarlet? Why did you leave me at the pier like that? If you knew you felt what I felt? Why did you try to make me feel crazy?"

"I love Scarlet. And I said I would marry her, so I did," Ian said. "I don't come from people who do otherwise. That's not me. But I don't love Scarlet the way I love you. I don't know how to be without you."

"Are you sure this isn't just about Xavier and me? That seeing us together did something to you."

"It did open my eyes. But that's not it. I know what this is—what I'm feeling."

"So what's the next step?" I asked this more as a dare than a desire. I didn't know what I wanted to do, but I needed to hear whether Ian had a plan. Maybe that would make me understand.

"Well," he started, looking at his duffel bag, "I can either sleep here or at the Marriott downtown where I made a reservation."

"Where do you want to stay?"

Ian turned back to me and pushed one of my curls behind my ear. "Right here," he said. "I don't want to go anywhere."

Ian and I sat up all night talking. He poured himself another Scotch and I sipped from the other side of his glass. Like we always did when we got drunk on my couch, we relived every moment we'd spent together since college. Only this time, Ian admitted to each time when he either wanted to reach for me or thought he was falling in love with me. And there were so many times. So many more times than I could've imagined. I always thought Ian was an amazing man. And finally I could admit that when we held hands on the beach during spring break or fell asleep on his couch when I helped him paint the walls in his first apartment, I pretended that we belonged to each other. I'd had no clue that he had been thinking the same thing. But the male mind doesn't work like the female mind. Ian said that knowing how much he loved me didn't make it easier to try to sleep with me or ask me out on a date. It made it harder. He didn't want a thing with me to be like a thing with everyone else. And if it didn't work out, he didn't want to go on the list of guys who'd done me wrong. And then never hear from me again.

We laughed about how many people had been right about us all along. Made a pan of brownies and fell asleep on the living room floor.

At some point in the night, though, my neck started hurting and then my back and then my knees and then I had to get up. I just couldn't find a comfortable position beside him.

I sat up and watched Ian sleep. His stomach rose and set with each breath. He'd already taken off his wedding band. A blond streak the width of a sandwich bag tie was the only sign of his past. I didn't believe what was happening. Couldn't have predicted it just twenty-four hours ago.

I took one of my chenille throws off the back of the couch and put it over Ian.

I went into the bedroom and got into bed.

I said my prayers for the first time in a really long time. I prayed for Grammy Annie-Lou. For me. For Scarlet. I knew that while I was in this dream place, getting something I really wanted, she was somewhere crying with a broken heart. It didn't matter what I thought about her. I knew the pain she was probably feeling. I didn't like the idea of anyone going through that.

I went to sleep and dreamed of King and me on one of our adventures. Only he was a puppy and I was a little older than I am now. We sat on a rock on the side of Winslow River that was farthest from the house where Grammy Annie-Lou, hanging sheets up on the clothesline, looked miles away. I fed King cornbread from my pocket. I pitched two rocks at one time into the river and watched the ripples cross one another.

I was awakened by Ian getting into bed with me.

He snuggled in close to my back and buried his lips into my neck. He kissed me gently.

"Is this real?" I asked.

"I hope so."

Ian was still there in the morning. I got up and looked at him like if I blinked he might be gone.

He stretched and said he was hungry. He asked if I needed to get to the office early because he wanted to take me out for brunch.

"Sure," I said and then we scrambled around the house, listening to music and getting dressed like it was something we'd always done together at my place.

We brushed our teeth. Smiled in the mirror at each other. He kissed me and said he'd meet me downstairs at the door. He was pulling the car around.

"I see everything is good this morning, Ms. Winslow?" Jeremy asked, pulling the elevator door open for me.

"Actually, it is."

* * *

I've never been married before, and I couldn't imagine being married to someone for thirty years, but I'm sure that being in love with your best friend must be what it feels like to be married that long. Having Ian at my place was like an extended sleepover with no parents and no rules. We'd stay up all night watching old movies and eating junk food. I never had to ask him for anything. He knew what I was thinking. I knew what he was thinking. When I was hungry, he'd call for pizza. When I got home, I'd have his bottle of Scotch. Every day, his pile of stuff in the corner grew larger. I didn't know if he'd been seeing Scarlet. I didn't ask about her. I didn't think he wanted me to and I didn't want to know. Every time I thought about her, I had to think of them together. I wanted to leave that in the past and move forward. Like Ian said so many times, he was where he wanted to be.

Two weeks or so after Ian moved in, I came home from work and wasn't expecting him to be back from the school. I opened the door to a loft filled with lit candles and smelling like Thai food.

"Ian?" I called. "What's this?" I put down my bag beside the door and was about to walk into the living room.

"Rach? That you? No! Don't come in yet!" Ian shouted.

"What?"

"Don't come in yet! It's a surprise. I'm not ready yet."

"Do you want me to go back outside?" I asked, laughing.

"No, just wait!" He sounded like he was rushing through the loft. "One more second."

There was a loud pop that sounded like he'd turned on the stereo with the sound all the way up.

"Whoops! OK. OK! You can come in now!" Ian called. "Rachel?"

"Yes?" I walked into the living room just as the first chords of my song, that India. Arie song "Ready for Love," began to play.

Ian was wearing an old FAMU T-shirt and blue jeans. Pictures of us in various stages of metamorphosis were set up all over the couch and taped to the window panes all the way to the ceiling.

"What's all this?" I asked, already tearing up.

"It's for you," Ian said, coming over to me and pulling me into the room. "I know it's not all that big—I'm not exactly raking in the dough right now—but I wanted to do something nice for you. An early birthday present."

"You didn't have to do this," I said. My birthday wasn't for two more weeks. I walked to the couch and picked up a picture of Ian and me waving orange and green pompons from the bleachers at our first homecoming game together.

"Actually, I did need to do this," Ian said. "You deserve this. You deserve all of it and more. I'm just happy to be with you. I'm happy you let me be with you."

Ian hugged me and pulled his face back to look me in the eyes. And the reality of something I'd been thinking about every day washed over me like a wave. Ian and I hadn't kissed since that day at the office. We'd pecked almost like cousins. He'd kissed my neck. I'd kissed his cheek. But that was in passing. While we were coming and going. We slept in the same bed every night, yes, but it was six hours of spooning and planning. Or saying how excited we were to be together, but then, drunk on Scotch and JD, we'd fall asleep and wake up in the morning like there was nothing odd about it. I'd told Journey and even Krista about it. They were in shock. They said something was wrong, but I defended it carefully and earnestly. I said we were waiting. There was nothing wrong with that. Sometimes these things just took . . . time. Krista had rolled her eyes unconvinced. "You put a man in my bed and someone's having sex. It can happen when he's asleep, but it's happening," she'd said. "Our relationship is about more than sex," I'd said. "We're working some things out right now. He's just left his wife. I don't want to sleep with a married man." Journey was on the same note as Krista one night online. She'd said, "Did you ask him if he minds that you're not sleeping together? And what's happening with the wife? Are they getting a divorce? Are they separated? Did you ask him about that?" I hadn't.

Ian wrapped his hand around the small of my neck and closed his eyes, coming in for a kiss.

I closed my eyes, too, but my neck wouldn't give way. It just wouldn't. It was rigid with fear. When I was seventeen, I played Effie White in a high school production of *Dreamgirls*. There was a scene where I was supposed to kiss Lucas Hamilton, the school nerd and top thespian who was playing Curtis Taylor, right on stage in front of the whole school. I couldn't do it. Grammy Annie-Lou said I stood there petrified, like one of those fainting goats that fall out stiff when they're afraid. That's kind of how I felt waiting for Ian's kiss.

He tried two more times, but I just got more awkward and more stiff.

I peeked at him and saw that he was peeking at me, too, and wincing just a little.

"Oh . . . I can't," he said, letting me go suddenly.

"What? You can't?" I asked like I hadn't been thinking and subconsciously acting out the same thing.

"I'm sorry, Rach. I really want to, but I—I can't right now.

"What do you mean you can't? Why?"

"It's Xavier. Being here, it's all I can think about. That he was here. That he was in this room with you. Kissing you just like I'm trying to do right now. Every night when I get into that bed in there with you, I think that he's been there. It's like he's still here."

I hadn't told Ian, but Xavier had e-mailed me twice asking if we could speak. I didn't respond because I didn't know what to say. If there was anything to say. But I'd felt X's energy in the loft, too. His toothbrush was gone, but I still had the organic toothpaste he'd purchased. And every place I'd been to in the city, even though I'd been there forever without him, it seemed like none of it mattered until I'd gone there with him.

"What about Scarlet?" I asked. "You don't think I think about her? About you two? She's the one you married. The one who has your last name. I'm just second. Not even second. I'm like a mistress or your whore."

"Don't do that," he said.

"What's up with her? We know where Xavier is. Where's Scarlet? Is she still at your place? My God, you haven't told me anything."

"She's fine."

"So you talk to her?"

"We had lunch a few times."

"What the fuck?" I pulled away from Ian. The song went off and then started playing again on repeat. "Why didn't you tell me?"

"Because it's nothing. I'm still here. Right? I'm where I want to—"

"Yeah, I heard that before. What's going on with you two?"

"What do you mean?"

"You know what I mean. Just level with me. Before you asked me to just talk to you like your friend; now I need you to do that for me."

"Nothing's happening."

"Are you getting a divorce? Getting separated? What?" I screamed.

"It's too soon to say."

"What?" I felt a chill. "It's been two weeks, Ian."

"Two weeks isn't a long time," he said.

"Yes, it is if you're living with a woman." I went and turned off the stereo with the remote. I started blowing out the candles.

"What? Wait! Stop!"

"You said you knew. You said you were sure."

"I am."

"Then why won't you get a divorce?" I didn't even know where this was coming from. I was building into a rage. My tears went from joy to anger.

"It's just two weeks. It's going to take time."

"You don't even want to touch me. We don't kiss. We don't have sex," I listed.

"You didn't seem too excited to kiss me just now either."

"I'm nervous!" I screamed.

"About what?"

"Whether you're staying." (Who the hell was speaking? Where was this coming from? Was I becoming one of those women? A mistress?)

"What?" Ian stopped me from blowing out another candle. "Wait, Rachel. Just wait a minute. I didn't mean for us to fight. I just wanted to have a good night together. For us to talk and maybe kiss. I wanted to celebrate us. To thank you. How did we get to this?"

"There's just so much going on right now. I don't know."

"Look at me."

I looked into his eyes. They looked the same as always.

"I'm Ian. I'm not here to hurt you." He grabbed my hand. "You know what—I think we need to relax. To just take a load off and breathe." He pulled me to the bar and went searching through the empty bottles.

"What are you looking for?"

He pulled the Patrón from the back of the shelf. "Shots!" he said.

"This is no time for shots."

"Just because you said that, it's the perfect time for shots." He set the bottle on the bar and got two double shot glasses.

"I have to work in the morning," I said.

"You own your own business. Call in sick." Ian

poured the shots and handed me one. "This shot is to *what's up.*"

"No lemons? No salt?" I asked.

"Fuck lemons and salt. Throw it back!" He banged on the bar and we took the shots. He started pouring again. "This shot is to *what next!*"

We took the shots. He poured again.

"You pick the shot this time."

I was already feeling the tequila. I said, "This shot is to *what the fuck!*"

We took the shots. He poured again.

The liquor rushed right to my forehead. I felt like I was balancing a heavy weave on my head. I was swaying a little.

"No, don't punk out on me now. Hands up!" He pointed for me to pick up the little glass. "This shot is to *whatever you want.* Throw it back!"

We finished the bottle with whats and ended up on the floor again, laughing.

I was telling Ian a story about Alarm Clock and Donnica's wedding. About the chocolate fountain and all the weedheads dipping everything from asparagus to shrimp in the chocolate.

He laughed and rolled over onto his stomach. The tequila was all in his eyes.

"Come here," he said.

"What?" I sounded like I knew what he wanted. The tequila was in my eyes, too. I could feel it.

"If you don't come to me, I'm coming to you," he said seductively.

I leaned over to his face. He came up a little, tilted his head to me, and opened my lips with his tongue. We started kissing and rolling around on the floor.

My shirt came off. I unbuttoned his pants. Felt his muscles for the first time.

We stumbled, embracing and kissing, pulling off clothes in a drunken dance to the bedroom.

I pressed my hand against Ian's penis.

He pushed me onto the bed like he didn't know me—like I wanted him to—and pulled off his shirt.

"I want you so fucking bad," he said, staggering and reaching into his pocket. He pulled out a condom.

I laid my head on the pillow. I looked at the blinds, the slats facing up to the ceiling. A little light was coming in from the moon.

Ian had turned around. His pants and boxers were down beneath his butt. He was shaking his head.

"You OK?" I asked.

"Just getting the condom on," he said. "I'm fine."

After a few seconds that felt like forever, he was talking to himself. Cursing.

"You need me to—"

"I'm fine," he said. "I just can't—"

"Maybe if I—"

Ian dropped his hands at his side to show his frustration. "Rachel, just don't try to help. I'm fine."

"OK."

He cursed a little more and then he took some deep breaths.

The alcohol was starting to wear off a little.

Ian sat on the edge of the bed and threw the torn condom wrapper to the floor.

"I'm too nervous," he said finally.

"But you were just hard," I said. "I felt it."

"I know, but now that we're about to do it—I think it's just my nerves."

"But we did shots. Aren't you relaxed?"

"Maybe I'm tired," Ian said. "And I didn't eat anything yet."

"True," I agreed, but really that was just because I knew I should. I laid there for a little while with goose bumps sprouting all over my arms thinking about what I could say to help Ian relax, but nothing seemed right.

"You want me to fix you a plate?" he asked, sounding as if I should be excited about the opportunity to eat. "I got some Thai tea, too. I know you like that."

"Sounds good, babe," I said.

"Great." Ian hopped up and pulled up his pants and walked out of the room without turning around.

After we ate, we spooned and Ian kissed me on the back of my neck. I don't remember ever going to sleep. I laid with him with my eyes open and on the light from the moon.

Ian and I had three more failed drunken sex nights before we settled on spooning without question. It was so tiring and so stressful to consider why it wasn't working for us in bed. And although Ian kept saying that he wanted us to be open about everything just as we'd always been, I knew not to push him about not being able to get it up. Really, I wasn't "getting it up" myself. Something just wasn't feeling right with us being together in that way. Every day I felt like it would be the day when it felt easy or natural, but my heart only twittered at the idea of talking to Ian, holding his hand, doing shots with him, and going to sleep.

A few nights a week, he'd fall asleep on the couch and I'd lie in bed remembering Xavier tearing away my underwear in the elevator. The look on Mrs. Jackson's face. I'd slide my fingers between my legs and be careful not to moan or move around too much.

We spent Thanksgiving in Social Circle with Grammy Annie-Lou. Saying it had been too soon, Ian hadn't told his parents about leaving Scarlet and he didn't want to go to New Orleans. I hadn't even told Grammie Annie-Lou about Ian getting married, so her dinner table was the perfect refuge. It did hurt me that Ian felt he couldn't tell his parents that we were getting together, but I trusted his decision and decided to focus less on creating new issues before we fixed what was becoming our biggest issue: the lack of sex.

My birthday, just a few days before Christmas, seemed like the right time. Krista's weedhead boyfriend Manuel sent a bag of hydro to the office for me the day before my birthday with a message from Krista that he had the good marijuana that was sure to leave any man (in his own words) "ready to cut Sheetrock."

I hadn't smoked "grass" (that's what they'd called it in the country back then) since high school, but I was willing to give it a try, thinking that if Ian and I could just get over the sex hump, we could be closer.

When I got home that night, I tossed the little clear bag of neon green grass onto the kitchen table where Ian was sitting and grading a stack of term papers, and told him what Krista's boyfriend had said.

"Why did he say that?" Ian asked. (Somehow I didn't think he'd be smart enough to pick up on why Manuel would make such a comment.)

"Just as a joke. He didn't mean anything by it," I said, knowing he really meant to ask if I'd told Krista about our bedroom misadventures, which I had.

Ian looked back at his papers.

"So do you want to smoke it tonight?" I asked. Ian had smoked marijuana through college and I knew he still smoked with some of his intellectual weedhead guy friends sometimes.

"Let's wait until tomorrow. For your birthday. We can smoke it then," he said. "I have to get through these papers. Grades are due online in the morning."

"OK," I said.

Ian stayed up all night grading papers and fell asleep on the couch.

In the morning, he came into the bedroom and kissed me on the back of my neck.

"Good morning, birthday girl," he whispered.

"Good morning." I turned around to him and smiled, still half asleep.

"I'm going to the office for a little while. I was thinking, do you want to meet for lunch later? Start off the birthday celebration at our spot?"

"Sure."

"Great. I'll see you there at 2:00 PM," he said. "And we can smoke your Viagra-laced weed tonight."

I laughed and rolled back over to catch my last few minutes of sleep. I'd taken the day off, but I had scheduled an early spa treatment.

* * *

I sat in the back booth at Fado for an hour waiting for Ian. Every time I thought to call him, I decided to give him a little more time. Furthermore, Shane kept bringing me free beers and even had a few sips himself in honor of my birthday. Got to love Irish men. They never miss a reason to celebrate.

Shane and I toasted a few times before I realized that two hours had gone by, when Ian finally called.

"Get your ass over here," I said into the phone. "I'm starving . . . and drunk. Where are you?"

"Um . . . just . . . I'm still in the office," Ian said in a low voice.

"Fuck! So you're standing me up on my birthday?"

Shane widened his mouth and rolled his eyes in mock disdain at my announcement.

"You'd better get over here, bro. Rachel is good and drunk!" Shane hollered over my shoulder into the phone.

We laughed, but there was silence from Ian's end. I suspected it was because he was with a student.

"I'm sorry, I can't make it," he whispered, lower this time.

"Oh," I said.

"How about later? Can we meet for dinner? I can make reservations at Bacchanalia."

"Bacchanalia for dinner on my birthday," I repeated, loudly enough so Shane could hear and he gave a thumbs-up. "Shane approves. What time?"

"Let's say eight," Ian said.

"Cool. I'll be there and not square," I joked.

"OK."

"Is everything OK?" I asked. He sounded so tense.

"Yeah. I'll see you later."

Later at Bacchanalia looked more like earlier at Fado.
I went home and changed into a short black minidress I'd been saving for months. I'd freeze my ass off in the December cold, but it would be worth it when Ian saw my legs out. Before I left, I rolled a clumsy joint with the marijuana and set it out on the coffee table beside the couch. "Here's hoping," I said, winking at it.

I stepped into Bacchanalia like applause was certain. I was sure Ian had gotten there early and had a bouquet of red roses waiting for me. There were flowers, but no Ian.

A waitress with green eyes and a bouncy ponytail led me to the table Ian had reserved. There was a beautiful arrangement of flowers sitting in my seat.

I picked them up and smelled them before placing them on the table.

"Would you like something to drink while you wait for Mr. Dupree?" the waitress asked.

"No. I'm sure he'll be here any minute."

Minutes went by. The tables around me started changing courses. I began to look odd sitting there alone.

The waitress came back with water and a new question.

"Perhaps a glass of dessert wine? Sweet for your birthday?" she asked suggestively.

"Sure," I agreed. I was beginning to get anxious and wanted to settle my nerves.

The tables around me were moving onto their third course. The couple sitting beside me asked if I would take their picture. I looked at my watch a few times.

Soon my wine was almost gone.

> **TO: IAN DUPREE**
> **TIME: 8:47pm**
> **Hey Babe. I'm at the restaurant waiting for you**
> **Where are you?**

> **TO: IAN DUPREE**
> **TIME: 9:13pm**
> **Hello? What's going on? Still here waiting . . .**
> **My bday will be over in a few hours. Hurry.**

> **TO: IAN DUPREE**
> **TIME: 9:36pm**
> **What's up?**

The waitress came over and asked very politely if I was expecting my guest any time soon and if I wanted to order anything. Hidden in her tone was a rush to turn the table over to another reservation. "I won't charge you for the wine," she said sympathetically. "And the flowers were on the house. Your date told us it was your birthday." She smiled and signaled for the waiter to come and pour me another glass.

> **TO: IAN DUPREE**
> **TIME: 9:50pm**
> **I am leaving here soon. What's going on?**

When I finished the second glass of wine, there was nothing to do but leave. The waitress had probably told the wait staff about my situation and they were all giving me the injured-baby-bird-on-the-side-of-the-road face. I plunked down a twenty on the table and smiled my way out to my car.

As soon as I put the key into the ignition, Ian wrote back.

> **FROM: IAN DUPREE**
> **TIME: 10:05pm**
> **I have a situation. I'm sorry.**

> **TO: IAN DUPREE**
> **TIME: 10:06pm**
> **Sorry about?**

> **FROM: IAN DUPREE**
> **TIME: 10:27pm**
> **I can't come.**

> **TO: IAN DUPREE**
> **TIME: 10:28pm**
> **Can't or won't?**

I sat in the car and waited another ten minutes for a response.

> **FROM: IAN DUPREE**
> **TIME: 10:39pm**
> **She called me.**

TO: IAN DUPREE
TIME: 10:40pm
And? Just say what's going on.

FROM: IAN DUPREE
TIME: 10:50pm
It's your birthday. I just feel like such an
asshole.

FROM: IAN DUPREE
TIME: 10:51pm
I can't do this anymore. I can't hurt two
people.

TO: IAN DUPREE
TIME: 10:52pm
What two people? Ian, what the fuck is
going on? Just say it.

FROM: IAN DUPREE
TIME: 11:00pm
I can't keep hurting her. She's my wife.

His words stung me to tears, the tears I should've
started crying hours ago.

TO: IAN DUPREE
TIME: 11:05pm
Then who am I? Are you hurting me?
The woman you said you loved?

FROM: IAN DUPREE
TIME: 11:06pm
Don't do that. This is hard for me. I didn't
mean to hurt anyone. Maybe I was just
being selfish. I made a mistake.

TO: IAN DUPREE
TIME: 11:08pm
You said you were sure.

TO: IAN DUPREE
TIME: 11:15pm
You said you loved me. I can't believe this.

FROM: IAN DUPREE
TIME: 11:50pm
We're having a baby. She just told me
today. We've been at the house talking.
We're going to try to work it out. We have
to.

I felt flattened. Beat by age-old wisdom. Ian was
my best friend. But he was also someone else's husband. And now he was acting like it.

FROM: IAN DUPREE
TIME: 12:01am
I know you hate me. But I didn't mean to
hurt you. I just can't not try. This is my
family. I have to be here. I'm so sorry.

FROM: IAN DUPREE
TIME: 12:03am
I'll come get my things in the morning.

11

Driving Off Into the Sunset

#losing . . . At sunrise, Ian showed up in my bedroom doorway with his bag packed and over his shoulder.

I was sitting in the middle of the bed, Indian style, with my laptop in front of my legs, trying to get Journey on the line. She wasn't there. I didn't know what to say to him.

He didn't seem to know what to say to me. He looked over at the window at the sun's rays coming through the blinds.

We listened for a while like two people expecting birds to chirp and to hear children hollering at one another as they walked to the bus stop. There was silence, though. No distractions from our reality.

"You want to go to breakfast?" Ian asked with a struggle for normalcy in his voice.

"No."

"OK." He sounded glad that I'd turned him down. "I left your key on the counter in the kitchen."

"OK." I was so desperately angry that I couldn't say anything else. That I couldn't fight this. But there was no reason to make him stay. I'd hate myself if I did. I'd hate him if he did.

We listened for the birds and children. Still silence.

"Rachel—"

I put my hand up to stop him. I didn't want to hear my name. This was difficult enough. Salt on my wounds. I couldn't hear my name from his mouth. That would just be like I was trying to make everything OK. Like I was pretending this wasn't what it was. Or like I thought he owed me some explanation. "Don't. Just go."

Ian looked down at his bag. "I didn't mean to hurt—"

"Don't!" I glowered at him.

"You're my best—" His voice was cracking the same way Xavier's had when he was at my threshold.

"Ian, stop it!" I said just as Journey took my Skype call. Her face popped up on the laptop screen. Ian couldn't see her, though. "Nothing you can say is going to change what's going to happen."

"But I didn't mean to—"

"You didn't do anything without me. We both did it. Everything. Our relationship. How else was this supposed to end up? How was anyone else going to survive in our lives with us the way we were? This had to happen." I started crying. "And I'm not sad that it happened. I'm sad that now things have to change. That they won't be like they were. But I know they shouldn't be."

"We can still—"

"No, we can't."

Ian exhaled and I knew what he was about to say.

"Don't say it," I said. "Don't say you love me. Just go. Go and be a good father. Be a good husband. Be a good man. Do what you promised you were going to do."

He sniffled and pushed his hands into his pocket. There would be no hug. No promise of to-morrow. This was the end of our good-bye.

I looked back at the blinds. The sun's rays were half gold and crimson. It looked like slivers of terra-cotta royal roses were spilling into the room.

When I looked back at the doorway, Ian was gone. I heard the front door slam.

I fell over on the bed and cried underneath the red and gold glow.

"You OK?" Journey asked after a while.

I curled up next to the laptop and turned her face to mine. My tears had fallen so quickly, there was a puddle of tears sinking into the sheet below my face.

"I tried," I said. "I had to."

"You're just a woman," Journey said. "You ain't perfect. Don't be too hard on yourself."

"I cried all last night." I wiped my tears and whispered into the laptop like someone else was there with me and could hear me. "And I don't think it was over Ian. It was over what we'd done. How much time we'd wasted. I keep feeling like I've lost so much."

"You can't charge your brain for listening to your heart."

"The crazy thing is that my heart wasn't so sad that Ian was going. My brain didn't understand it, but my heart was fine. It was kind of thinking about something else."

"What?"

"Xavier. I wished he was with me."

"Where is he now?"

"Back in Chicago, I'm sure," I said. "I told him to go away. He's not the type to stick around where he's not wanted. I guess Tante Heru counted on that in any man." I looked down at the sheet. The tears were just a wet spot now.

"You could call him."

"I hurt him. I don't think there's any coming back from that."

Bird called on a cold December morning to tell me that he couldn't think of anything else to do to the truck. He sounded sad. Told me to come by the shop with something to hang from the rearview window.

"Isn't she beautiful?" Bird said when I got to the shop and found the red truck pulled out front like it was on display for everyone driving by to see. It was so shiny and bold. It looked like someone had opened a can of candy apple red paint and just dumped it on the hood. The white seats inside looked like they'd never been touched and never should be.

"She?"

"Yeah. The truck is a she. Every car is a she."

"Why?"

"Because she'll always have her hand in your pocket, but you won't care, because she'll always look so good on your arm." Bird popped out his left arm like he might if he was escorting a woman into a room or hanging it out of the window of a car.

I laughed so hard for the first time since Ian had left my place. I hadn't heard from him. I hadn't heard from Xavier either.

"What you gonna do with the truck?"

"I don't know yet. Maybe I'll drive it," I said, knowing this would entertain Bird. I'd taken a cab to the shop and planned to drive back home.

"Whoooo! You're a woman after my heart. Now you know that every man everywhere you go is going to ask you about this here truck. Won't be able to let you drive by without stopping you."

"Really?"

"This truck is about to be like sugar in front of a baby." He patted the hood softly and blew the truck a kiss. "The best gift in the world. That's why I wanted to have it ready for you by Christmas. Figured it would be the only thing you needed under your tree."

"It's perfect," I said.

Bird took me around the truck and showed me all the bells and whistles he'd included. He sounded like he was describing a woman he loved or a dream he wanted so badly to revisit.

Once he was finished and we were sitting in the front seat—me behind the steering wheel and him in the passenger's side with a grin, I almost wanted to give him the truck. But I knew it had to come

home with me. I'd decided that I couldn't give the
truck back to Chauncey Billups.

"So what you got to hang from the mirror?" Bird
asked. "My father used to say you don't own a car
until you hang one thing, and one thing only, from
the rearview mirror. It's like naming your baby."

I pulled a thin golden necklace from my pocket.
An oval-shaped locket with ivy engraved over the
top hung from it. I handed it to Bird.

"What's this?" He opened the charm.

On the left side was a picture of my father and
King that I'd taken with my first Polaroid camera
on the front steps of Grammy Annie-Lou's house
in Social Circle. The truck was to my right in the
grass when I'd taken the photo. Still new and glis-
tening. A promise. The tires filled with air and
ready to go anywhere. You couldn't see the truck
in the little picture, but I knew it was there.

"It's my father and my dog," I explained to Bird
of the picture in the left frame.

"What's going here?" He pointed to the empty
right frame.

"There is something there," I said. "It's my
baby."

Bird didn't asked me anything else. He took the
locket and slid it over the rearview mirror.

"That's fine travelin' company, Ms. Lady," he
said soberly. "You ain't never going to be lost with
these kinds of passengers."

We watched the locket dangle for a minute and
find its place.

"Just promise me one thing," Bird asked.

"What?"

"Don't leave this locket hanging from the mirror. Somebody's bound to crack the window to get at it. And then I'm gonna have to go to jail, because I'm going to find that person and put my hands on him."

"You're so crazy," I said, laughing. "How about this—I'll keep it in the glove compartment?"

"Yeah, because I didn't want to ruin the moment, but you might want to just get a palm tree air freshener or something to hang from the rearview window," Bird said, getting out of the car and walking around to my window. "You have to be careful in this truck. Can't leave it just anywhere. Can't take it just anywhere. And don't stop at any red lights in the hood."

"I know. I know."

"Might want to keep it in a garage through the winter. Paint's still new."

"I know," I said. "Hey, what are you doing for the holidays?"

"Going on a three-week cruise to Alaska. Christmas and New Year's."

"Really? A cruise? I didn't peg you for the kind of man who'd enjoy being on a boat that long."

"Got me a new girlfriend. She ain't never been nowhere, so I put a little money in her bank account and told her to take her man someplace nice."

"That's wonderful," I said. "I'm sure you two will have a great time."

"We will. She's the kind of woman who will make sure of it. What about you? What you getting into? I'm sure you'll be at the mayor's ball or the White House by New Year's Eve."

"Don't be too sure," I said. "I'll probably be doing the same thing I did last year."

"Well, don't break too many hearts out there, pretty lady," Bird said.

"I'm sure I won't."

12

"Auld Lang Syne"

#Oldacquaintances. New Year's Eve 2011. Bird was somewhere on a boat looking at whales swimming by in the Alaskan oceans. I was on my couch considering if old acquaintances should be forgotten. It seemed as though I had entered into a season of perpetual repetition. Recycling old curtains with no value and hanging them in old windows that had been broken beyond repair. The result? Rain on the inside. Drafts. Snow. Humidity. Torrential downpour all over my life. Winter. Summer. Spring. Fall. Indoors. Five hundred twenty-five thousand six hundred minutes. Three hundred sixty-five days. A whole year and I was right back where I began: two hours before the conclusion of the first year of the second decade of the twenty-first century and I was alone again. The pizza was on its way. The wine was on the table. The DVD was ready to go and I was in the living room about to pop my pills.

That song, that horrible, horrible cliché of a song that everyone loves to sing on New Year's Eve, "Auld Lang Syne": it asks if we should move on, forget the old acquaintances, those little moments with people and things that happen in the five hundred twenty-five thousand six hundred minutes, the three hundred sixty-five days that make up the years of life. But it always assumes that the answer is no. The words are rhetorical, but the music, and how people sing it—decked out in party gear and donning colorful hats and their best jewels—is nostalgic, hinting that the old acquaintance is to be remembered longingly. What did I have to remember longingly? I started the year out of love, fell in love, was denied love, fell in love again, lost it, found it, and lost everything. Everything I had. As if I'd put it all up for grabs on a Vegas craps table. Now there was nothing. The same silence I'd started with. Only now it was much more depressing and nothing to even make a smart, chiding comment about. That past needed to stay where it was. To die. I could do that. Leave it all behind and make a resolution never to retrace my steps again. It was time to move on with me. With or without someone.

I loved love. I really, really loved love. At first flirty smile—love. At first sexy scent—love. The first moment you see him and you just know from somewhere in your navel that you must have his babies—love. Defy your mama—love. Defy your daddy—love! And who gives a damn if neither one of them ever speaks to you again because "he" is in your life and nothing else really matters right now, does it?—love. Cherry on top—love. Hand-holding on the Ferris wheel—love. Staying in bed all day and you don't even care that your underarms smell like onions and his breath smells like onions (because he's been kissing your underarms)—love. Red roses and chocolates on February fourteen—love. *Love Jones* with Nia Long standing out in the rain crying just before Larenz Tate sweeps her up into his arms—love. Sappy—love. Yes, clichéd—love. And we don't care if it is clichéd because it's our fairy tale and it can be whatever and however we want it—love. Just—love.

But I couldn't help wondering whether it was all worth this pain. Maybe that kind of love wasn't for me. Maybe, like that old myth said, I was meant to help others in their love, but never have one of my own. Maybe there was no man who could live up to the words of that song. Maybe I couldn't. I'd tried e-mailing Xavier twice. To apologize. To see if maybe, just maybe, I'd made the worst mistake. I missed him so much. But he never answered. Maybe he felt I was the old acquaintance that should be forgotten.

I looked at the little blue NyQuil pills on the table. This couldn't be my reality. Not again. I didn't want to take them, but I couldn't stand the idea of being alone. Not again. I wanted to miss this. To fall into oblivion and wake up in the second act of my life where I'd figured this all out. Alone and at least content. At least satisfied with me. Maybe I was what I'd been missing. Maybe I was the man of my dreams. Maybe the world had made me that way.

I reached for the pills. Grabbed the glass of wine. I was about to pop them into my mouth, but then the doorbell rang. I was expecting the gold-toothed pizza man with my delivery.

"One second," I said, putting the pills back onto

the table. I went to get the fifty dollars I'd left on the table.

The bell rang again.

"I'm coming!" I answered, running to the door. "One sec—" I opened the door, ready to hand Goldie the money and get my cheesebread.

"Hey, Rach." Xavier was standing there, holding a suitcase.

"X?" I just jumped on him. Dropped the fifty dollars and jumped right on him.

"What? What's this? What's up?" he asked laughing. "Guess you're glad to see me."

He picked me up and carried me into the loft.

I was crying the saltiest tears on his shoulder.

"What are you doing here?" I asked, my voice broken after every word.

"I came to sweep you off your feet," he said, holding me up in his arms in the middle of the living room floor.

"Sweep me off my feet?"

"If you'll let me." He let me down and looked into my eyes. "If you'll let me sweep you off your feet, I'd like to do it. Will you?"

"Uhhh . . . Delivery for a . . . Winslow?"

We turned to the doorway. There was a skinny kid in a Morehouse T-shirt balancing a box of pizza on one hand.

"Oh, that's for me," I said, wiping my tears.

Xavier picked up the fifty dollars and handed it to the guy before taking the pizza.

"Keep the change," I said.

"Wow! Thanks!"

I was about to close the door, but asked him, "Hey, where's Goldie—the other pizza guy?"

"That fool had a date," he said.

"Awesome."

I closed the door, turned around, and leaned up against it. Xavier had already opened the pizza box and was sitting on the couch, flipping through channels on the television.

"Come sit down, girl!" he said. "I want to watch the ball drop with you."

"I don't usually watch the ball drop." I walked over to the couch and looked at Xavier, chomping down on the pizza like he'd never left.

"I see." He looked at pills. "You sick?"

I coughed a little. "Just a slight cold."

"Hum . . . Guess I won't be kissing you tonight." He laughed.

"Kissing me?" I repeated. "X, what are you doing here?"

He clicked off the television.

"I missed you. I was sitting in my place this morning and I thought, I can't go into the next year without her. I can't make a new start without her," he said. "So, that's what this is. That's why I'm here."

"I see."

"Do you want that?"

"I told you to go away. I just thought you would stay away. . . ." I said. "I mean . . . you were away. But now you're here."

"Do you want me here?" He took my hand and kissed it.

"Yes. I do."

"Good! Because you know what they say—"

"Whoever you're with at the stroke of midnight on New Year's Eve is the person you'll spend the next year with," we said together.

Shelly Ellis returns with the explosive first book
in the Chesterton Scandals series.

Don't miss

Best Kept Secrets

On sale in September 2015!

Chapter 1

LEILA

Leila Hawkins paused as she mounted the last
concrete step in front of the double doors of the
First Good Samaritan Baptist Church—one of the
oldest and largest churches in Chesterton, Vir-
ginia, her hometown. Nestled on Broadleaf Av-
enue across the street from rustic Macon Park, the
house of worship had hosted many a baptism, funeral, and nuptial inside its brick walls in the one
hundred and some odd years of its existence. And

since 1968, a stark white sign had sat along its exterior, highlighting a Bible verse chosen by the honorable reverend or the assistant pastor when the reverend was ill or on vacation. Leila stepped aside to let a couple pass as she squinted at that sign, which hung a foot away from the doors and several feet above her head.

A FOOL GIVES FULL VENT TO HIS ANGER, BUT A WISE MAN KEEPS HIMSELF UNDER CONTROL, the sign read in big bold letters. PROVERBS 29:11.

Her eyebrows furrowed.

What the hell . . .

Was someone reading her mind?

Who cares if they are?

She grabbed one of the church's stainless-steel door handles.

She was on a mission today and she wasn't going to be deterred from it. She was giving "full vent" to her anger, whether any celestial being liked it or not. Leila was crashing this hifalutin wedding, and only lightning bolts or locusts would keep her away!

She walked into the vestibule, then tugged a heavy wooden door open, preparing herself to be met by a hundred stares, finger pointing, and indignation the instant she stepped inside the sanctuary.

"Hey! You're not supposed to be here!" she waited for someone to shout at her.

Instead, she was greeted by a light melody played by a string quartet and the polite chatter of the two hundred and some odd guests who were taking their seats in the velvet-cushioned pews.

No one stared at her. Hell, they barely seemed to notice her!

The tenseness in her shoulders instantly relaxed. Her white-knuckled grip on her satin clutch loosened. She reminded herself that she was walking into a wedding, not a gladiator pit.

"You're here to talk to Evan," a voice in her head cautioned her. "Not to fight with him. Remember?"

That's right. I'm just here to talk to him, to have a conversation with an old friend.

And if Evan chose not to be polite or listen to her, then and *only then* would she go off on him.

She looked around her.

The sanctuary was filled with splashes of pink and lavender, which Leila remembered were the bride's favorite colors. Roses, hydrangeas, freesias, and lilacs decorated the pulpit and pews, filling the space with their alluring scent. Ribbons and ivy garland were draped over anything and everything, and free-standing candelabras were along each aisle and by the stained-glass windows.

Leila felt an overwhelming sense of déjà vu. She hadn't set foot in this church since her own wedding day ten years ago. As she gazed around her, all the memories of that day came rushing back like a tsunami: the anticipation and nervousness she had felt as she waited for the church doors to open, the happiness she had experienced when she'd seen her handsome groom waiting for her at the end of the aisle, and the overwhelming sadness that had washed over her when she had looked at the wedding guests and had not seen her then best friend, Evan, among their friendly faces.

But she had known Evan wouldn't come to her wedding. Stubborn Evan Murdoch had told her in the plainest way possible that there was no way he would stand by and pretend that he was happy about her nuptials.

"That son of bitch is going to break your heart," Evan had warned her over the phone all those years ago when she'd made one last-ditch effort to ask him to come to the wedding. "He's going to drag you down. And when he does, don't come crying to me."

Leila wasn't sure what had made her angrier: that Evan had given her that dire, bitter prediction on the eve of her wedding—or that his prediction had come true. But today she would have to put aside all that resentment and anger if she was going to get Evan to do what she needed him to do for her mother. Her mother . . . a proud woman who had juggled multiple jobs and saved every dime she had for decades to gather the money to put Leila through school and give her a reasonably happy life. Leila had tried to repay her by purchasing her a two-bedroom bungalow in a middle-class neighborhood where they still held summer block parties, where neighbors still waved and said hello. But now Leila's mother would lose her home in a few months without Evan's help.

Leila's grip on her purse tightened again.

She'd argue. She'd beg. She'd do what she had to do to get Evan to listen to her.

For Ma's sake, she thought.

"Bride or groom?" someone asked, yanking Leila from her thoughts.

"What?" Leila asked.

She turned to find an usher leaning toward her. An officious-looking woman stood behind him with the kind of pinched face reserved for those who waited at the counter at the DMV and dentists' offices. A clipboard covered with several stacks of paper was in her hands. The woman discreetly whispered something into her headset while the usher continued to gaze at Leila expectantly.

"Are you with the bride or groom?" He gestured toward the pews. "On which side would you like to be seated?"

That was a tricky question. The bride hadn't invited Leila to the wedding; neither had the groom. But Leila certainly knew the bride better. Paulette Murdoch, Evan's sister, was someone Leila had once considered a friend—almost a little sister.

"Umm . . . uh, bride . . . I-I guess," Leila finally answered.

They noticed her hesitation and exchanged a look that Leila couldn't decipher. The woman behind the usher whispered into her headset again and waited a beat.

What? Leila thought with panic. *What did I do wrong?*

The woman stepped forward, plastering on a smile that seemed more forced than friendly.

"I'm sorry. Would you mind giving me your name?"

"Uh . . . why?"

"I just want to make sure you're seated in the proper area." The woman then pulled out a pen and pointed down at the stack of papers. Leila could see several names listed along with check marks next to each of them.

You've gotta be kidding me, Leila thought.

They actually had a guest list for the church! What did they think? Someone was going to sneak into the wedding?

"You are sneaking into Paulette's wedding!" the voice in her head chastised.

But still, this was ridiculous! Leila wondered if the guest list had been Evan's idea.

Wouldn't want the unwashed masses to wander in off the street, would we? Leila thought sarcastically. *Wouldn't want the poor people to stink up the place! Only the best and the brightest for the M&Ms!*

M&Ms or Marvelous Murdochs . . . People had been muttering and snickering over that nickname for decades around Chesterton, using it to derogatorily refer to the Murdochs—one of the most wealthy, respected, and (some said) stuck-up families in town. Of course that was better than their old nickname, the "High Yella Murdochs." That name had faded once the Murdochs became more equal opportunity and let a few darker folks like Evan's mom into the family.

"Well, my . . ." Leila paused, wondering how she was going to get out of this one. She most certainly wasn't on the list. "My name is . . . my name is, uh—"

"Leila! Leila, over here!" someone called to her. Leila turned to find her childhood friend Colleen waving wildly. Colleen sat in one of the pews toward the front of the church.

Saved by the bell!

"Come on, girl!" Colleen shouted, still grinning. "Sit by me!"

"I guess my 'proper area' is up there, then?" Leila asked.

The usher laughed while the woman with the clipboard continued to scrutinize her, not looking remotely amused.

"Go right ahead," he said, waving Leila forward. She walked down the center aisle to Colleen. As she did so, she ran her hands across the front of her pale yellow dress. It was an old ensemble that she had thrown on at the last minute after raiding her closet. She hadn't wore it in years, certainly not since she had given birth to her daughter. It felt a little tight and she worried that it wasn't very flattering. The ill-fitting dress only added to her already heightened anxiety.

"I haven't seen you in ages, girl! I didn't know you'd be at Paulette's wedding," Colleen cried, removing her heavy leather purse from the pew and plopping it onto her ample lap. She shifted over, causing an elderly woman beside her to glance at her with annoyance. Colleen then adjusted the wide brim of her sequin- and feather-decorated royal purple hat. "I saw you come in, but you didn't notice me waving at you. What were you thinking about, staring off into space like that?"

Leila pursed her lips as she took the seat nearest to the center aisle. "Just took a little trip down memory lane, that's all."

"*Memory lane?*" Colleen frowned in confusion. Suddenly, her brown eyes widened. "Oh, I forgot! This was the church where you got married too, isn't it?"

Leila nodded.

"Ten years ago last month! Girl, I remember," Colleen continued. "It was a beautiful day, wasn't it? And you had looked so pretty in your gown." She patted Leila's hand in consolation. "I'm so sorry to hear about you and Brad, by the way."

"Don't be sorry," Leila assured.

I'm certainly not, she thought.

Not only had Brad broken her heart, like Evan had predicted, but that man also had put her through so much pain during the course of their marriage—between the lies, philandering, his get-rich-quick schemes, and his all-around bullshit—that he was lucky she hadn't thrown her wedding ring down the garbage disposal in outrage. Instead, she had pawned it to pay for a hatchback she'd purchased for her move from San Diego back to Chesterton. She'd had to get a new car after her Mercedes-Benz was repo'd thanks to Brad neglecting to mention that he hadn't made any payments in four months.

"So it *is* final then?" Colleen asked. "It's over between you two?"

"Almost. The divorce should be finalized in a few months, I guess."

Leila certainly hoped it would be. But frankly, it was no telling with Brad. He had been dragging his feet on the divorce proceedings, saying that his focus was instead on his criminal case. He faced charges for fraud and money laundering because he and his partners had bilked several wealthy clients in Southern California out of more than twenty million dollars with some elaborate Ponzi scheme.

Thanks to Brad, his lawyer, and the California court system, Leila's life was still in limbo. She felt like she was *still* swimming her way out the whirlpool Brad kept sucking her into.

"Well, I'm glad you came back here," Colleen said. "We missed you. I know I certainly did. I'm sorry your divorce is the reason why you came, but . . . you tried your best, right?"

Leila nodded then turned away to stare at the front of the church, wishing desperately that Colleen would drop the topic. She didn't want to think about Brad right now. She had enough on her plate today.

"You put up with more than most wives would," Colleen continued, oblivious to Leila's growing discomfort. "It's a wonder you lasted as long as it did. I know I wouldn't have!"

Leila's smile tightened.

"All that lying and cheating—and now that pyramid-scheme nonsense! That man has dragged you through the mud, Leila. Right on through it!" Colleen shook her head ruefully. "Girl, I would have taken a frying pan to the back of that man's head *years* ago!"

It was bad enough to have a wreck of a marriage, to find out that you were sharing a bed every night with a liar and a hustler. But it was ten times worse knowing that everyone in town also knew— and Chesterton was a town that loved its gossip. She was sure her failed marriage and Brad's criminal charges had been gossip du jour in every beauty salon, church gathering, and coffee shop in Chesterton for months!

Of course, Evan had discovered the truth first, but he hadn't needed the town gossips to tell him. He had figured it out himself. He had seen through the varnish and spotted the shoddy workmanship underneath. He had seen the *real* Brad back when she met the smooth-talking Casanova her junior year in college. Though Brad had blinded Leila with his sweet talk, worldliness, and charm, Evan had called him on his bullshit. But she had been too naïve and lovesick at the time to listen to her then best friend. She wished now that she had. It could have spared her a lot of disappointment, agony, and heartbreak in the long run. It could have spared her from severing ties with Evan and the humiliation she was suffering today.

"The flowers are beautiful," Leila said with a false cheeriness, trying to change the subject from Brad. She looked around her again, taking it all in.

Paulette Murdoch was probably deliriously happy with how the decorations had turned out. The décor fit her to a T.

"I knew everything would be this nice though," Leila said. "Paulette's dad never spared an expense, *especially* when it came to his little girl. I've been away for a while, but even I remember that much."

Colleen shook her head and leaned toward Leila's ear. "Not her father, honey," she whispered. "All this was arranged while he was sick in the hospital and after he died seven months ago. It's Evan who dished out the money for this wedding. He controls the purse strings now!"

Of course he does, Leila thought sullenly. Evan controlled everything. He held all the cards, which was why she was here today.

The last note of the melody the string quartet had been playing ended and the violins started to play *Canon in D Major.* The chatter in the sanctuary ceased as the church doors opened. The groom and his six groomsmen strolled toward the front of the church, near the pulpit, in single-breasted tuxedos with pink calla lilies pinned to their lapels.

The groom was a handsome man. He stood at six feet, had ebony-hued skin, and wide shoulders. *Just Paulette's type,* Leila thought, remembering when Evan's little sister had described her ideal man more than a decade ago as Leila painted the teen girl's toenails.

Leila watched as the bridesmaids began the processional. They were all wearing satin gowns of various designs, but in the same shade of lavender. They clutched bouquets of hydrangea, freesias, and roses. The adorable ring bearer and the flower girl made their way down the center aisle next. The little girl reminded Leila of her own daughter, Isabel.

Suddenly, the music changed again. This time it was Vivaldi's *Spring*. Everyone took their cue and rose from the pews in anticipation of the bride's entrance.

Seconds later, Paulette stood in the church doorway, and she took Leila's breath away.

Leila couldn't believe this was the same unassuming teenager she had last seen ten years ago. This woman was beautiful and regal. Her long, dark glossy hair cascaded over her bare burnt-copper-toned shoulders. Her curvy figure was accentuated by the mermaid cut of her strapless wedding gown, which was decorated with Swarovski crystals and lace. A cathedral-length veil trailed behind her dramatically.

Paulette looked so beautiful, so stunning, so absolutely—

Perfect, Leila thought as she stared at her in awe.

And holding Paulette's satin-gloved hand was Evan. Being the new family patriarch, it only seemed right that Evan would give the bride away today. Judging from the grin on his strikingly handsome face, he seemed proud and happy to play the fatherly role.

Evan hadn't aged much in the past decade, but he certainly looked more handsome and distinguished than Leila remembered. He had the same coppery skin as his sister and was even taller than the groom. The glasses he'd often worn during childhood were gone. Leila was happy to see he had finally given them up for good. She had always thought he had the most soulful dark eyes that shouldn't be hidden behind thick, plastic lenses.

As the brother and sister walked down the center aisle toward the altar, a lump formed in Leila's throat. Her heart ached a little. This was the man whom she had once called her best friend. Once, they had been so close. She had been able to turn to Evan in her darkness moments, to confess to him her worst fears. Now he wouldn't even return her e-mails or phone calls. He hadn't met her daughter. He had gotten married five years ago and she had found out about it months later. She hadn't even met his wife!

Leila stared at the front pew, looking at the faces of the folks who sat there, wondering if his wife was among them.

She and Evan were practically strangers now. What the hell had happened to them?

Time . . . distance . . . silence, she thought.

But they could still make it right, she told herself, filling up with the warmth of the moment. They could put the past behind them. They could make amends. The guy standing in front of her didn't seem petty or angry. Maybe she had just misunderstood him. Maybe they just misunderstood each other. Once she told Evan why she needed his help, he would listen. She knew he would!

As Paulette and Evan drew closer, Leila grinned at the bride, whose loving gaze was focused solely on her husband-to-be.

Meanwhile, Evan's eyes drifted to the wedding guests. He nodded at a few in greeting. Finally, he noticed Leila standing in the pews near the center aisle.

"Hey, Magoo," she mouthed before giving him a timid wave.

Magoo. It was the nickname she had given him back when they were kids. Whenever he hadn't worn his glasses, he had squinted like the cartoon character, Mr. Magoo. His nickname for her had been "Bugs" after Bugs Bunny, thanks to her bucked rabbit teeth, which had thankfully been corrected over time by a good set of braces.

When Leila waved at him as he walked past, Evan did a double take. Leila watched, deflated, as his broad smile disappeared. His face abruptly hardened and his jaw tightened. The dark eyes that she had once admired now snapped back toward the front of the church. Evan looked more than irritated at seeing her standing there in the church pew. He looked downright furious.

The warm, mushy feeling that had swelled inside of her abruptly dissolved. Her cheeks flushed with heat. Her heart began to thud wildly in her chest again.

"There goes that fantasy," the voice in her head scoffed.

She should have known it wouldn't be easy. Evan was obviously still cross at her and even more so now that she had sneaked into his sister's wedding.

Fine, she thought angrily. *Be that way, Evan.*

But she wasn't giving up. She was still going to find a way to talk to him today—or yell at him or plead with him, whatever was required. She would find a way to plead her mother's case.

Chapter 2

EVAN

"What the hell is Leila doing here?" Evan snarled as he stood at the bar in the hotel's immense and elegant ballroom.

"Paulette said she doesn't remember inviting her," his equally handsome brother, Terrence, replied. "Maybe there was a mix-up." The younger man adjusted the bowtie at his throat. "Hey, is this thing on straight? It feels crooked."

"There was no goddamn mix-up! I can't believe Leila had the balls to just . . . to just *show* up!"

And to think, Evan had initially balked at the idea of having a church guest list when the mother of the groom had made the request. She had explained that she wanted to make sure the VIPs, like Mayor Crisanto Weaver and his wife, were properly seated in the church, but Evan suspected that the meddling mama really wanted to make sure no undesirables made it into the wedding. Evan had thought it was not only in poor taste but outright rude to ask people to give their names as they entered the sanctuary, though now he was starting to have second thoughts about that.

The list didn't work anyway. Leila still made it in!

Terrence lowered his hands from his bowtie. "I know you're pissed, Ev. But just chill out, all right?" He shifted a shot glass toward Evan. "Here. Have my drink. Maybe it'll calm you down."

Evan highly doubted that. He was too hot with anger to be cooled down right now.

Terrence nudged the glass again with the tip of his finger, easing it closer to his older brother. "Go on."

Evan hesitated for only a few more seconds before he raised his shot glass to his lips and downed his drink in one gulp. He then slammed the shot glass down on the bar's granite countertop and grimaced. *"Ugh,* what the hell was that?"

"Tequila," Terrence answered as he sniffed the shot glass. "Why? What was wrong with it?"

"It tasted like shit!"

"No, it didn't." Terrence held up two fingers to the bartender behind the counter, silently conveying that he wanted a double. "You are such a pussy now, man! There was nothing wrong with that drink. You've just lost your taste for liquor. That's what happens when you act like a monk and stop drinking alcohol."

"You know why I don't drink," Evan said tightly, silencing his brother. "Charisse drinks enough for the both of us," he muttered.

In fact, seeing his wife, Charisse, slur and stum-

ble her way around their home had put Evan off
drinking for years. The taste of the stuff he had
just imbibed told him he wasn't missing much.

"She's lucky I don't have her ass thrown out,"
Evan said.

"Who? Charisse?"

"No, not Charisse! Leila!"

Terrence tiredly closed his eyes, which were a
shade of caramel that he had inherited from their
father. "So we're back to Leila, huh? Ev, we all
know how you feel about her, but Paulette said
she's okay with her being here. So why don't you
just—"

"But what if *I'm* not okay with it?" he asked in-
dignantly, pointing at his chest.

"Yeah, I figured you'd say that. I told Paulette
you wouldn't like it. She said . . . and I quote . . .
'It's my wedding day and Ev will just have to get
over it.' "

Evan blinked in amazement. Did he hear him
correctly? *"Get over it?"*

Terrence shrugged. "That's what she said."

Evan turned his menacing gaze to the parquet
dance floor, where his mutinous sister and her
new husband danced under the misty glow of an
orange spotlight. He gritted his teeth. *Get over it?*
So this was the thanks he got for the more than
two hundred thousand dollars he had spent on
this little shindig?

Paulette had nearly fainted when she'd seen her
Vera Wang wedding gown at the bridal shop and
she'd just *had* to have it. Had Evan balked when
he'd seen the fifteen-thousand-dollar bill months
later? *No.*

Had he complained when the wedding guest list got as long as his arm? *No.*

Had he objected when he'd heard about the ice sculptures, four-foot chocolate fountains, performance artists, and fireworks display planned for the reception? *No!*

And why had he simply opened his checkbook and wordlessly written check after check?

Because I wanted to make my little sister happy, Evan thought irritably. Whatever Paulette wanted on her special day, he promised he would give it to her. Even their crusty father would have done as much. But how had Paulette repaid Evan's graciousness? By siding with the one woman he had avoided for almost a decade, the one woman who had betrayed him and broken his heart.

"Look," Terrence began, reaching for his own shot glass, "Leila is one out of I don't know how many guests here tonight. I wouldn't worry about her. You probably won't run into her again anyway."

"But what if she's here to start some shit? What if she's here to ask about——"

"But what if she's not? Maybe she came because she just wanted to see Paulette get married."

Evan squinted in disbelief. "You don't really believe that, do you?"

"Yes, I do, and I'll bet you a hundred bucks that I'm right. If I'm wrong, then you get a hundred bucks and we'll have her escorted out. Until then, just forget that she's here and go enjoy yourself. Do some schmoozing." Terrence smirked. "You're a Murdoch. It's what we do best."

Evan gazed around the darkened ballroom, his expression grim. That was easier said than done.

Even if he didn't see Leila, he knew she was probably out there sitting at one of the banquet tables. Feeling her presence in the room ruined his evening, though he kept telling himself that such feelings were nonsense.

"Just misplaced anger," a voice in his head said.

Maybe, he conceded.

The person he was really mad at was Charisse, who hadn't bothered to stay sober enough to at least make it through the entire wedding. She had sat bleary eyed during most of the ceremony, hiding her hangover and her bloodshot baby blues behind tinted sunglasses. After a few drinks during cocktail hour, she was back to her outgoing self, laughing and charming everyone. But, of course, she had started to go downhill by the time the bride and groom had their first dance. She had been constantly tripping over the hem of her evening gown. Her words had become more and more slurred. She had been on the verge of getting full-on drunk and making a real ass of herself when Evan had her spirited away.

His half brother, Dante, had agreed to drive Charisse home. Dante had only connected with the family less than a year ago, not too long after their father's death. He was eager to be accepted into the Murdoch fold and wanted to be helpful. Thank God he had offered to handle Charisse!

But now Evan had another headache to deal with, thanks to Leila Hawkins crashing his sister's wedding. He could feel the tenseness winding up inside him, making the muscles in his neck and shoulders rigid. His eyes darted anxiously around the darkened room, anticipating the moment when he would spot her again. Would she come up to him and tap him on the shoulder? Would she corner him and confront him in the open? It was like he was preparing for battle.

"Hey, sexy," a female voice said from over Evan's shoulder. He turned to find one of Paulette's brides-maids smiling up at him. She laid a warm hand on his arm. "Wanna dance, baby?"

"There you go! A distraction, Ev," Terrence said. "Just what the doctor ordered! Go out there and get your groove on, boy!"

"Uh, I'm married," Evan muttered to her, hold-ing up his ring finger and ignoring his brother. He returned his gaze to the ballroom.

"So! I'm not asking you to run away with me! I'm just asking you to dance," the bridesmaid per-sisted. She wrapped an arm lazily around his shoulders. "Come on! Dance with me!"

Evan narrowed his eyes down at her.

Her name was Angie. Or was it Amy? *Something that begins with an A,* he thought.

Loose curls had fallen out of her chignon and one lock hung limply over her heavy-lidded, glazed brown eyes. One of the straps of her satin dress was hanging off her shoulder, revealing the lace bra underneath.

If he had wanted to dance with a drunken woman tonight, he would have just asked his wife for a twirl on the dance floor.

"Look, why don't I do this?" he asked, gently shifting the young woman toward the bar counter. "Instead of us dancing, why don't I get you a cup of coffee?" He then motioned to get the bar-tender's attention.

"I don't need a cup of coffee," the bridesmaid argued. "I said I wanna *dance!*"

She then shoved away from Evan and turned, snagging the heel of one of her stilettos in the hem of her dress. She stumbled forward with arms flailing wildly.

"Oh!" Terrence shouted. "There she goes!"

Both brothers caught her just before she tumbled.

"You got her?" Terrence asked, shifting her toward his older brother.

Evan nodded, slowly bringing her back to her feet. "Yeah, I got her."

The bridesmaid gazed up at Evan and Terrence woozily. She slumped against the older brother's broad shoulder. "I don't . . . I don't feel so well. I think I'm gonna be sick."

"*Sick?*" Terrence exclaimed. He eased back and pointed at his tuxedo. "Oh, no! Not on this! *This* is a Tom Ford."

"You're a real prince, Terry," Evan murmured sarcastically. He then returned his attention to the bridesmaid. "Let's get you out of here. I'll get you to the ladies' room. All right?"

She closed her eyes and weakly nodded.

Evan guided her across the crowded ballroom to the double doors, drawing a few curious stares from wedding guests. There was nothing he hated more than making a scene. Having a woman besides his wife clinging to him was bound to cause some talk, but he couldn't let her stumble drunkenly around the reception, or worse—lose her five-star dinner right there on the parquet dance floor. Like with Charisse, it was better to spirit the bridesmaid away to a place where she could recover privately. Terrence was obviously no help, so Evan would have to take care of this himself.

Evan stepped into the carpeted foyer with his arm wrapped around her waist and her arm draped around his neck.

"I'm really going to be sick," she murmured again.

"I know. I know. I'm working on it," he grumbled, glancing frantically around him.

He struggled to remember where he had last seen a women's bathroom. Finally, he saw a few women streaming out of a door on the other side of the foyer's winding staircase. He walked toward them and started to ask if one of them could help him, but when the women's bathroom door opened again, the words halted in his throat.

Leila Hawkins stepped out of the tiled bathroom into the foyer. She dropped a compact into her clutch purse, snapped the steel clasp shut, and looked up to find Evan staring at her. Her mouth fell open in shock.

"Evan," she whispered breathlessly.

Shit, he thought. This was the last person he wanted to see right now!

His jaw clenched. "Leila."

As much as he hated to admit it, Leila was as gorgeous and sexy now as she had been ten years ago. The only thing that was different was her hair. It was shorter now, chin-length and cut in a fashionable bob. He also noticed that she was wearing heels, something she had never worn when they were younger because she had said she didn't know how to walk in them.

Her honey-hued skin glowed under the foyer's chandelier lights, and she looked elegant and alluring in the simple pale yellow cocktail dress that hugged every delectable curve in just the right place.

She doesn't have a right to look this good, he thought.

He'd prefer for her to be a hunchbacked cyclops, or at least to have gained forty pounds or more. Then he wouldn't have to worry about reacting to her like the way his body was responding now.

"I'm glad I ran into you, Ev," Leila said as she took a step toward him. "I mean I'm glad we . . . we ran into each other. I wanted to talk to you about . . ." Her eyes shifted to the drunken bridesmaid at his side. "Is she okay?"

"No, I'm *not* okay!" the bridesmaid garbled against his shoulder.

"She's had a little too much to drink," Evan explained now that he was cornered. "I was trying to get her to the bathroom."

"I can take her," Leila volunteered. She grabbed the bridesmaid's hand. "Let's get you into one of those stalls, honey."

Evan watched as Leila guided the hapless young woman through the swinging door. He heard the loud retching and dry heaving a few seconds later and cringed. He could have left then. His intoxicated charge was now in capable hands, but he would feel bad if he didn't stick around to see if the bridesmaid survived.

The young woman and Leila emerged from the bathroom fifteen minutes later. Angie (or Amy . . . he still couldn't remember her name) looked more sober and slightly less ill, but still seemed out of sorts. Leila had an arm wrapped around her protectively.

"I think I'm going to say good-bye to Paulette and go home now," the young woman mumbled, wiping her mouth with a wet paper towel. "I've had enough fun for one night."

"I think that's a good idea," Leila said.

The bridesmaid looked at Leila, then Evan. "Thank you for your help—the both of you."

"No problem," they answered in unison. They then glanced at one another. When their eyes met, they broke gazes.

The bridesmaid walked back toward the ballroom doors, looking worn and tired.

"Do you think she'll be all right?" Leila asked, watching the bridesmaid's retreat. "Does she have a safe way to get home? I hope she's not driving."

"I'll have my driver take her home. He can come back later to get me."

Leila turned to him. "That's very nice of you."

When she beamed, something inside his chest warmed instantly. He shouldn't still be reacting to her this way.

Not after all these years. Not after what she did.

Leila had long ago proven that she couldn't be trusted.

"I'm not being nice," he answered firmly, so that there was no misunderstanding that he was a pushover anymore. He could tell from the look on her face that his tone had caught her off guard. "I don't want her driving home and getting into an accident. Something like that would end up in the paper, probably on the front page. Paulette doesn't need that type of drama around her wedding."

Leila's smile disappeared. "Yeah, Ev, because it's less important that the poor girl might plow into a tree and kill herself, than whether her accident might ruin the vibe at the wedding or"—she mockingly raised her hand to her lips and widened her eyes—"bring shame to the Murdoch name."

Sarcasm. He should have expected as much from Leila. It was a shield she had always used in

the past. Well, he had a shield too—a formal
blandness he reserved for business meetings and
acquaintances he wanted to get rid of quickly.

"Well, thank you very much for your help earlier. It was a pleasure seeing you again," he lied,
buttoning his suit jacket, then gesturing toward
the double doors. "Now, if you'll excuse me, I
should get back to the reception."

Just as he turned to head back to the ballroom,
Leila grabbed his arm, making him pause. "Evan,"
she said softly. "Evan, please . . . please wait."

Her touch ignited a small spark inside him that
he hadn't felt in quite a while. His pulse quick-
ened, and his skin tingled on the spot where she
touched him. He wanted to take her hand within
his own, tug her toward him, and kiss her. Instead,
he forced himself to pull his arm out of her grasp.

"What, Leila? Look, I'm supposed to be hosting
this thing. I can't just disappear and—"

"No one's going to think you're a bad host if
you disappear for a few minutes! No one's going to
look down on you for taking time to talk to me . . .
me, Ev." She pointed at her chest. "Someone who
used to be your friend!"

"The operative words are 'used to be,'" he said
coldly, making her cower as if he had hit her. He
began to walk away again.

"What did I do?" she asked as she trailed him,
taking fast steps to match the strides of his longer
legs. "What the hell did I do to you to make you . . .
you cast me out like this? You treat me like I'm
some leper!"

"Keep your voice down," he snapped as he
turned back to her. They were drawing stares from
a few of the guests who lingered in the lobby.

"No, I'm not keeping my fucking voice down! I've tried doing this quietly and privately! I've tried emailing you . . . *calling you!* But you never responded! I need your help!"

Of course she does, he thought bitterly.

Terrence owed him a hundred bucks! He knew Leila had shown up here because she wanted something, and he suspected he knew what that something was. But Leila had always needed his help. She had always needed *him*. In their friendship, he had been the one she would lean on when things went wrong: when her father walked away from her family, when her mother lost a job, or when one of Leila's boyfriends broke up with her. But Evan would be damned if he'd be the shoulder for her to cry on or the shrink for her to drone on and on to today. He wasn't that guy anymore.

"My mother is going to lose her home! Look, I fell behind on the payments. I mean . . . well, Brad *and* I fell behind. I thought he had it covered, but he didn't. Anyway, Murdoch Bank owns the mortgage now and—"

"I don't want to talk about this," he said as he neared the double doors. "Not here. Not now."

"But all we need is one word from you! If—"

"I told you that I don't want to talk about this! This is a wedding, Leila. Not now!"

"If you would just make one call—"

"What did I just say?" he boomed.

"But you don't understand!"

No, he understood perfectly well. He knew that her mother was in default of her mortgage and the bank was now taking her home. Almost more than two dozen other mortgage owners at Murdoch Bank were in the same situation.

Evan had inquired about the loans when the stories first started to appear in the local newspaper about how several homes in one neighborhood in Chesterton with mortgages all owned by Murdoch Bank had either fallen into arrears or were in foreclosure proceedings. The neighborhood also happened to be on land that a major corporation wanted to purchase to build a new shopping center in town. The reporter shared a few of the homeowners' conspiracy theories that the bank was in cahoots with the corporation to push them off the land to make way for the brand-new center.

When Evan's father, George, had told him two years ago that Murdoch Conglomerated was acquiring the local savings and loan bank, Evan had thought it odd. Banking didn't really fall under the company's portfolio. Their company focus was usually foods and retail. Why did his father want to purchase a bank? But when the news stories came out soon after George's death, all the pieces of the puzzle had fallen into place. His father wanted that shopping center so that Murdoch Conglomerated could open a new store there. The houses were an obstacle to his goal and he had found a sneaky way to get around it.

But, of course, George wasn't a stupid man. What he did may have been unethical, but it certainly wasn't illegal. All of the homeowners were behind on their mortgages. The bank had every right to use its own discretion to try to reach some settlement or simply allow the homes to go to foreclosure. Evan had no desire to micromanage and tell Murdoch Bank what to do. He had enough to worry about with his own duties as new CEO of Murdoch Conglomerated.

"Do you want me to beg, Ev?" Leila yelled, drawing more onlookers. "Is that what you want? Because that's what I'll do if it'll mean you'll—"

Her words were cut short. This time he grabbed *her* arm. He practically dragged her across the carpeted foyer to a secluded spot near a trickling water fountain. He finally let her go with a shove.

Evan glanced over his shoulder, making sure they were no longer being watched. "Are you trying to embarrass me? Are you trying to embarrass Paulette?"

"No, I'm trying to make you listen, damn it! I can't let my mother lose her house!"

"So get your husband to take care of it. He's the big shot. Let him pay off her mortgage!"

Her face crumpled. That was a low blow and Evan knew it, but he couldn't help himself. She had cast her lot with Brad and it had turned out ugly. Now she had gone running back to Evan like he'd always known she would.

Leila crossed her arms over her chest. "If Brad had the money, believe me, I'd ask. Unlike you, I'm not too proud to humble myself to help a friend!"

He fixed her with an icy glare. "You said what you had to say. You asked the question you wanted to ask and the answer is still no. So now I'm going to ask you as politely as possible to leave."

She raised her chin in defiance. *"Or what?* You're gonna have someone come over here and toss me out?"

"No," he said menacingly, taking another step toward her. "I'll toss you out myself."

"Yeah, right! Like you'd ever get your hands dirty, you self-entitled son of a bitch!" She shoved him aside and walked off. "Tell Paulette I said congratulations," she muttered over her shoulder.

Evan then watched Leila stomp toward the hotel's revolving doors, leaving him both stunned and furious.